MARTIN KNIGHT was born in Epsom, Surrey. He is the author of many books, including working with footballers George Best, Peter Osgood, Dave Mackay and Charlie Cooke and Bay City Rollers founder member Alan Longmuir on their autobiographies. He has also written novels and several books in the true-crime genre.

JUSTICE
KILLER
MARTIN KNIGHT

LONDON BOOKS
39 Lavender Gardens
London SW11 1DJ
www.london-books.co.uk

First published by London Books 2023

A catalogue record for this book is available
from the British Library.

ISBN 978-1-7396983-2-4

Printed and bound in Great Britain
by CPI Group (UK) Ltd, Croydon, CR0 4YY

Typeset by Octavo Smith Publishing Services

JUSTICE KILLER

MARTIN KNIGHT

LONDON BOOKS BRITISH FICTION

To Harry Brown

CONTENTS

1	Old Wally	11
2	Buried Memories	21
3	Bubbles	32
4	Stuart	39
5	A Killer	52
6	Jan	63
7	Dad	76
8	Janice and Helen	84
9	Frank	96
10	Bubbles Bursts	111
11	Black Spot	124
12	Holly	138
13	Uncle Phil	146
14	Is Anybody There?	156
15	Mother's Day	170
16	Gents	176
17	Howard Plume	187
18	Contacting The Dead	195
19	Inspector Scull	210
20	Ned	221

1
OLD WALLY

STUART HINDS – THE horse-faced, manky-toothed teenager with the smooth stump for a forefinger – had never completely left my mind. I had departed Bridgnorth decades ago, and my family had only lived in the town for a couple of years, tops, but Hinds and the murder of poor, dear old Wally Tombs still pains me now when I am in middle age and many miles mentally and physically from 1970s Shropshire.

It had been a big news story back in the bleak midwinter of 1974. It had been on the news, with BBC Midlands cameras in the town for a couple of days where detectives had set up a 'murder hut' outside the school in the hope that pupils would drop in and offer information. I expect it was almost a welcome diversion, at least for everyone outside of Bridgnorth, taking their minds off strikes, power cuts, three-day weeks, plummeting *Financial Times* indices and the weary roll-call of familiar cheerless names that filled our news bulletins: Feather and Gormley, Scanlon and Scargill, Heath and Wilson. Power jockeys all of them. Men, always men, in and out of meetings, refreshed, our newscasters assured us, with beer and sandwiches. As if we gave a toss what they bloody well ate and drank. They spoke their own, meaningless to me, language – artificially elongated sentences liberally peppered with words such as demarcation, solidarity, thresholds, bargaining and comrade. Weaponised acronyms assaulted our senses daily, threatening havoc: ASLEF, COHSE, TGWU, NGA, NUR, TUC, NUS, NUT and IRA.

The IRA, particularly, was a malevolent spectre overshadowing day-to-day life. The posh Surrey town of Guildford had been blown up, for God's sake. Litter bins had been sealed or ghosted away, even in Bridgnorth, because IRA men dressed up as you and I were apparently in the habit of planting explosives submerged deep down among the Embassy cigarette packets and Golden Wonder crisp bags. We were a population cowed, worried where the next bomb would ignite. Fortunately, us boys had Noddy Holder, Brian Clough, Trevor Francis, Kevin Keegan, Barbara Eden off *I Dream Of Jeannie* and Elizabeth Montgomery from *Bewitched* to keep us focused. The girls had David Essex, the Bay City Rollers, Michael Jackson, Donny Osmond and David Cassidy to divert them from the frightening undercurrents.

I had triumphantly got my ugly mug on the telly, on *Nationwide*, no less, barging in among the daily parade of grey Sketchley-cleaned and pressed three-piece suits and grizzled sideburns, when I had walked backwards and forwards past the murder hut dozens of times, pretending I was unaware of the cameras trained on it, hands thrust deep into my side pockets and trudging in the slush, looking at the ground, wearing my leather-backed donkey jacket which cloaked my school uniform beneath.

'There I am,' I squealed delightedly at Mum, pointing at the television and bouncing in the armchair.

'Yes, there you are indeed, Paul,' she replied, unimpressed. 'Look at the state of you in that ridiculous jacket. People will think you are there to dig up the road. Why you can't …'

It was then – seconds later – that the brief thrill of television celebrity that I had been basking in caught in my throat. For the first time I saw a picture of the murder victim flash up on the screen. I had already heard the murdered man was a pensioner and that he had been named as Walter Tombs and he lived near our school. That much had been said on the radio and on the TV the day before, but this was the first time I had seen a photograph. And I realised then that the name Wally was short for Walter.

'Bloody hell, Mum, I know him. I know him. That's the old man, Wally.'

'You know him? And do you mind? Your language is appalling. We don't use words like that in this house.'

We *did* use words like that in that house. She meant *I* was not permitted to use words like that in that house. Dad uttered far worse.

'He calls himself Wally, and he lives in Telford Road. I told you, he give me the medal. Remember? He's a nice man ... he was a nice man.'

'That man. Oh yes, I remember. The man who said he was a famous footballer. I remember. He *gave* you the medal. Not *give*, *gave*.'

For a year and a half before the murder I had walked Telford Road twice a day on the way to and from school. In the summer old Wally had a habit of taking a striped canvas deckchair into his front garden and just sitting there until it became too nippy. I would nod, and Wally would smile, as did some other boys, and occasionally we would chat, especially on the way home when I wasn't late for anything. Wally said he was eighty-five years old, and to me he looked it. When he lifted himself out of the deckchair to come to the fence it seemed to take a terrific amount of effort and mind–body coordination, and I wished he would not try. Then, when he leant on the fence, his shoulders heaved up and down as he summoned breath from within, and when he filled his pipe with tobacco and struck a Ship match with trembling hands, it seemed to take an age, and I always worried that the old man would expire in front of me. He smelt, not offensively, of pipe tobacco and the insides of cupboards.

Wally told me that he had played professional football for Crewe Alexandra and that the big clubs had been interested in him, but the First World War had interrupted his career, and by the time he came home from France he was too weak and too old to resume his football career. I tried to look him up in books but could find no mention and assumed that the old codger was probably making it up or becoming confused. I had asked him who was the best player he ever played against, and Wally enthused about a man called Bloomer. He said Bloomer was over forty when they were on opposing sides in a wartime exhibition match, and he was still by far the best player on the pitch. He said this man Bloomer scored seven goals that day. The comical name Bloomer and the seven goals in one game indicated more imaginings to me. I didn't bother to consult my *Rothmans Football Yearbook* about him.

'Do you collect medals, son?' Wally asked one warm day.

I did now.

'Come on in then – you can have mine.'

At fourteen or fifteen years old I knew I should not go into strange men's houses, and I knew why. It had been drummed into me from an early age. Don't accept sweets from strangers. Don't get into cars. Definitely do not enter strange men's houses. But Wally was no stranger now, and besides, I was biggish for my age, fit and could box a bit, so I believed that this old man had little chance of overpowering me should he be a child-molester, pervert or serial killer.

The house stank. Musty, damp and dark, the natural light suppressed by drawn moth-eaten curtains. The walls were stained yellow and bare. A clock was stopped on the mantelpiece, and the fireplace had balls of newspaper stuffed into it. Where a television should have been, in the corner of the living-room, was a radiogram. A single misty light bulb apologised overhead. An unlit lamp with a shade with hanging tassels stood in one corner, and up against one wall was a bureau with a warren of drawers and compartments. Wally was bent over it scrabbling among broken watches, buttons, trinkets, utility bills, bus tickets, aged receipts and assorted junk.

'Here we are,' he declared eventually, holding a strip of purple-

and-orange cloth between his trembling finger and thumb with what looked like a half-crown coin hanging on the end.

'Do you want it? Have you got this one?'

'Don't you want it, Wally? What did you win it for?'

The old man pondered. I noted flecks of saliva clinging to wisps of silver hair on his chin, which he had missed when shaving. 'Won it? I won it for not dying, I suppose, boy. Ent for nothing else. What do I want it for? When I croak the totters will be in here in a flash, and they'll have it, and they'll flog it. Rather you have it if you like this stuff.'

'Thanks, Wally,' I said, taking it from the old man and turning to leave the house.

'I've got another somewhere, lad. Same as that. I'll try and dig that out for you. I am sure it was here, too, in this drawer.' Wally rummaged again.

I never went in Wally's house after that afternoon, although I exchanged greetings and small talk with him when we did see one another, but, as winter advanced, Wally was not out in the garden so often. I guessed that his health had also deteriorated further. The downstairs curtains remained closed most days, but once or twice I saw the meals on wheels lady open them up. Truthfully, I had not given the old man much thought again until I heard about his murder.

I had barely known anyone who had *died*, let alone been murdered. There was the girl who fell off a horse when we lived in Newbury, but I only knew her by sight, and, of course, there was Grandad Bert who had died 'from his lungs' – but what did he expect smoking three packs of untipped Senior Service a day? That was what Mum said – uncharitably, I thought – about her own father. I asked Mum if I should go to the police and tell them that I knew Wally and had once been inside his house. She was hesitant and said we will ask your dad when he gets home.

'Don't be so bloody silly. Keep out of it.'

A strange reaction from my parents, I thought. Showing a

reluctance to engage positively with the fuzz like they were persistent offenders when in reality neither of them would dare even contemplate parking on a yellow line, even on a Sunday.

Stuart Hinds was arrested the day after my TV debut. It was all around the school. Stuart had left just six months after I had arrived there as a new boy two years before. He was two school years above me, and, although I knew him, Stuart would not have known me. Everyone knew the Hinds family. There were six boys, three girls and (some said) three fathers at least. They were what Mum called a 'rough' family. Stuart was the youngest son and was mythical for having sparked out a teacher from another school when he was being ejected for loitering in their playground, allegedly waiting to attack this other school's equivalent of him. He was a bully. The teacher he assaulted, I was told, was a tiny, bent-over old man. Almost sixty, I heard!

Stuart's upper forefinger on his right hand was missing following an accident when, as a small child, he had been putting the chain back on his pushbike; his brother, who was perched on the saddle, suddenly pressed on the pedals and tore Stuart's finger clean off. The story goes that the brother put the severed bloody digit in his mouth while he pedalled furiously to the hospital with Stuart on the crossbar. However, the hospital was unable or unwilling to reattach it, probably not keen to handle the body part with congealed Sugar Puffs and blood all over it. This minor disability gave Stuart exalted status in the playground and on the mean streets of Bridgnorth. Inexplicably, it was seen as a badge of his toughness, as if the finger had been chewed off by Hell's Angels in a public-bar brawl rather than in an unfortunate childhood mishap.

When I joined the school I learnt, as schoolchildren do, to be wary of Hinds, and our paths rarely crossed, but I had heard about the time he'd beaten up Moss (naturally nicknamed Stirling) – a boy in the year above me and the year below Hinds – whose only crime was to be good-looking, smart and in possession of the first pair of oxblood Ivy loafers to clatter across the school playground; naturally, he attracted the giggling and fawning girls. This had been shocking, as Stirling was charismatic and suave, the kind of boy who glided through every situation intact. To see (or hear) about him being battered and utterly humiliated somehow made it worse than the usual sad, downtrodden victims getting their routine beatings.

Most days after Hinds had left the school he would hang around outside at lunchtime eating chips from a vinegar-sodden paper bag and generally basking in his notoriety. The oldest boy. Manifestly unemployed, boosting his self-esteem by surrounding himself with kids smaller than him who knew their places in the pecking order. He now wore a chunky gold sovereign ring on the stump of his finger, purchased no doubt with his new flow of dole money. Hinds made a point of scratching his nose with it or holding his cigarette between the stump and the middle finger. It was hard not to stare. Why would the police be arresting him, though? He was a hard nut, perhaps. A troublemaker, for sure. A hooligan. A bully. Known to the police, but surely he could not be the murderer of an old man? It must have been a mistake.

It quickly emerged that Stuart Hinds's dabs were all over Wally's house. It was also said that neighbours had stated that Stuart was a regular visitor to Wally's place, and this had started when he had been at school and was walking home like me. The police, in time, alleged that Hinds had been stealing from the pensioner over a long period, and when Wally had challenged him he had flipped and stabbed the old man repeatedly. Stuart admitted to being in the house on the day Wally died but denied killing him. When he had left, he maintained, Wally had been sat in his chair, smoking his pipe and listening to the radio.

Even without an admission of guilt, the police felt the circumstantial and forensic evidence and motive was sufficient to secure a conviction, and Stuart Hinds, just eighteen, was tried several months later at Shrewsbury Crown Court for the murder of Walter Tombs, aged eighty-five. After the trial, details of Wally's death were reported in the papers and on the television, and they gave me nightmares. Literally. They disturbed and distressed me. Cast a shadow over my entire childhood. Poor Wally had been stabbed with a weapon – which was never found but was believed to have been a large knife – a total of twenty-six times. Most of the wounds were to the torso, but one stab wound had pierced the eye, penetrating poor Wally's brain. I pictured his rheumy old eyes and someone plunging a knife into them and squeezed my own eyes shut in a vain attempt to banish that diabolical image. I stood in my bedroom and simulated a stabbing motion with my torch twenty-six times. It takes an age. Try it, you'll be shocked. Wally, the old soldier, would have experienced unimaginable agony and sustained terror. I cried for him for the first time when I reimagined his final minutes. It would not be the last.

It had taken months for the case to come to the court, and then it was all over in a couple of days. A jury found Stuart Hinds not guilty. His mother had testified that at the time the police believed Wally was murdered Stuart had been with her watching television at home, and one of the programmes they had viewed was *Coronation Street*. Stuart was able to remember the plot line although his mother couldn't. He described a reconciliation between characters Billy Walker and Deirdre Hunt in the Rovers Return pub. They were the on-off, loved-up young couple. The prosecution contended that Hinds might have watched the programme at Wally's house. The old man did have a television in his bedroom, the court heard, although he died in the front room and no prints from Hinds were found in the bedroom. Despite the cumulative evidence and the stench around him, Hinds walked free. A cowardly jury found him not guilty. I did not understand how they reached such a verdict and still don't. Stuart made no statement on the steps of the court afterwards, as innocent people often do, brushed aside the cameras, pulled his collar up and disappeared into the back of a waiting Morris Marina.

'I wonder who done it then,' I mused to my mother and father as we all sat together one evening in the sitting-room after the verdict had been reported on *News At Ten*.

'*Did* it, Paul,' Mum corrected.

'The police will have to start again,' I shrugged.

'Of course, the bloody little tyke did it,' Dad snorted testily. 'The police won't be starting again. Don't worry about that. When they say they are not looking for anyone else that's copperspeak for he did it. More fool you, jury, for acquitting him. That's what they are really saying.'

'But how did Stuart Hinds know about that programme?'

Dad threw me his *I give up* look. 'Somebody told him? One of his brothers? His mum? His mates? Come on, Paul. Get with the programme.'

I nodded. I hadn't thought of that. 'What will happen now?'

'Nothing. Sweet Fanny Adams will happen. This, I'm afraid, is the world we live in,' huffed Dad, angrily shaking the creases out of his broadsheet *Daily Express*.

'Well, Stuart Hinds will have his conscience to wrestle with. He will probably leave the area. It will blight his life, for ever,' my mother interjected.

'Will it fuck!'

'Alan! Language! No wonder I can't stop him swearing,' Mum said, nodding over at him as he sat deep in thought. Troubled. I should have gone to the police despite what my dad reckoned. When they said Wally had been attacked with a large knife, I knew which large knife it was. The bayonet. I remember seeing it leaning up against the wall in the hall. I assumed it was another war memento. It crossed my mind to ask Wally if I could have that as well. I wish I had now. Poor Wally had died on the end of a bayonet. But not a bayonet brandished by a German soldier on the blood-soaked fields of the Somme along with his youthful comrades but a bayonet brandished by a scumbag wanker who never cleaned his teeth. I should have told the police.

Stuart Hinds did not leave the area. He was still in Bridgnorth when Dad got a new job in north London, and we moved to Barnet several months after the trial. I passed him on the bridge over the river and looked away, fearing meeting his cold eyes and possibly having to speak, and then one final time in the newsagent's a few days before we left when I went to cancel my weekly delivery of *Shoot!*. Stuart was in front of me buying ten No. 6 cigarettes. I quickly feigned interest in a *Country Life* magazine and turned away from him. He scared me. I hated him for doing what he did to defenceless old Wally, but I was shit-scared of even coming on to his radar.

'I wish I didn't have to serve him. Scum,' complained the young female assistant when Hinds was safely outside the door, dramatically looking at the hand that had dropped the change into Stuart's as if it were now infected.

'We'll ban him then, next time, Julie, shall we?' chuckled her boss Mr Wyman, the newsagent. 'Tell him we don't serve killers. I'm sure he'll understand.'

2
BURIED MEMORIES

THE TELEVISION WAS blaring, demanding my attention. Knots of revellers closed in around the camera to create the illusion of larger crowds, filling the screen with inane smiles, jostling one another, attempting to penetrate the nation's consciousness and living-rooms. Hoping some producer somewhere would spot their charisma and select them for the British version of *Friends*. They were waiting for the cue to unleash contrived jollity in exchange for their five seconds of fame. Windswept presenters tried to convey a sense of occasion while simultaneously battling both the weather and the press of the crowds. Breathlessly pretending they were barely able to resist being overcome by the urge to join in the festivities, and that they were seriously elated. The screen divided into eight windows, and light shows and fireworks competed in London, Birmingham, Edinburgh, Cardiff, Glasgow, Plymouth, Newcastle and Norwich – and Big Ben chimed.

Let's all meet up in the year 2000 ...

Jarvis Cocker's lyric rattled around my brain. Jan loved the song and sang snippets of it to herself as she pottered around the house. That line mainly and something about Debra and wood-chip on the wall. They had played it earlier on TV along with '1999' by Prince, before it finally passed its official sell-by date. I looked it up, 'Disco 2000' by Cocker's Pulp came out in 1995. Little did Jan know then she wouldn't be here only five short years later. Jan will not be meeting up with anyone in the year 2000.

It was a new year and a new century, but instead of celebrating the dawning of a new age, really celebrating, not contrived nonsense, the media chose to ruin it by predicting disaster. Computers were supposed to crash, causing mayhem; trains would derail, and other countries, less prepared than Britain, would collapse, or so the BBC had predicted. I, more out of a mild sense of unease at not doing so than any other reason, raised a glass and then swallowed a large mouthful of the Sancerre I had poured an hour earlier. The phone rang. An excited young voice rode over a cacophony of noise and jubilation in the background. I heard the pips go and a ten-pence piece drop into the ether.

'Happy New Year, Dad.'

'Happy New Year, Angel. Where are you?'

'I told you, we're in the Blacksmiths. You should have come down.'

'I'm fine, Holly. Honest. How are you getting home? Do you want me to come and pick you up? I haven't had a drop.'

'Dad,' she shouted, no doubt a finger in her ear as she called from the busy pub payphone, 'Dad, we've only just started in here. I've gotta go. There are people behind me. I love you, Dad. Happy New Year!'

This was my first New Year's Eve alone, ever. Life is a series of firsts. In the beginning those firsts are a delight of discovery and wonder, but then there comes a point, perhaps in middle age, when those firsts become portentous and depressing. The first sight of your bald patch in a barber's mirror held up behind you, the first time you realise you are not waking up with an erection every morning, the first time you realise you prefer Radio 4 to Capital. Later still, the firsts become terrifying. The first hip operation, the first decision not to get a new dog because you don't know if you will outlive it or not. I had had my first birthday as a widower, and now this was my first New Year. My Jan had died on 17 March 1999.

Life now was like one of those Christmas advent calendars I had delighted in as an excitable kid. Except, in reverse. I remembered the delicious permission from Mum to prise open the cardboard window with my nail and work loose the milk chocolate behind to pop into my watering mouth. Christmas another day nearer. Suspense and delight. Now, it was all about closing those windows.

The advent-calendar notion first occurred to me when we drove to York, to Dave Hallet's funeral, a couple of years back. The Hallets had been our neighbours when we lived in York for a year or so in my early childhood. A bond had been formed between our two families, and we visited each other regularly, although the gaps between meetings widened as the years rolled by.

Dave was the son, a couple of years older than me. Me and Dave were very different but sat comfortably together. Dave was loud. Slaughtered a drink. Followed rugby. Got fat. Never too interested in women. Got fatter. In his mid-thirties he developed diabetes. I went up to York to see him.

'Aye, you best come up, pal. My toes are falling off.'

And they literally were. We laughed about it, but I looked at his florid face and watched him swing around his bachelor kitchen like Long John Silver on a crutch and thought, this shouldn't be happening to you. Not at just turned forty. Not yet. Life begins at forty, doesn't it? Dave seemed unperturbed and did not alter his daily routine of graft in the chocolate factory, seven pints in the Golden Fleece back bar and a four-course meal preceded by the demolition of a poppadom mountain in the Taste Of Bengal. I enjoyed visiting Dave. Felt refreshed doing the obligatory Micklegate Run pub crawl with him in a city which seemed so much more relaxed and friendly than London or even South Croydon and the surrounding suburbs. He was a funny fucker. Once when we went to an Indian restaurant he summoned the waiter over.

'Is this food gluten free?' he demanded to know with a straight face and after he'd eaten most of it.

The waiter was unsettled and fetched his boss who was

apologetic and pointed to a disclaimer about food intolerances in the small print on the menu.

'So, it's not gluten free?'

A pause. Heads from other tables turned expectantly.

'No, sir. It is not.'

Another pause.

'Good! I fucking *love* gluten.'

The waiters relaxed and started to laugh along with the rest of us. It was one of Dave's many party tricks.

After his toes had gone they took Dave's foot, and he became wheelchair bound. It was a torrid and rapid decline. The last time I spoke to him on the phone he said, 'Next time you come up it will just be my head on the sofa.' He had a black sense of humour, our David.

The funeral, or rather the wake, was fitting. A stream of rugby pals and locals took the stage in the back bar of the Duke Of York and regaled the mourners with tales of Dave's drinking exploits and gastronomic feats. Stories of vomiting from cars and accidentally splattering a passing cyclist, wetting beds in seaside towns and so on. How we all laughed as Dave's red carpet to ruin was gleefully unfurled. I had no real idea what a local legend my childhood friend had become. I glanced over at Dave's parents, back together for just one day. They had divorced in later life. It was an event that shocked my parents, I could remember. Made them realise there were other avenues open to them in their own not entirely happy union. Vi and Charlie Hallett were smiling and laughing at the ribald memories of their late son, but I couldn't help thinking that it would be nice if somebody stood up and said a few words about what a decent, kind, thoughtful chap Dave was rather than recalling the day he drank seventeen pints of Tetley's and still rode his bike home from the pub. I should have done it, but public speaking terrifies me. Coward that I am.

On the way back, driving down the motorway, I realised a door on my advent calendar had closed. Not so much the loss of a loved one, I was getting used to that, but I knew I would never visit York again. Never in my life. There was no need now Dave was not there. And I found that, strangely, more depressing than the loss of my pal in a way. I loved York. The people were just so genuine. They called me a Cockney, which I'm not, and a 'southern softie', which maybe I am, but they meant it affectionately. I remembered evenings in the Painted Wagon and the Old World nightclub after hours to end the night and chatting up tough-but-tender Yorkshire lassies as Billy Ocean's 'Love Really Hurts Without You' pounded away. Dave coming across the dancefloor holding a Whitbread Best beer tray with four pints balanced on it, the strobe lights illuminating him. He swung his hips in time to the beat. He was still a good-looking chap then, and the girls liked him, but he would not permit romantic liaisons to interrupt his drinking trajectory.

Holly had wanted me to come to the pub with her and her crowd. Many of these girls knew me from when they were kids, and it would not have been awkward, but Jan and I always went out together on New Year's Eve, and I just couldn't face it. At times like this the pain throbbed so hard. Everybody said I was coping, and I was. Holly had suggested she move back home for a while, but I told her not to be so ridiculous. But the utter despair, the absolute fucking pointlessness of living and the anger sometimes poleaxed me, causing me to slip into the kind of vegetative state that cannot be meaningfully conveyed. You either managed it or you didn't. If you did not, you topped yourself. Jumped the queue. Committed sewage pipe, as one of my hod-carriers used, oddly, to term it. By now I had realised I was a suicide-in-waiting. This is no cry for help. No whine of misery. It was a fact. A mere fact. I had no wish to live my life without Jan, but I had a duty to a daughter who had just lost a mother and hadn't even come of age yet. I vowed to hang around until I felt it was tolerable for me not to. I did not know if that would be a year away, a decade or, maybe, never. Perhaps something natural will get me first. But the thought that this was *the plan* comforted me. Gave me hope. Knowing I would eventually, sooner rather than later, take my own life gave me a reason to carry on living. It is a secret get-out-of-jail-free card that I carry around. Life can do its worst, but it won't beat me. I will beat *it* by opting out. Ending it. Proving I don't need its questionable gift. I am not part of it any more. I am in the departure lounge but have not boarded the plane yet. I am under no illusion that me and Jan will be reunited in some delightful, idyllic afterlife. I know religion is bollocks. Bollocks constructed in every society at the beginning of humanity to discourage people from killing each other. To encourage good behaviour. To rein in evil impulses. Religion, whatever strain, is, in my eyes, an intricate and ingenious deterrent device that has got out of hand. Those who started it had no idea how seriously people would take it.

According to the experts – like that absolutely slimy, perma-tanned fraud of a doctor on daytime television – there are five stages of grief: denial, anger, bargaining, depression and acceptance. Well, I seriously weave plans in my head to waylay the good doctor as he leaves the studio one morning and batter him as he reaches into his pocket for his car keys, spilling his blood all over his shiny blue Crimplene suit. I grab his silly paisley tie and smash his head on the bonnet. I … doesn't matter … but I guess we can conclude I'm stuck at the anger stage.

I wondered whether *my* computer had crashed. I failed to see how the so-called 'millennium bug' was going to burrow from thin air into my hard drive yet thought I should check. Y2K this and Y2K that. I was sure it was a scam perpetrated by the software industry to scare everyone into buying more virus-protection packages – but best check. I had taken to the computer age with ease for an old-school, hairy-arsed builder. I was an early adopter, having bought one of Alan Sugar's first green-screened 'home computers' some years back and quickly progressing to newer and more versatile models. Jan did all my invoicing and accounts with QuickBooks, Holly had used the Encarta encyclopaedia software for her homework as a kid and I had embraced the treasure trove of the internet with enthusiasm. I started keeping a diary and writing up memories from my childhood. It was a wonderful thing. I am not really much of a political thinker or a philosopher, but I cannot see how the World Wide Web will not ultimately enhance democracy and improve society. How will authoritarian states such as China keep things from their people when everything is there at a click of a mouse? How will some Muslim countries continue to treat their women as second-class citizens when they (the women) can see how most of the rest of the world lives and behaves? Computers and the internet are, on balance, a force for good. I am sure of that. I really hope I am right.

My first Amstrad encouraged me to write more and more. I wasn't writing with any serious intent to be published, purely to satisfy myself. I could compare something I wrote today with something I wrote a year ago and could see the improvement in grammar, fluency, structure and use of words. I was shit at school, had no real interest, and the books they introduced us to held no attraction. The first novel I read not under curriculum duress was *The Rats* by James Herbert. I saw a bloke reading it on a bus, and the cover featuring a huge black rat, her jowls dripping with blood, grabbed me. I bought a copy and devoured it like the rats devoured hapless civilians in the story. I bought a *Collins Pocket English Dictionary*, and I carried this in the top pocket of my Levi's jacket, much to the amusement of the boys on site, who would laugh as I looked up every word I did not know – and there were plenty. After *The Rats* I read *Jaws* by Peter Benchley and then Ken Kesey's *One Flew Over The Cuckoo's Nest*. I've not stopped since, and even now I refer to my little dictionary. I don't find it discombobulating at all. It's still a thrill when I find a new word. I try to insert them into what I am writing. Sometimes it's obvious, like just there.

The computer fired up just fine. Everything intact and smooth. No juddering or smoke. The world had not ended. I began to browse. Hours of the day and night can be eaten up surfing the 'information superhighway', as the papers had dramatically labelled the new-fangled internet. I loved the randomness. I could start by looking up an old actor or footballer and find myself three hours later reading the proceedings of a 1790 Old Bailey murder trial. Wally Tombs came into my mind, I know not why, and for the first time I typed his name into Yahoo!. Nothing. Then I remembered his full name was Walter, and I tried 'Walter Tombs, footballer'. There was one entry, and it was from a Crewe Alexandra fan site: 'Walter Tombs. Full back. Born Newcastle-Under-Lyme, 1889. Debut versus Brierley Hill Alliance 1912–13. Total appearances 43.'

Further investigation revealed that Crewe had not been playing in the Football League at the time but were in a Birmingham league that fed the Football League Second Division and was the equivalent of the second or third tier today, I guess. Old Wally's claims were true after all, and this shred of information supported his statement that the war had interrupted and ended his career.

It turned out that the other man Wally had mentioned, Steve Bloomer, was an absolute superstar with Derby County, and the internet produced a feast of information on him. I wondered why I hadn't picked any of that up when I was a kid, as Bloomer would have still figured in the public memory. Now I just knew it was true, too, that Wally had been skinned alive by this legendary striker. This belated confirmation of the old man's claims added to the tragedy of his story, and I felt waves of guilt for not having believed him and grief and anger all over again at his terrible, brutal demise.

Back in 1974 his small place in sporting history was all but lost, no reports of his murder had ever mentioned him being a professional footballer, but with the advent of the internet and the efforts of an obsessive football fan his existence had been resurrected. I reflected on how his murder was, for now at least, erased and how those people who had made it into the newspapers before the internet era have dropped out of sight, but those who appeared in the media post-internet are findable for ever. This could be good or bad depending on why your name figured in the records in the first place.

Armed with a birth date and place I skimmed across to a First World War archive site and keyed in Walter Tombs. There he was again. His life re-forming before my eyes: 'Tombs, W.G., Sapper, Royal Engineers, 1914. Discharged, 1919.'

So, he hadn't returned from France until 1919, when he was thirty years old, which would explain why was unable to fully resurrect his footballing career. Later searches on various ancestry sites would reveal that Wally had been a railway worker at Crewe and had volunteered when war broke out along with just about everyone in his yard. He had a brother, Henry, a year younger, who had perished in 1916. He never mentioned that. How tragic. I wondered if the other medal that Wally was going to give me all those years ago was Henry's. A fuller picture formed of Wally in my mind: an athletic, patriotic, working-class young man who was quick to answer Lord Kitchener's call and, through no fault of his own, survived the bloody conflict. I remembered Wally telling me he got his medal for that. Surviving. He was almost apologetic about it. I think that's how many old soldiers felt after seeing so many of their comrades and friends suffer and die. That's why they rarely talked about it. There was no glory in their eyes.

Wally had probably gone back into the railway yards after the war and at some point moved to Bridgnorth. I guessed that he had never married. Perhaps the war had caused him to miss that boat, too. There were no relatives or children that I could remember named or quoted in the newspapers back in 1974–5, and I don't recall him mentioning any family to me. I closed my eyes and re-created his living-room in my mind. I could see the mantel-piece again. There were no photograph frames of family or anyone. I could see the bayonet, though, propped up against the wall. I remembered now him nodding over to it and saying that when I was older he'd give it to me. Funny I remembered that promise only now, years later, but not in the months afterwards. It's amazing the power and trickery of memory. The murder weapon was never found, at least as far as I was aware.

Wally was a decent, lonely old man who ended up being butchered in his home by a robbing piece of fucking shit. I looked up that piece of shit. Nothing in the search engine. He's dead. Drugs. Would have got on smack. It wasn't about in Bridgnorth in 1974, at least not among the plebs like us, but it would have been ten years later, and Stuart Hinds was a man who would have found heroin. If he were alive he'd have been in trouble. He'd have been in prison. He would have made the papers. He would have drifted. Seaside town where nobody knew him or his past. Just try 192.com. Not that Hinds would be on the electoral register ...

'Hinds, Stuart, 12b Blenheim Court, Bridgnorth, Shropshire. Approx. age: 42–44.'

A bolt of adrenaline surged through my veins, then I felt rage. The mug is still there. The arrogant misfit. He hasn't even moved. He hasn't even had the decency to die a drug-addled death. He's swerved being murdered himself or gurgling on his own vomit. He lives with a lady called Sharon. Perhaps he has to be on the electoral roll in order to collect benefits? Fucking hell. There is even a phone number. Who needs private detectives in the internet age? I seethed quietly. The bayonet and the knowledge that Hinds appeared to be living a quiet, domestic life incensed me. Back in my armchair, with the television broadcasting from Scotland, where, the BBC link man assured us, they know how to celebrate New Year better than us in England, I pictured Wally clearly and remembered the V-necked red sleeveless woollen sweater the old warrior wore the day I went inside his house. Marvelling again at how things are buried in the memory, and sometimes they re-emerge. I remembered Wally offering me a drink of milk from a misty bottle with a tide mark, but I had politely declined when I saw him sniffing the bottle. I tried to imagine the grisly scene as Hinds attacked him. Did Wally scream? Did he beg for mercy? Was the piercing of his eye at the beginning of the attack or at the end? Forcing myself to replay what I knew had happened unlocked those vulnerable childhood fears and worries, and I started to cry loudly because I knew there was no one to hear. I rocked in my chair and wailed. I longed for Jan to hug me. But she was not here.

That horrible, sleazy arsewipe had literally got away with murder. Had a life. Waltzed around town as if all he had done was smash a few windows. Had a wife. Still has a wife. I don't have a wife. My wife has died. Where is the justice? Did Hinds ever think about Wally Tombs? Did he ever wonder about the man he killed? Did anyone ever challenge him about it? What about his mum? She knew he'd done it. How did she live with herself? The older brothers and sisters – what did they do? Blood is thicker than water and all that, but surely there would have been fall-out from having a violent, bloodthirsty, murdering teenaged scumbag in their family? And why was Wally coming into my mind so forcefully now in the opening hour of this new century? Was he asking for revenge? No, not revenge. He'd been a gentle man. Was Wally asking for justice? Was that to be the only remnant of his life – a single line on a fanzine page? Was I duty bound to at least take Stuart Hinds to task? Was Wally talking to me?

Something, I wasn't sure what, was forming in my mind. I felt a purpose. Seconds later, after taking a piss, I was back in my captain's chair and on the internet looking up accommodation in Bridgnorth.

3
BUBBLES

GARFIELD DESIGN & BUILD ran itself, had done now for a few years – and even after Jan died the business continued to flourish. I still came into the yard most days but never hung around too long and would instead drive around to the various jobs if I felt like it, but Bubbles ran the show, and I had complete trust in him, as did Jan. Bubbles – aka Franklin Constantine Lane, albeit not very often – had been taken on as a labourer when he was only sixteen. I remember well him walking on to a job down Banstead way with his emaciated face framed by an unruly mop of tight, black, curly hair, which I gathered had led to his childhood nickname. His sunken cheeks and knowing eyes put me in mind of Phil Lynott. His pectorals bulged under a loose-fitting, mucky, torn 'Frankie Says' T-shirt.

'Got any work, mate?' the kid asked almost aggressively, Yosser Hughes style.

'For what?' I had said.

'For me.'

'Doing what? I meant,' I said, now bristling at the kid's brusqueness and arrogance.

'I'll do whatever you want.'

'You're not learning a trade then? Brickie? Chippy? Sparks?'

'No, not yet, but I want to learn to be them.'

To be them. Bubbles was keen not to close off any avenues. As luck would have it we were a labourer down on the job, and I gave him a start and instructed him just to do what he was told. At the end of the week the main bricklayer on the site reported back that the boy was a 'diamond'. Worked his bollocks off, he said. Ran up and down the ladder with a hod like a young Max Quarterman. That was rare with the youngsters, even then. I kept him on.

I had had no idea that Bubbles was only sixteen. He looked like a thirty-year-old who hadn't quite thrown off his boyish looks. Those sunken cheeks hinted at a drug habit to me, the random tattoo dots on his fingers and arms evoking borstals and approved schools, and his eyes betrayed a knowledge of the darker side of life, a knowledge that would normally only come from a hard life led. Bubbles, it transpired later, was living in a children's home up the road that day he walked into our lives, having been there on and off since he was very young. He confided to me he had been in 'trouble' but never elaborated.

Pine Forest Children's Home was a few miles out of Croydon, where suburbia leaked into the countryside. It had been there years, since Victorian times, and had taken boys and girls from broken homes or never-formed homes across south London. He had an 'auntie' and 'uncle' and shared a re-created family unit within the home with other kids from London. He had had the last couple of years of education at the local secondary school. When they left education they were told they were now on borrowed time. It was a *children's* home after all. They were expected to get a job and then find accommodation, and it was that sudden edict that had led Bubbles to our house-extension job in the leafy roads of Banstead that sunny afternoon in 1986. Years later he told me we were literally a couple of streets away from where he lived, and I was the first person he had asked for work. How the world turns.

My bricklayer was right, Bubbles *was* a diamond. He was a natural grafter with a keenness to learn and please, and after a while his earnestness and vulnerability had bought out Jan's maternal instincts. Bubbles was soon eating meals with us, and eventually he came to live at our house. We encouraged him into technical college where he learnt bricklaying, carpentry, plumbing and plastering and at the same time he grew taller and stronger, filling out nicely and rapidly becoming our most valued employee.

When he was twenty he left our home and took a flat in South Croydon, determined to stand on his own two feet, but his loyalty to us remained undiminished. A couple of years later still he married a girl he had known at Pine Forest, Marcella, and two lovely children followed. As Bubbles's ability grew he was able to relieve me of more and more of the daily workload, and the only tasks he was not ready to take on were the book-keeping and the pricing of jobs. Jan took care of the former and me the latter.

Jan, a few years back, suggested that I make Bubbles a partner in the business. She said that she didn't think he would strike out on his own, but it was in our interest as well as his to tie him into the company more formally. Jan's foresight humbled me. She also said it was the right thing to do. Jan was shrewd, quietly ambitious, but she liked to do that right thing, and that was another reason I still adore her. Adored her. We made Bubbles a director and allocated shares to him. When we told him over a takeaway meal and a bottle of Lambrusco he had sobbed into his serviette, and we followed suit. It was a sweet moment.

When Jan died, Bubbles was almost as upset as me, and the two of us now avoid too much contact through fear of stimulating each other's raw anguish. Bubbles worked extra hard to ensure that I had as much time as I needed to adjust. As far as he was concerned, if I never wanted to set foot in the yard again I needn't. He once said that Jan and I had saved him from an uncertain future and educated, nurtured and cared for him. He was for ever in our debt, he insisted.

'I'm going away for a couple of days, Bubbles. Going to see Mum, and I have a few other bits and pieces. Will you be OK? I've got the mobile if you need me.'

'No problems, Paul. Take your time. See you when I see you.'

It was a typical brief-and-to-the-point conversation between us.

Although I hadn't clarified it yet to myself, I guess I was planning revenge. What form of revenge, I was unsure. I would let destiny take its course. A few hours later I pulled the Jag into the car park behind the Black Horse in Bridgnorth and walked into the pub. I had never been inside before, although I passed by it regularly for two years of my life. The newsagent's where I last saw Stuart Hinds was almost next door. I asked if there were any rooms available, although I was pretty sure there would be this time of year. There were. Under the name Brian Jarvis, I booked for one night and paid in cash. I used the name Brian Jarvis because he had been an anodyne character in *Crossroads* when I was young. I figured it was one that would not arouse suspicion, and I knew I would not forget it and get caught out. The lady then showed me to a neat, tidy room in an extension block behind the pub. As I fetched my bag from the car boot I could see the River Severn lapping the rocks at the bottom of the car park, and I stood still for a minute watching the river and wondering exactly what I was doing there. My heart pumped. Butterflies danced excitedly with one another in my gut.

In the evening I ate in the bar area and then moved on to a stool at the counter and struck up a conversation with the barmaid, who was the same lady who had booked me in earlier. It is strange how environments change perceptions. When she had booked me in and led me to my room I had not really noticed her. We were involved in a transaction. Now in the smoky, convivial atmosphere of the pub, and her pulling pints, she had become feminised. I noticed the freckles speckling her arms. I saw how her breasts expanded when she pulled the pump handle back and her deep-blue eyes. More spaced-out freckles adorned the bridge of her nose, reminding me of a song-thrush egg. Between her serving other customers, I managed to get her talking about the pub and its history and the town. She said the place was very popular with fishermen in the summer, after the barbel in the Severn, and said the football on the big screen in the games room brings in the locals during the week. I was surprised at how easily I lied about who I was and what business I had in Bridgnorth. Apparently I was a salesman and had meetings in Wales and was staying over before my next unspecified stop. I sold kitchens. As I fibbed away, I thought of my dad. He would most definitely have drunk in this pub. He would have come in here and refreshed himself after a day on the road flogging typewriters.

'Actually,' I volunteered casually, 'my father lived here for a while in the 1970s, but he and Mum were divorced, so I never visited.' The barmaid or landlady, who revealed that her name was Angie, nodded. 'I'm not sure where he lived exactly, but I'm sure it was Bridgnorth. I remember him telling me about an old man that lived near him that got murdered. Stabbed, I think, in his own house.'

'Yeah, that's right. The old man lived just down the road from here. I remember that. Everyone remembers that. It was all over the papers and on the box. My aunt lived in the same road.'

'They got someone for it, didn't they?'

'Yes, they did, but he got off in court. He did it, though.'

'Did he? How do you know?'

'Because he told everyone he did it. That's how I know. He was proud of it. Well, he used to be. He doesn't mention it now.'

'What? He's still around?'

'As large as life. He lives three minutes' drive from here. Doesn't drink in here, thank God. He drinks in High Town. High Town is up there,' she said, pointing out of the window and over the bridge. 'You have to walk up the cliff or take the funicular railway. He walks past here most days.'

'If he got off, why did he tell people he did it?'

'Double jeopardy. Is that what they call it? You can't be tried twice for the same offence? Not sure how our mad system works.

He thought it made him look "hard" that he killed someone. Even if it was an old chap. He used to say the man attacked him. Made a pass at him, if you know what I mean. People feared him because of it. Still do a bit, I suppose. I don't. I think he's a prick.'

I liked her spirit. I would never form another serious relationship with a woman, but I was not oblivious to a female's attractions. She was assured and sparky. I looked at her hand for a wedding ring. There was a ring, but then again, there was one or more on every finger and even her thumbs. I guessed she was ten years younger than me.

'And his mates, they just accept him? Accept what he did?' This bothered me.

'He doesn't have mates or friends, does Stuart Hinds, just accomplices.'

I smiled at her turn of phrase. Pleased she confirmed the name because if I had let it slip out I would have revealed that the murder was more than a vague memory to me. She pulled another foamy pint and handed it to a man who was waiting alongside. When he walked off with it she explained further, lowering her voice, leaning into my close proximity revealing a hint of cleavage.

'He's pond-life. Lowlife. A see-you-next-Tuesday. Excuse my French.'

There was a fleeting sexual frisson as she spelt out that word cryptically and bowed her head towards mine. We both felt it. I smiled. Good girl. I changed the subject. I had enough information. Got what I needed and did not want Angie to have any reason to remember this exchange or me. She had done most of the talking, and I made sure that the minute or two on Wally was sandwiched and buried in a whole lot of other routine stuff. I felt a bit reckless knowing that it was not sensible to talk about Stuart to anyone. But Angie must have dozens of conversations a day. Hundreds a week.

I went to bed warm and fuzzy courtesy of the Old Speckled Hen Angie had recommended, thinking only of Stuart Hinds and how even in death he had abused poor Wally, saying that he had made sexual advances on him, and then I felt my adrenaline surge at the knowledge that Hinds was lying in his bed, too, only a few streets away, and blissfully unaware that Wally Tombs was about to re-enter his life.

4
STUART

17 MARCH 2000 was the first anniversary of Jan's death, and I went to see Bubbles at the yard where we half patted each other on the back and half awkwardly had what they're now calling a man-hug. (When I see man-hugging on TV and in films that are set in the past, even times as recent the 1970s, I switch off because the authenticity has gone out of the window. Men did not do that then, so stop rewriting history.) Afterwards I met Holly for lunch at the bottom of the market, and we had a long embrace and short cry over the woman that had been the centre of both of our lives for so long. When Holly laughed, as she often still did, thankfully, I could see Jan so clearly, and it made me ache for my soulmate. Just to see her again, if only for one more time.

'Why don't you come over the flat tonight, Dad?' Holly said, my bottled-up despair threatening to uncork explosively across the dinner table.

'No thanks, Holly. No offence, but I'm going to go home and have a quiet time in. I want to be alone. Sounds a bit Greta Garbo, doesn't it? But I like just being there. It feels right ...'

'I know, Dad,' said Holly, resting her hand on my forearm and blinking back tears.

'Are *you* going to be OK?' I asked.

'I'm out tonight ... with the girls ...' Holly hesitated, a little embarrassed and guilty that she was going to be enjoying herself on this milestone day in life post-Jan.

We pecked, I paid the bill and walked Holly back to the estate agent's office on Catherine Street where she worked and walked further on to the NCP. Instead of returning home I headed out to the M25 and, ultimately, to Bridgnorth. I had filled up with petrol earlier because I had already decided that the less CCTV tape I guested on the better.

Three hours later I arrived at my destination, having driven in a leisurely fashion to avoid even the slightest chance of being flashed by a speed camera. I parked in a residential road about three miles outside of Bridgnorth town centre and close to where we used to live. As I got out of the motor I put on a puffer jacket that a labourer had left on site a few years before, and which I had not previously worn but had kept because I thought the man might come back for it. Sometimes they did. I fiddled with my sweatshirt before zipping up the jacket and putting on a baseball cap that I had never donned, but which, again, had appeared in the office. It was nondescript, black, with no logo. Locking the Jag with a depression of my thumb on the remote control I started walking, knowing it would take me about one hour to arrive outside the Black Horse. This would make the time approximately 6.30 pm, and I was banking on the fact that Stuart Hinds would not have left his house and crossed the bridge for his Friday-night piss-up before then. I hoped, too, that I would recognise a man I had not seen for a quarter of a century and not since he was a gangly, spotty youth of eighteen. I was reasonably confident that I would. Some things never change, and, besides the missing forefinger, Hinds had that long horse face, I recalled, and his hair, if he still possessed it, was lank, lifeless and black.

It was 6.45 pm when I first passed the Black Horse, and I did not linger, not wanting the barmaid Angie to register me should she be looking out of the window, and I walked across the bridge over the River Severn and then back again on the other side of the road. I did this several times. I spied a camera high up on a lamp-post and avoided passing directly in front of it, but I could see no others, although this did not mean they weren't any. I still did not know exactly what I had in mind beyond confrontation, I really didn't, but my instinct was that I should limit any obvious signs of my presence in Bridgnorth on this night. Every person that came towards me I scrutinised as discreetly as I could. I knew I was looking for a man in his early/mid-forties so was able to discount many of the pedestrians who passed me, and I kept my head down and hands thrust in the puffer-jacket pockets as they drew level.

After forty-five minutes or so of walking to and fro over the bridge and beginning to accept that I was assuming lots of things and probably had been on a wasted journey a man approached who I thought could be him. My insides stuttered. My arse muscles tightened. The man's walk had an arrogance and swagger; he literally threw one shoulder forward then the other and that distinctive gait that first alerted me in the distance triggering a fragment of memory, and as he drew close I decided he was the right age range. I had a strong feeling that this could be Hinds. As we drew level, I looked hard at him, and fortunately the man was looking vacantly ahead and did not notice me. I had a few seconds to decide. The face was longish but not quite as equine as I remembered it. His hair was straight and dank and was gathered at the back into the once-fashionable male ponytail. He was sporting a badly manicured goatee beard. More like a patch of burnt grass on his chin. It could be him. It might not be, though. If I followed the man and it was not Stuart Hinds, then the whole journey, the whole episode, would have been wasted, as I could not be sure who would have passed over the bridge in the meantime. *Que será.* I swung around in one neat movement, worthy of a scene from an old British Scotland Yard B-movie, and discreetly followed my target.

The ponytail bounced as the man strode into the funicular railway carriage and plonked himself down on the wooden seat thrusting his legs forward opposite a young woman in a short skirt, parka and hooped earrings. She looked out of the window to the side of her, straight at the red-brick wall built into the cliff face rather than acknowledge her fellow passenger's demanding presence. I sat on the same side as the girl, one empty seat away, and fixed my line of vision away from the face but on the man's hands, which remained defiantly planted in his green flying-jacket side pockets. At the top of the cliff, as the doors opened a couple of minutes later, the man was the first out, and I allowed the girl to step out before me. He produced some change from his pocket and paid the lady in the booth, but, although I could see flesh, I could not make out whether a finger was missing or not from the hand proffered. In addition, I could not for the life of me – now I thought about it – be entirely sure if it was Hinds's right or left hand that was missing a forefinger.

When I had lived in Bridgnorth twenty-five years earlier, I had rarely ventured to High Town, and I did not know the streets like this man obviously did and found it a little difficult to tail him as he weaved in and out of roads and alleys before disappearing inside a small pub with two frosted bay windows. It was a cold night, and a log fire blazing inside gave those windows an inviting, warm, Dickensian-Christmas-card glow. I did not follow the man in, comfortable that I knew where he was, and busied myself looking in some shop windows and wandering up and down the street. I did not want Hinds to clock me and was worried he might if there were only a handful of customers inside the public house. Looking at my watch I noted the time was now past eight, and having seen some people enter during the previous fifteen minutes and suddenly concerned there might be a back entrance he could leave by, I decided to go in. I had to know for sure if I was stalking the correct person.

Fortunately there were several customers, more than I'd realised, and my entering did not cause any heads to turn. I positioned myself at the far end of the bar and ordered a pint of Carling. As I sipped from the straight glass, overdoing my concentration on the lager, I lifted my head and surveyed the bar area. It was not the sort of place I envisaged Stuart Hinds drinking in. A tactile couple in baggy woolly jumpers lounged on the comfortable seats in front of the fire; regulars, I guessed, as the woman had her bare feet tucked underneath her body. Her shoes were parked on the stone floor. A corpulent middle-aged man with a florid face in a bold pin-stripe suit was holding court at the bar encircled by three soberly besuited underlings, who nodded enthusiastically at the end of each of the older man's profound sentences. I would guess he was a senior partner in a local solicitor's practice, and the three men were clerks or trainees. There was a further small group who looked like students: intentionally ripped pullovers and T-shirts with boring slogans, torn jeans, no tattoos and loud laughing. This was a time when you could tell a student from a young worker by the presence or not of tattoos. An old man sat alone and upright at a table looking dolefully into the middle distance with a pint of bitter neatly central on his table, and another man on the table next to him was reading a tabloid newspaper.

A fruit machine whirred, whizzed and chimed in the corner, and in front of it, standing legs apart and jabbing it as if in a confrontation, was my target. The ponytail confirmed that. His jacket was off, revealing a Ralph Lauren polo shirt and skinny arms decorated with time-faded tattoos, possibly scratched on with a schoolboy compass and Indian ink. A newer, professionally made tattoo with colour, depicting a dagger poked into a flower, adorned his upper arm. That annoyed me. If this were Stuart I could see meaning in that. His full straight pint glass was on top of the machine. Likely his second. Possibly his third. I knew this was the moment and glided down the bar to stand behind the man while his attention was solely on spinning the oranges and lemons. I had a clear view now of his right hand as he punched down on the HOLD buttons, and his forefinger was much in evidence. The other hand was holding a burning cigarette, and I had to crane my neck to the left to view it. The man obligingly brought the cigarette up to his lips to inhale as the reels spun furiously and the machine juddered noisily. He was holding the cigarette between his forefinger and his middle finger. Except there *was* no forefinger. Just a stump. A stump with a gold band around it. Stuart Fucking Hinds.

Elated, excited, scared, I moved away and sat down behind the machine and a tree-trunk pillar, heart thumping furiously. The beat resounding all over my body, not just my chest. I gulped greedily on my pint. We could not see each other in this position, but I could see the door, and that was all that mattered. Half an hour and probably another pint later Stuart Hinds pushed that door open, and I saw his swaggering form pass the window. I quickly followed as he headed downhill. Soon he veered left into a pub called the Black Boy, and again I waited outside. I looked up at the sign that swung above the entrance. It was a picture of a chimney sweep, and I thought of *The Water-Babies*, a book that my teacher had read to the class at infant school. I entered.

A band was playing somewhere in another bar inside; I could hear a female voice, struggling to be heard above over-amplified guitars, singing 'Hotel California' ...

He said, 'We haven't had that spirit here since 1969.'

But this bar I was in was packed, more the environment Hinds would be at home in, I imagined. The clientele was more youthful than the last pub and considerably younger than Hinds, with groups of males and females eyeing one another in a romantically curious manner. A pick-up joint. It was now around 9.30 pm, and the collective voice was rising, with arms gesticulating, jaws grinding and heads being thrown back in over-exuberant laughter. Stuart Hinds joined a group of men in their thirties, but only after he had first bought his drink alone. The body language signified they knew him, but there was no back slapping or shaking of hands. These lads didn't seem overly pleased to see Stuart. Eventually he moved over to a corner where a fat man in a lumberjack coat and jeans was sitting on a stool. The man offered Stuart a cigarette by pushing his tobacco tin towards him along the bar. Stuart leant on the bar but turned away from the man and looked at the girls bunched immediately in front of him and was commenting from the side of his mouth. Occasionally the lumberjack laughed. I knew he was making comments like 'I'd give that one ... What I could do to that ...' and so on. I noticed that some men nodded at Stuart, and he responded in kind as they edged in at the counter for service. A couple of young women even spoke to him as they passed by on the way to the toilet. I hoped that Stuart was not going to meet anyone who would be walking home with him later. If my quarry pulled, that would be the end of whatever was going to happen tonight.

Did these people, who obviously knew Stuart, know that he had brutally murdered an old man? Did they know he shoved a bayonet into an eighty-five-year-old's eye, piercing his brain? It was a small town – people must know. Why do they even tolerate him? Why is he not shunned? What about poor Wally Tombs? Is this what it has come to? A merciless murderer of old folk can walk around unmolested, and people talk and share tobacco with him. Was it so long ago that it doesn't matter? Or are people genuinely scared of him? Has murdering an old man made him 'hard'? I would like to think he wouldn't get such an easy ride in Croydon but could not be sure. I could not be sure of anything these days. Morals and standards that had generally helped keep a reasonable level of order for centuries had gone out the window. Our governments – and they are all the same – allowed it to happen. Stuart Hinds wasn't hard, I could see that. Long streak of piss. I knew I could put him down with one single punch. He might carry a blade, but he would not get a chance to use one on me. The more I looked at him, and as the third (or was it fourth?) pint of slowly drunk lager slid into my bloodstream, the more I wanted to deliver that blow.

The last-orders bell rang. A mad rush to the bar, and Stuart pushed his empty glass towards the nearest barman first. He must have had eight pints with this one, yet there was not an ounce of fat on him. Typical. I only have to have a couple of pints and a curry, and I'll put on three or four pounds, although I do work at keeping trim. I got up and left and walked slowly towards the bottom of the hill figuring that Stuart would not be walking back up the hill and away from home when the pub chucked out. I stopped and watched the pub from a doorway. Ten minutes later a gaggle of revellers burst out the door, one of whom was Hinds, who walked backwards as he said his goodbyes to the lumber-jack, who headed uphill in the opposite direction. I started walking, and now Hinds was unwittingly following me.

Soon we were out on the bridge, and the Severn was pushing through noisily. Growling, almost. A group of girls tottered along on high heels, clutching tiny handbags barely bigger than purses, on the other side of the road. I knew it was time to act. I had no fear just excited anticipation. I stopped dead and waited for Hinds to catch up with me. This was the first time that Stuart Hinds registered my presence. Ever. I turned.

'Hello, Stuart,' I said.

'All right?' replied Hinds dismissively without stopping and passing around me. He obviously had me down as someone who knew him but whom he did not recognise. Maybe someone he'd sold drugs to once. Unimportant. Irrelevant.

'I'm talking to you, you cunt.' I had to pull him up quickly. Stuart stopped and spun around. His face did not register anger or fear, only confusion.

'What d'you say?'

'Do you want a row? A tear-up? You piece of shit.'

The sheer unexpectedness of the situation had thrown Hinds completely.

'You what? Who are you? What's your fucking problem?' Stuart looked around him, hoping there was somebody he could enlist for help, or maybe he was checking I was alone. Perhaps he thought it was an ambush.

'You scared, Hinds? I thought you were a hard man. Are you going to fight me or not?'

Stuart looked around. He was not panicking, but he was struggling to know how to respond. There were two men coming up behind, and for a minute I thought that he might ask them for advice, but they passed us without anyone saying a word.

'I'll tell you who I am in a minute. Are you going to have a straightener with me or not? I always had you down as a bottle-job, Hinds ... just like the rest of your family ... grasses and cowards ... all of them ...'

That last comment galvanised Hinds; the mention of his family signalling to him they were all in this together.

'I'll fight you,' he shrugged. 'You're one of the Howards then?' He was wracking his brains and suspected now I was a member of another family that he or his brothers had probably upset somewhere along the line.

'No. Let's go down there.' I motioned to some steps down to the riverbank just past the bridge. 'We don't want a nicking.'

I was pleased at how easily I had dived headlong into street-speak and how the aggression tumbled out of me. Years of working on sites and with many rough, tough builders had attuned me to be the sort of person now who would demand the attention of Stuart Hinds.

If he hadn't been emboldened by seven or eight pints, I really felt that Hinds would have run, but he walked down the steps first. We stood in the shadow of the pillar of the bridge next to the river. Hinds had his legs apart like when he was at the fruit machine. His fists were clenched. He was coiled.

'What's it all about then, mate?' he asked, opening his arms and the palms of his hands, his tone faintly conciliatory. This was foreign territory for him. He was vulnerable, and he knew it. Hinds could have a row, I imagine, but he liked the odds to be in his favour or to be in a pub where fights would likely be broken up quickly and he could grandstand while ostensibly being restrained. This stranger was weird, he thought. Or that's what I thought he thought. I was about the same age. In good nick. But hard for Stuart to suss out my build in the puffer jacket. I didn't look *bad*, though, and that provided some comfort to Hinds, I imagine. He knew the *bad* people. He knew how they looked and how they moved. *Bad* men can see it in each other. He thought he wasn't facing a seriously bad man.

'I'm Wally,' I smiled.

'Wally who?' Hinds returned, his eyebrows knotted, nervously biting down on his bottom lip.

'Wally Tombs. You murdered me. Surely, you remember. You stuck my own army bayonet through my eye? Remember, Stuart?'

Stuart stepped backwards as if to get a better look at me and clenched his fists tighter, his eyes bursting wide open and his body tensed. It was like my revelation had electrocuted him.

'What you on about?'

The bit about Wally's bayonet had freaked him. The murder weapon was never found, and only he knew what it was. Only he knew that he had slaughtered the old man with his own First World War bayonet.

'Yes, I'm Wally, Stuart,' I continued calmly poised to leap on my prey should he make a move to run.

I unzipped my jacket, held it open and thrust out my chest to reveal Wally's war medal pinned to my sweatshirt. 'Recognise this? I gave you the other one, didn't I? Or did you thieve it? I'm old. I can't remember. My memory does not serve me so well. No, I gave it to you, I'm sure. Now why did you kill me, Stuart? I'd really like to know. What did you do with my bayonet? Throw it in here?'

I nodded at the river gurgling hungrily besides us.

'The old cunt ... I didn't kill him ... it was self-defence ... he was an old queer ... he was trying to rape me ... I was a little kid. Who the fuck are you?'

'Stuart, Stuart,' I interrupted showing him the palms of *my* hands. 'This is me you are calling a cunt. This is me you are calling an old queer. This is me you are claiming tried to rape you. These are serious allegations. They are not very nice, are they, Stuart? They are not true, Stuart, are they? I was there, remember?'

His Adam's apple bounced up and down in his scrawny neck as he swallowed repeatedly. Stuart Hinds tried to speak, but no words came out. He looked up hopefully at the bridge. I believe he wanted to call out. My calmness and confidence was frightening him. My knowledge terrified him. How could this bloke know about the medal and the bayonet? he was thinking. Old Bill never even knew the old goat owned it. Stuart's mind must have been whirring. Adrenaline battling the alcohol. His brain searching for a logical explanation. He did not know where this was going. He had been plunged into a nightmare. I wondered if he had had this nightmare before or something very much like it.

'Are you Old Bill? How do you know all this? I mean, what makes you say this?'

'I'm not a police officer, Stuart, as you well know. I won't tell you again. I'm Wally, and if you cannot give me a satisfactory explanation for murdering me, I shall have to kill *you*.' I grinned manically at him, feeling power and purpose rise up inside me. Hinds stepped back. He pissed himself. Not completely through fear probably. Perhaps he had been dying to go and could hold it no longer. Warm urine rolling down his leg and darkening his blue jeans may have given him seconds of comfort.

'Well? Why did you do it? I was old then and could never have hurt you. I could barely get around the room, remember? I was only ever good to you.'

'I never did anything. I wasn't there. I was found not guilty.'

'But, you just said I tried to rape you. It was self-defence.'

'I wasn't there.' Hinds was firming up. Getting his act together. Grasping the situation. Did he think that he was being set up to admit to the murder? Was this some grandson of the old man? Old Bill? There was something weird and very dangerous happening. He needed to shape up and get out of it.

I was guessing about the bayonet and the medal, and I didn't know he was going to say any of this, yet my words were hitting home like dartboard bullseyes. The blood had disappeared from Hinds's alcohol-tinged cheeks. His fists were still clenched, but they were shaking. He was suddenly very, very sober. He knew this could not be Wally Tombs. He had killed him. This was a man of about his own age. But how did he know all this? What was happening? Fuck. Fuck. Fuck.

Whack! I jumped forward, crouched down and unleashed a punch from the knee up in one swift movement which connected under Hinds's jaw and lifted him clean off the ground. His legs buckled beneath him, and his eyes shot up into his forehead. As he crumpled on the floor I dragged him into the river at the bank next to us where it was shallow and sat on him with my knees in the small of his back. I grabbed Hinds's pathetic ponytail and wrapped it around my fist like a bandage, intending to smash his head on to one of the rocks as soon as he began to show resistance.

I jerked his head out of the water and hissed, 'Are you going to apologise for killing me? For doing that to me?'

Hinds tried to arch his back like he was on a bucking bronco in a Benidorm bar throwing the drunk off, but I drilled my knee in the small of his spine holding the ponytail rein tightly. His arms thrashed in the water, and I grabbed one and bent it up his back with my free hand.

'Keep still or I'll break your fucking arm,' I whispered.

Hinds started to shout, 'Fuck off. Cunt! Fuck off. You're killing me. Fight fairly!' Each exclamation climbed a decibel as panic gripped him and the realisation he was being murdered dawned. Fight fairly? What, like you did with an emphysema-ridden old war hero? Shut the fuck up, I thought. Shut up. Stop shouting. Someone will hear. I shoved his head downwards into the water again, more to quell his noise than anything else – tightening my grip on the ponytail – and this time I did not allow his head to rise.

5
A KILLER

MAMA, JUST KILLED a man ...

You couldn't make it up, and I'm not. Queen were singing to me over the car radio within minutes of steering the Jag out of the residential streets of Bridgnorth and on to the motorway home. Mama, I *had* just killed a man. You are correct, Freddie.

Carry on, carry on, as if nothing really matters.

This was all so surreal. What had happened was meant to have happened. Of all the lyrics, in all of the world ... *this* song at *this* time. Knowing that Wally had given Stuart the other medal or he had pinched it out of the drawer. Everything was spot on. How I had gone to Bridgnorth in the first place not knowing what I was going to do. What were the chances I would see him on the bridge? I had been guided and gifted. I felt no guilt, no fear, no pleasure. It was meant to be. It just was.

If it had been solely about revenge I would have driven a screwdriver through Stuart Hinds's eye, deep into the socket, but I could not do a thing like that. I am not a gratuitously violent man, after all. It was about justice, justice for Wally Tombs. It was a natural thing. Nature. I hadn't planned to kill the man, but I *had* planned some revenge. Poor Wally had been let down by the police, the courts, society, us. He had been left to the mercy of the likes of Hinds – unscrupulous, violent, ruthless, evil, a useless individual, scum; one of not so many in 1974 but all too common now – and he had got away with murder because Wally was old and invisible. Well, he hadn't now. He was dead, too, and in his final minutes he would have registered that justice was being meted out at last. I told him when I yanked his head out of the water briefly. What goes around, comes around. He had died quickly. Very quickly. I thought he was faking it. When I let his greasy ponytail go and took my knee off him and stood back I was expecting him to spring up. Spring up and run, and if he had I would not have chased him. I had terrified and damaged him, and he had suffered. He'd be scared for the rest of his days. He would have lived in constant fear I would return. I would have been his own personal Grim Reaper lurking behind every door, about to enter any pub. Hinds would not have reported the incident to the police. I had stared down at his lifeless body and quickly squatted down. I could hear voices on the bridge. Girls. Shouting. I lifted Hinds's head out of the water again. His eyes were wide open but not looking, not there, like a fish on a slab, and there was no doubt that he was dead. Very dead.

Adrenaline coursed through me then. I felt high and, unlike Stuart, very much alive. Slow down. Mustn't get flashed. I marvelled at how easy it had been to kill Stuart Hinds. It had been easier than moving an old fridge from a kitchen to a skip. Easier than crossing a busy road. It had been a piece of piss. The alcohol had made the wanker no match for me. The punch had been a good one and the key to what happened next. I knew I could punch and knew he would hit the deck. If he hadn't, I was ready with a swift combination of nut, fist and boot to finish him off.

I remembered the first time I struck someone properly outside of a boxing ring and the sense of empowerment I felt. Me and Patty Molloy had gone to the Greyhound in Croydon to see Generation X and watched dumbfounded and transfixed at the punks springing in the air and spitting at one another as they watched Billy Idol, the peroxide-blond singer, admiringly. You couldn't forget Billy. Once seen, never forgotten. I didn't think much of the spitting and was ready to lump anyone who spat directly on me. On the way back to our car parked in a sidestreet we were waylaid by a couple of older boys who asked if we had change for a bus fare. One of the boys tried to put his hand into my pocket, and I just flashed my fist upwards and under his chin with all my might, and he keeled over. Pat Molloy looked at me with a whatthehellareyoudoing? look and ran away.

I was left standing alone facing the other lad, who said rather disingenuously, 'What did you do that for?' and knelt and tended to his friend. I said nothing and walked away. That was the first time. Secretly, I had wanted to do it again. It had been a great feeling. Exciting. Powerful. My punch was my secret weapon. It was like walking around knowing I had a gun in my pocket and I was a responsible gun owner. I wouldn't punch unless provoked. For some years I yearned to be provoked. Once I met Jan those violent urges subsided, but now they were back with a vengeance. I think back to people I should have hit. People who should have been dealt with. But they are few, as I was with Jan from an early age. My vengeance is often aimed at people who have never wronged me personally. Like the smarmy doctor on TV or Stuart Hinds.

Today I pray some local lowlife burglar gets in my house. I would show no mercy. They (I hoped for two) wouldn't be tying me up, they wouldn't be terrifying me, I'd be doing it to them. I'd bind them up and knock them about a bit. Then I'd get the electric drill from the garage and walk towards them with it humming and whirring.

'Boys, meet Bosch. He hates robbing, druggy toerags ...'

Of course, I wouldn't do anything fatal with the drill, but you can be certain they'd never rob another house.

Earlier, in my second year at school, I got bashed up. I cannot claim it was bullying, the boy was the year below me – a mere twelve years of age – and about the same height and stamp. His name was Steve Jenkins, and his brother was in my class. We were sitting on the school field one lunchtime, and for some reason Steve was sitting next to me, and I dipped my hand into his packed lunch-box, took out his last egg-and-cress sandwich and bit a big chunk out and replaced it. I was not hungry and guess I wanted to make others who were also there laugh and thought that with Steve being a year younger normal deference would apply.

'What did you do that for?'

'I couldn't resist it, Steve. Egg and cress is my favourite.'

Steve looked around at the four or five sitting on the grass. I could see he was angry. He got to his feet and raised his fists high like an old-fashioned prize fighter. I laughed at him.

'Fight me,' he demanded.

This exchange had taken a strange and unexpected turn. I got to my feet and reluctantly raised my fists, and Steve started to dance around me like Cassius Clay. My eyes followed him, bemused. I threw a punch, which he slipped easily, and then another, which he blocked. Amazingly, the very efficient lunch-break bush telegraph had been activated, and I could see and feel boys from all over the school field descending on us. A chant of 'Fight, fight, fight' emanated from the gathering mass. I was still not connecting, and each miss was making me look increasingly stupid. I attempted to throw my arm around Steve's neck and draw him into a headlock, but he shook free.

'Now, now. Clean fight, gentlemen, please,' said one of the older boys.

And then it was over in seconds. Steve flashed into me with a flurry of well-aimed punches. One straight in the solar plexus which caused me to throw my head forward, delivering it to my opponent on a platter for the obvious uppercut, and then a succession of blows to the head that hastened my descent to the ground. I got on one knee to get up, but Steve stood over me fists raining down like he was hammering a fence post into the ground. I curled up into the foetal position until somebody, mercifully, called, 'Break it up. He's had enough. He's not getting up.'

There was limited blood, and I was helped up by some boys, but the embarrassment and shame were almost unbearable. To be beaten up by a boy from the year below was unimaginable.

His brother came up to me in class in the afternoon and apologised.

'It's my fault,' I said, and I meant it. I knew it was. I had tried to humiliate the kid, and he had done nothing wrong. I had essentially tried to bully him and come a cropper.

Steve Jenkins had set about me like a seasoned pugilist, and I decided I needed to equip myself for any future mishaps and joined a boxing club I was vaguely aware of that operated out of a local youth club. One evening about a week later I strolled in.

Old Frank Mills was the trainer, and he took me under his wing. He was a grey-haired, grizzled man in his sixties who wore a thick fisherman's flecked-wool roll-neck jumper and jeans with unfashionably high turn-ups. Some of the boys said he was related to Freddie Mills, the former boxing champion, but he laughed it off when I asked him.

'Freddie And The Dreamers, more like,' he laughed.

'Hello, Sunny Jim,' he smiled that first evening I walked in. 'You come to learn to box?'

He knew. Frank sparred with me that first day and immediately started building up my strength on the bag and with weights. I soon hit a growth spurt, too, and within a few months I had become big and strong for my age. Frank said I was a natural and had skill and determination. He started to spend a lot of time with me and encouraged me to come into the gym more and more.

He coached me about the 'tool-box' and how you needed all the tools, not just some of them, to really succeed in boxing. He also instructed me about mental strength and humility and not to take advantage of weaker opponents. He probably would not have been happy, had he known, about what I later did that night in Croydon, but I was being mugged, for God's sake. We didn't call it mugging then. That was a term imported from America with uncontained glee by the red-top newspapers a few summers later, and at one point the Yanks even sent over their Guardian

Angels to try and stop it flourishing on our tube lines. The Angels caught my imagination, and for a while I wanted to enlist. The summer lasted longer than the Angels did.

Frank developed me to a degree that I could compete at the Amateur Boxing Association junior level, and with a couple of other boys we travelled to tournaments around the country. If I didn't knock a good opponent down in the early rounds I was quite likely to lose. I rarely won on points. But I stopped a lot of boys. I won a couple of belts and cups. In Essex I was put up against their county's schoolboys' champion, a kid called Hales. He had a big reputation. I was the underdog. Frank instructed me to be very careful, as this kid would try to knock me out in the first round, and the key was to avoid him at all costs and let him wear himself out in the first few rounds and then outbox him. We touched gloves, and I think I floored him within fifteen seconds. He didn't get up. I looked over, and Frank was shaking his head in despair, but a smile played on his lips.

Old Frank discouraged me from going in for the knockout. He said my job was to 'beat them, not beat them up'. He tried to instil in me a more defensive technique and improve my stamina. He said I should also remember that people want to see a fight 'not an execution'. I didn't agree with that. If my best chance was quick and early, then I'd go quick and early. I didn't mind training, but I was never going to allow training to dominate my life. Knowing that, Frank and I could both see I was not going to get to the next level, and my boxing career fizzled out. I had no regrets, and me and Frank never fell out. He said I was the best two-round boy boxer he had ever coached.

As the car gobbled the lines in the road on the M40 returning from Shropshire I wondered what would happen next. Who would find Stuart Hinds? Would murder be obvious? Had my blow marked him? Was his jaw broken? Would the police think he was drunk and had fallen in the river? Did anyone see us there? Or on the bridge? Well, there were the lads who had passed us and the girls on the other side of the road. But would they remember? Everyone was pissed. Were we on tape? If I was arrested or quizzed, what would I say? I would not be able to tell the police that I was avenging a murder from twenty-five years ago. Or would I? Maybe I should. Maybe the attendant publicity would make others think twice before committing such an act? What would Holly think? I jolted. Twisting in the gut. What *would* she think? Her father a murderer. Her mother dead. I mustn't get caught. But I should have taken more care. I couldn't have taken more care. I didn't know I was going to kill the scum. Yes, you did. Why did you park your car miles away outside the old family home? Because if you were questioned afterwards as to why you were in Bridgnorth you'd say you were on a nostalgia visit. It had been easy to kill Stuart Hinds, yet it could have been perfect. If I had known I was definitely going to kill him I'd have made sure I would never have been caught. Next time I'd be more careful. Plan it. What did I mean – next time?

I was shocked after I killed Stuart Hinds. Shocked by how nothing really changed. Shocked by how unshocked I was. I didn't feel different. I didn't feel I was bad. I didn't feel like a murderer. I didn't feel good either. It was almost as if it didn't matter. It was something I had done and that was that. No need for dramatics. I had righted a wrong and committed a wrong in doing that. But I didn't feel like a bad man. I felt like a good man.

The rest of the world, or at least Bridgnorth, thought it didn't matter, too, it seemed. The next day I watched the TV news but soon realised that even if murder was suspected it would not make national headlines. I had scanned the online version of the *Bridgnorth Journal* newspaper forensically in the days and then weeks after the incident, but to no avail. Finally, about three months after my visit and when I had almost stopped thinking about it, I found the following small item in the *Shropshire Star*:

BRIDGNORTH MAN DROWNED FOLLOWING
DRINKING SESSION

The senior coroner for Shropshire, Telford and Wrekin has recorded a verdict of Death by Misadventure in the case of Stuart Gene Hinds, 43, an unemployed welder of Blenheim Court, Bridgnorth. Mr Hinds was found drowned in the River Severn at Cross Bridge on the morning of Saturday March 18th. The coroner commented that Mr Hinds had alcohol in his blood equivalent to more than three times the drink-drive limit.

Sharon Hinds, wife of the deceased, told the court that her husband had shown no signs of depression and that she firmly believed that he had not committed suicide.

And that was that. Not even the police suspected foul play, even if his wife did. They were looking at suicide, more than anything. Surely the autopsy found bruising to his jaw? Apparently not – or if it had been spotted it was attributed to his journey into the water. Somebody must have seen us. If not below the bridge, on the top. It was academic. The case was closed. Nobody had publicly connected Hinds's death to Wally Tombs, and now he was gone, too. Perhaps the police had decided not to break a leg in investigating Hinds's death. He certainly would not have been the most popular man among those trying to hold the line on law and order in the area. I was amused his middle name was Gene. Felt sure his mother must have been a fan of the rock and roller Gene Vincent, who also met an untimely end.

I had planned my contingency should the police find their way to me. I would say that I *did* plan revenge on Stuart Hinds. That I *did* go to Bridgnorth with the intention of confronting him. That I *did* confront him, and we went down to the river to have a tear-up. My story would then diverge from what really happened. I would say Stuart called Wally and old queer and deserved what he got and said, 'Do you want some, too?' and lunged at me. I will say I punched him as he came forward, and he fell back into river. At that point I ran off. I think the most I could be charged with would be manslaughter, but I doubted it would even come to that. If I did have to face a jury I could not see decent men and women convicting me.

It was all so easy, and within a few weeks I – the killer – was not even giving it a second thought. I'd got away with murder because I was meant to. I firmly believed that. Wally Tombs had been avenged, and his memory was no longer the aching sore it had been. My taking revenge on Hinds had been destined, and it had been right. And that was that. Justice had been served. The only shame was that I couldn't shout it from the rooftops. Someone had kicked back. Me. If the establishment would not uphold justice then we the people would. Well, I would. I'd done my bit. Done. Dusted. I like to think that in his dying moments Stuart believed that it was Wally who was killing him. Wally had come back as a younger man and avenged what had been done to his older self. What else could he have thought? That made me feel very, very satisfied. Those awful visions I had about Hinds butchering Wally went. That's the truth.

There was a pang, I'll admit, when I read *Sharon Hinds, wife of the deceased*, hitting home that I had murdered somebody's husband. That didn't sit well. For a minute or two. There might be kids. Children I had made fatherless. Did they run up to him and jump into his lap? There might not be children. If there were I doubt it would have been 'happy families'. More likely he and Sharon were smackheads and any maltreated children rescued by the state years ago. It was war, and in war there are casualties. When the RAF bombed Dresden those men could not have thought about the women and little children they were killing and maiming. They could not. There was a bigger picture, and they had to focus on that. Stuart Hinds had stabbed a defenceless old man, a war hero, through the eye with a bayonet. He deserved to die, and that was all there was to it.

My having dealt with Stuart emboldened me, if I am honest,

and I wanted to right more wrongs. It had been so bloody easy. I was frustrated that I couldn't tell anyone, not so much for my ego but because I wanted people to know that crimes like his do not pay. It will catch up with you in the end despite the supine justice system in place in our land. If everybody knew that Wally Tombs's murder had been avenged, eventually, it would act as a deterrent for some, at least. The killing of one rancid bastard would deter other rancid bastards. I would have saved lives if people just knew.

During my lifetime I had witnessed the end of capital punishment, and we were at a point now where a life sentence barely makes double figures, and if you manage to serve your sentence with good behaviour you'll be out in half that time. We had gone from stringing people up for murder to letting them serve six, seven or eight years in relative comfort. Breaking up rocks on Dartmoor was now a distant memory. Prison sentences were more palatable than they had ever been.

What sort of society are we where we tolerate this approach to those who decide to kill? Especially those who kill for thrills, fun and to satisfy a sexual urge. What thought goes to the loved ones, families and friends of those whose lives have been taken? The least we can do for those left behind and for the victim is to ensure that we impose a proper punishment. It's not ideal, an eye for an eye, but the alternative we operate now is sick, and we have become inured to it.

I had one last dream with Wally in it. The thing about dreams is that when you're in one you don't know it's a dream. It's real. I was in a northern working-men's club. I don't know why. I have never been in one. Games of cribbage are being played. It feels like the 1950s as flat caps are in abundance and the smell of pipe and rolling tobacco permeates the place. Sitting alone is Wally. He's younger and carrying some weight, and I just know this is how he did look when he was this age. I am convinced of that. One day I will see a photograph and prove it to myself. He's wearing a blazer and a shirt and tie, and there's a crease like the edge of an axe in his trousers that ride high up his leg, and on his feet are the heaviest, shiniest tan brogues – Church's or Loake – you have ever seen. Wally calls me over with a curled finger.

'I know what you did,' he said.

'Are you pleased?'

'No, I'm not, boy. I am certainly not pleased.'

'Why?'

'Because two wrongs don't make a right, and besides, *I* was going to deal with it when the time was right.'

I was deflated and confused, but it was kindly said. He wasn't cross. He patted my hand as he said it. And then, inexplicably, he stood up and glided effortlessly between the tables dancing, tap dancing, like Sammy Davis Jr and Fred Astaire combined. Nobody looked up from their beers, from their cribbage boards, nobody took a blind bit of notice. And Wally was graceful, right over the other side now, one hand on his hip, tapping away. With the other hand he had pulled a handkerchief from his blazer breast pocket and was waving it above his head. Make of that what you will. This astral image of Wally, smiling cheekily, trying to catch my eye, spinning the handkerchief over his head, has replaced in my mind the imagined one of his mutilated eye socket and the real one of his heaving chest as the old man tried to catch his breath while he leant on the fence. Mercifully.

6
JAN

I WAS EIGHTEEN, nearly nineteen, when Jan and I first met. James Callaghan was the beleaguered prime minister as the country thrashed around in an economic mire while John Travolta and Olivia Newton-John were providing musical and filmic escapism for many. Washed-out Kodak snaps from the period show I wore a flared collar, lairy shirt and bomber jacket, strutting around like Tony Manero in *Saturday Night Fever*, except without the tins of paint (or the looks).

I had been working for Del Casey, the builder. He had originally taken me on casually and off the cards a while back, later employing me more regularly under the Youth Opportunities Programme when that was brought in. YOPs allowed Del to have the benefit of my labour while the government covered a chunk of my meagre wage. For them it was one more number off the unemployment register and for me it was slightly better than signing on. A few years later UB40's 'One In Ten' would help shame the politicians into trying to do something about jobless, hopeless and aimless youths.

It wasn't a good time for the older generation either. Dad's employer had gone bust. They sold typewriters for Remington, Singer, Imperial and others. Operating from the middle of the country, they placed machines all over the United Kingdom. Dad was assured in his role as sales director, and when he was made redundant they took his self-esteem as well as his living from him. It was awful to see.

'I'm fifty,' he lamented. 'Who will employ me? I'm finished.'

Listening to my dad say that and holding back his tears tore me up inside. Mum seemed unsympathetic at the time, but I guess she was only trying to buck his ideas up.

'You need to snap out of it, Alan. People will always need typewriters. People will always write letters. You can sell. You know that, and other employers will see that. It's a blow, but it's not a knockout blow.'

How little my mum knew. She was right, he got other 'positions', but his tenures became shorter and shorter, and she was wrong because people didn't always need typewriters, and a thing called the word processor eventually came along. Dad was not going to retrain. Dad was right, career-wise he was finished at fifty.

I had agreed to go and work for Del while I decided what it was I really wanted to do with my life. The situation with Dad taught me that trusting your career to employers and companies was foolhardy, leaving you in a precarious situation, even if you did think you were valued and got feted annually at the Salesman Of The Year dinner. I could see these so-called secure jobs with pensions that we were taught to aspire to were not what they seemed. I resolved to control my own destiny but had no idea how.

'You decided what you're going to do?' Dad had said months earlier with his back to me, as he stood in the lounge rearranging golf cups in the cabinet.

'No, not yet.'

'Well, you can't doss around for the rest of your life.'

'I haven't even left school properly yet, Dad.'

'You need to take an apprenticeship. Or get in with a big company on the clerical side.'

I curled my lip.

'You can pull a face all you want. But don't think you can live here for nothing.'

'Working for a big company hasn't worked out so good for you, has it?'

His aside, which I took as an accusation of poncing off them, had made me want to hurt him verbally. Dad stepped forward and went to smack me around the head with his open hand. I blocked it instantaneously with a raised arm and threw a punch at his chin, pulling it theatrically at the last millisecond. I brushed his chin. Then I turned and left the room, and the incident was never mentioned again. I don't know if he told Mum. I doubt it. I didn't. I was ashamed and felt sorry for him. I should have apologised.

I worked hard for Mr Casey because I found that way it made the day go quicker, and once he'd got wind of the new YOPs scheme he asked me if I wanted to 'come on full time', which I already thought I was. Nevertheless, my money jumped, and as I still had not found what I wanted to do with my life I agreed.

I hadn't intended to stay with Del Casey for long, but it seemed to suit me. When they laid me off now and then as work dried up I got a start on a building site from an advert in the evening paper or from down the pub. Brickies, even young ones short on experience, were always in demand. It wasn't what I wanted to do, but I was self-sufficient and paid Dad the housekeeping money he craved.

The little gang I was with had a start on an extension in Hadley Wood. Del was rubbing his hands because it was a big three-storey job and the customer had pots of money. Had to have living in Hadley Wood. Spike Milligan and various Spurs and Arsenal footballers lived up the road, Del reckoned.

'Lots of opportunity for add-ons,' Del Casey observed greedily.

It had not taken me long to work Del out. His main aim was to maximise the take from each job while doing the least amount of work, often at the cost of the end relationship with the customer. Attrition was a feature of almost every job. This client in Hadley Wood, however, was no pushover. Indeed, Mr Jacobs was the sort of customer that Del Casey detested. He was on his case. Inspecting the work daily. Having weekly budget meetings. Debating how overruns could be retrieved. Limiting the extras.

'Fucking Jewish. They want to squeeze out every last penny,'

Del complained because he had come up against someone who was preventing him from doing exactly that.

I was unsure how my boss had arrived at the conclusion the customer was Jewish, but he seemed to know. I didn't think his wife could be. She was small and blonde and, if anything, looked Nordic. She had been the perfect customer's wife. Delivering tea and ginger-nut biscuits at almost hourly intervals. Smiling and chatting. Tapping her feet to Boney M. emanating from our cement-encrusted transistor radio lodged on the windowsill.

'I would fuck that,' Joey Casey (Del's son) remarked most days.

He said this as if he was being generous with his highly sought-after sexual favours or was particularly fussy about who he had sexual intercourse with, when I was sure, in reality, he would be unlikely to spurn any female. Joey was a dosser. Resented knocking up muck. Preferred to be elsewhere. Numb and snappy in the mornings from amphetamine abuse the night before. To my utter shock his dad did drugs with him. Where and from whom they would source their speed was a regular subject of conversation during tea breaks.

'It's old, but she's still got it,' Joey would say about Mrs Jacobs, rocking his hips backwards and forwards simulating sexual intercourse when she walked out of the room.

I became more and more annoyed as he referred to our kind and attentive customer as *it* and *that*.

Mrs Jacobs did still have it, I had to agree. I did not have a regular girlfriend or even an irregular one. I had lost my virginity to my first and only girlfriend awkwardly in Trent Park a couple of years before, while her fat old family Labrador tried to join in the fun nuzzling my ears and neck as we writhed in the grass. I had sustained a smidgeon of a sex life with her for a year or so afterwards, either on the floor or the sofa at her house and later in my Ford Escort, but we had mutually allowed our romance to fizzle out, there being no overpowering attraction or strong bond between us.

Mrs Jacobs often wore a thin, neat, black polo neck – which accentuated her shape – a pair of leggings that ended just over the knee and open sandals. She didn't seem old to me. There was a hint of crow's feet around her eyes when she smiled, but this added to her allure. She smiled a lot, and I felt sure she smiled at me the most. But there was no definitive flirtation. She was the house owner, and I got on with the job.

Inevitably I had to watch and slink into the background, embarrassed as the relationship between Del and Mr Jacobs deteriorated. Mr Jacobs became frustrated and angry over budget and time overruns, and Del, likewise, over what he saw as Mr Jacobs's intransigence. Mrs Jacobs and I exchanged knowing looks while all this was going on. Our eyes had clearly transmitted the message to each other that we did not necessarily approve of either man's stance. Del and his son pulled off the job and moved on to the next one leaving me alone to deal with wrapping up and the numerous 'snagging' jobs that Mr Jacobs insisted were carried out. I was the snagging boy.

'Call me, Jan, Paul,' said Mrs Jacobs after she had invited me into the kitchen to drink the tea she had just made us. The weather was turning, and she motioned me to come inside. 'Short for Janet.'

That morning she sat on a high kitchen stool chatting, laughing and kicking her legs out like an excited little girl. I was amazed at how tall her refrigerator was and how it dispensed ice cubes and iced water like a vending machine. She asked me about my life and told me a bit about hers. Her husband Gary was the in-house lawyer for a mining company based in London. His work took him all over the world, especially South Africa. Gary's family did not really enthuse over their marriage as she was a 'gentile' and he a Jew, but they had come around to the idea. I couldn't believe that people still allowed all this Bible stuff to govern their personal lives. They had been married sixteen years. She was thirty-seven years old. Her husband eight years older. There were no children. They would have liked to have had children, but it just hadn't happened, and she doubted if it would now.

I cannot be sure if it was that first long conversation in the kitchen (three cups of tea each were slowly consumed to lend our bonding some legitimacy) or one of the other tea breaks that followed in the ensuing days, but I think I fell in love with Jan that first occasion.

'You should work for yourself,' she announced one afternoon. 'You're a hard grafter. You know what you are doing. You deal with the suppliers better than your boss does, and you have customer-relations skills,' she laughed as she said this and put her hand on my arm. 'No, seriously, you should. Why don't you?'

'I've never considered it,' I replied. 'I'm too young. Nineteen. People don't take you seriously. I'm not much more than a kid. I don't have any money. A van. You need money …'

'Nonsense. What money? Mr Casey took money off Gary from day one. The customer provides the cashflow. Hire a van, and then buy one with the profit from your first job. You'll do a good job. You'll get recommended. Mr Casey makes a living – a good one, I should think – and I bet he doesn't get his work through word of mouth. He gets his work because he's there. Am I right?'

I nodded. Flattery emboldened me. This little elfin lady made it all sound so easy. Her confidence in me was exhilarating.

Lengthening tea-and-chat sessions were off the agenda within a few weeks, as Del pulled me off and on to the next job. Regretfully, I said goodbye to Jan, and she wiped her hands on a tea cloth and offered me her hand. I wasn't sure whether to grasp it, shake it or kiss it. I took it awkwardly and she laughed and clasped mine with her free one.

'You remember what I said, now. Next time I see you I want to see you in a truck with Paul … what's your second name?'

'Garfield.'

'Garfield? That's an unusual name. I've never met a Garfield. Are there any famous Garfields?'

'There was a famous Hollywood star called John Garfield. Have you heard of him? He was before my time. My mum remembers him.'

'Never heard of him. Before my time, too – believe it or not! Next time I see you I want to see PAUL GARFIELD in big letters on the side of your van.'

'OK,' I smiled weakly, walking backwards to the front door. I wanted to say more but had no idea what. When I got into my old Escort I could see in my rear-view mirror that she was still standing on the doorstep, seeing me off. Waving. I felt strange. Really, really strange. She was old enough to be my mum. Twice my age. But I was churned up and devastated that I might not see her again. I nearly cried.

Jan was in my head from that day on. I found myself attracted to her strongly. The men and boys on sites would sometimes talk about the 'Divorcee and Singles Nights' they attended. They weren't even married, let alone divorced. Yet they went to these things because the general idea was that divorced and separated women were desperate for sex and would supply it with no ties. 'Grab-a-Granny' they sordidly called it. How successful they really were, I questioned. I had learnt to believe only about 10 per cent of the stuff you heard on building sites. The point was, when they talked like this, I did not understand why they would want to grab grandmothers in the first place. There were plenty of discos and pubs bulging with young women and girls who were on the market. To want to have sex with women in their thirties, forties or even fifties had struck me as strange.

Until now. Jan shimmered. Now I could see that everything about her was beautiful. From her feather-cut hair to her sculptured hands. Her pert little bottom and breasts. Not a trace of make-up. Everything about her was natural. Healthy. Right. She was to be worshipped, not lusted after. Joey's remarks nagged at me, and I wanted to defend her honour and smack him. But she was married. Rich. Out of my league. She *had* shown an interest in me. I had sensed some attraction on her part. But could I be sure? Was she just a nice person? Bit lonely, maybe? Liked a chat?

Against my better judgement, I went out with Joey Casey and his mates one night around this time 'on the pull'. The venue was Tiffany's in Purley. In my mum's time it had been the Orchid Ball-room, now it was riding the disco boom, and single girls and boys – their hormones tuned up – turned up on a Saturday night in their droves. Joey said you had to ask girls to dance. I watched him approach a girl, and she said yes, and they stood a few feet apart jigging from side to side to 'Native New Yorker' by Odyssey. I thought how ridiculous they would look if there were no music. They never held each other and at the end walked backwards to their own little clusters.

'And? What was that? You looked a right earole.'

'Well, I've broken the ice, ain't I? When the slow ones come at the end you dive in for the smooch. Get among them, mate. Then you snog 'em and then, who knows? He who dares. Onwards and upwards.'

He motioned to my glass and made the tipping motion then strode off to the bar to fetch more pints of foaming Tuborg. More drink was spilt in here than drunk, testament to this was walking to and from that bar on the sticky carpet. It was like wading through Marmite.

The opening bars of 'Can't Get Enough Of Your Love, Babe' and Barry White purring through the speakers and washing over us all like luv lotion was the signal that smooch time had arrived. Joey sprang up and practically yanked his target on to the dance-floor. His mates did the same, and I was left standing alone as people floated past me. Couples clinging to one another turning slowly like a plate in a microwave. Girls, liberated by alcohol, were nestling their faces into their dance partners' necks, some were even openly kissing like they had known each other for years, and adventurous hands were resting on and even squeezing receptive soft buttocks. I felt like a prat and contemplated going to the toilet or buying another drink.

We've shared love and made love (well, well, well) ...

I saw a girl looking at me, and she did not look away when she saw me looking back. A faint smile twitched on her lips. We were both tiptoeing around potential rejection. Like diving off the higher board at the swimming baths for the first time, I jumped. I found myself in front of her.

'Would you like to dance?'

'OK, then,' she shrugged but smiled encouragingly.

We walked slowly on to the dancefloor, and as I rested my hands carefully and politely on her hips, she joined her fingers around the back of my neck drawing me closer until our fronts were touching. Barry ran out of steam and stopped singing. I let go. I moved to untangle. I was terrified something fast would come on like 'Under The Moon Of Love' by Showaddywaddy, and I'd be expected to rock 'n' roll jive. Hands on hips. Thankfully, the opening bars of 'Rock Your Baby' by George McCrae floated in to the rescue.

'Don't you like this one?' she asked.

'Love it.'

By the end of the record it was as if we were a long-standing couple. Our bodies pressed up against each other, and somehow our tongues ended up twirling inside each other's mouths. I soon had an erection that was battling to escape my pants and trousers, and when she felt it against her she pressed against me harder. It remains one of the most erotic moments of my life. George was the final record of the night. The lights came on at the end as couples unlocked, blinking away the strobe lights flashing in our vision, we were both not disappointed at the appearance of each other in the unforgiving unnatural natural light.

'I enjoyed that,' she said, smiling knowingly, referencing our little trouser secret, I thought.

'So did I,' I replied relieved my erection was subsiding just a bit.

'I live in Mogador,' she said. 'Do you want my phone number?'

Mogador sounded like somewhere Dr Who might visit.

'Yes, please.'

She took a pen and a bus ticket from her handbag and wrote Julie and a number on it.

'Thanks. I will call you in the week, Julie.'

'Well, I look forward to that ... what's your name?'

'Dave. Dave.'

Why I said Dave I don't know. It was a quick reaction. I could understand if I was married or in a relationship. I just panicked.

Back indoors I lay on the bed – the beer I was unused to drinking in large quantities still swilling around my insides like a wave pool – and studied the bus ticket. It was for a journey from last week in central London. I guess Julie worked in the City. Probably in a bank. She was really pretty and seemed a nice girl, and I fancied her. However, I screwed the ticket up and lobbed it into the wire wastepaper basket across the room. Kicked off my shoes, closed my eyes and thought only about Mrs Jacobs. Jan.

'Fucker,' Del Casey senior growled as he hurled the telephone receiver across the desk and left it bouncing by its curly lead mid-air. Mr Jacobs had again refused to pay the final instalment of his bill.

'He says he ain't paying until we come back and do the snagging and finish the patio.'

'We haven't really started the patio,' his son pointed out.

'And we are not going to,' Del said. 'There's no money left in the job.'

'If we do the patio then you'll get the rest of your money,' I said.

'It costs. I've lost a packet on this wanker. He's trying to ruin me. He's squeezing my goolies. I've a good mind to go round there and rip the fucking extension down.'

'I'll finish the patio and the snagging. I'll do it evenings and weekends. It won't take too long,' I offered.

Del needed some convincing. I said I'd do it for nothing.

'You're after his old woman, you are,' sneered young Casey.

'Fuck off. I'm trying to help. We don't want to make an enemy of Jacobs. He'll be delivering leaflets saying we're cowboys, then where will we be?'

'Yee-haw.'

'He's got a point,' said the father, thinking pound notes.

'Yeah, yeah,' Junior nodded knowingly. 'Paul's after drilling the old woman. Just admit it, mate. Who offers to do work for nothing?'

I shrugged, knowing my eagerness had given me away, but I tried to portray indifference. But the blood rushed to my head, and I had to look away and then down at the floor. I nearly lost control, and it was scary. Del, his son and 'Roger Whittaker' – the other labourer, who had a beard hence his unimaginative nickname, who hadn't said a word as usual but was laughing – had no idea how close they were, all of them, to being spread across the office that day. I was thinking about uppercutting big-mouth son between the legs and into his groin – no more grabbing grannies for him – and then throttling his old man with the telephone wire until the blood vessels in his eyes burst. Roger Whittaker, knowing what was best for him, would be halfway back to Durham town.

Destiny. If I hadn't gone back and finished that patio my life would have taken a very different course. That first week and weekend Mr Jacobs was away visiting a platinum mine in South Africa, and Jan and I bonded some more. On the Saturday she drove into Barnet and collected a Chinese takeaway, and we ate it together. She produced a bottle of wine from the fridge, and we drank it. It was the first wine I had ever tasted. I liked it. Jan asked me about girlfriends. I told her about the only one I had had. She hinted that she was not entirely happy with her husband by being slightly disparaging about him. Things were moving fast. Then Mr Jacobs returned home, and the relationship reverted to strictly professional. We were getting our first practice at deception.

During the following week Mr Jacobs was away again, this time in England, but a mid-week trip. Jan fetched Chinese again for when I had finished my collar at about 9 pm and it was getting dark. I noticed she had changed into a cheesecloth shirt with a black bra visible underneath. Had she done this deliberately to attract me, or was I reading too much into it? It's a minefield.

At 10 pm I said I'd best go. Jan suggested that I move my van a couple of roads away and come back on foot. She said it would stop tongues wagging, and we could then open another bottle of Sancerre. There was now no doubt now that something was going to take place! I tried to do this in a leisurely manner but could barely contain my excitement. That heart-drumming sensation of sexual expectancy made me weak at the knees. As I walked back into the drive and pushed at the open door, I cursed my erection already demanding attention.

I was feeling awkward and not up to the occasion. If, indeed, it was an occasion. I could still be wrong. I leant forward on the sofa to obscure the swelling of my genitals. She passed me a glass, and instead of sitting in the armchair joined me on the sofa. She started to talk hurriedly about having to set the video for something her husband wanted her to tape.

'Oh, forget it,' she garbled. 'It'll be repeated. Do you find me attractive?'

'Pardon?'

'Oh, nothing. It's the wine. I'm tiddly.' She moved away slightly and laughed at her own impudence.

'Yes, I do. Very attractive.'

'You're not too bad yourself.'

'Thank you.'

'Thank you.'

'Thank you.'

'Thank you.'

We were both giggling. I leant over to her, and she opened her arms wide in an over-dramatic receiving gesture, and I climbed upon her kissing her furiously. She licked my face back like a dog and bit my ear lobe. We were naked in record time and rolling on the floor. When we had finished – or rather, when *I* had finished, which was only a minute or three after the first kiss – Jan lay there and sighed, 'Thank God, that's over with.'

'Oh,' I said, lost for words. Crestfallen.

'No, no, you idiot. Thank God we did it. It had to happen sooner or later.'

And it happened again three more times that evening before I slipped out into the night. Walking on air, drained but filled with elation in a way I had never before experienced.

7
DAD

EVENTS MOVED AT an astonishing speed thereafter. Love was declared. 'Love Is In The Air' was our song. I cannot listen to it now. If it comes on I have to leave the room. Every word, every bar conjures up the power of our love that only got stronger and has now been taken away. John Paul Young's voice taunts me with what has gone. What has been taken. I cannot rationalise what happened to Jan. She was clean-minded and clean-living. Fit in body and spirit. Kind. Decent. Giving. Caring. But she was snatched and butchered. Yet the earth crawls with disgusting scum who will live out their lifespans, harming and destroying along the way.

Dreams were shared. Trysts were had. In the February of 1979 Jan left her husband. She told him that she had fallen in love with Paul – the builder, the young one, the snagging boy – and he was filled with disgust rather than rage. His first question was whether we had done it in their bed. She answered honestly that we had not and to spare his feelings lied that it had never happened in the house. He called her a whore. A child-molester. A bitch. She said she did not want a penny from him. Later, much later, and following a quick divorce where she made no claim on any of their assets at all, he very fairly sent her a cheque for £25,000. In return he wanted a solicitor's letter saying she would make no claims against him in the future. Jan would have been happy to have done that anyway. Mr Jacobs was not a bad man, and I hope he found contentment.

My now-estranged (from one another) parents were surprised

by the relationship. Jan was not much younger than my mother. Dad was bemused but got on well with Jan. Proud of his son at pulling such a classy, mature woman. Scandalously, his own new girlfriend was even younger than Jan. She was from Thailand. Dad had met her on a golfing trip. Mum and Dad's last holiday together had been to Clacton. Things were changing in the world.

It was a shame I didn't have much of a relationship with my old man. My parents separated emotionally long before they did physically and legally. I knew inside that they stayed together for my benefit, and sensing this as a teenager was not a good feeling. My dad was a hard person to live with. He had been brought up a certain way and expected his domestic life to mirror that. They didn't have a joint bank account, which was the cause of many whispered arguments in the house. My mum had to ask my dad to 'give' her money. He never asked her how her day was. I wasn't surprised when Mum left him within a couple of years of my leaving school.

I never understood why they got married in the first place; they were so different. Dad was older and had a sales 'position' with a car. In those days – the late 1950s – that really meant something. Her friends were mainly dating apprentices and office juniors. Dad elevated Mum into a different world at a very young age. The age difference set the tone of the relationship. Dad was the senior partner. His needs, his desires, his wants came first. Don't get me wrong, Mum was no shrinking violet and would argue her corner, it's just that after about ten years of marriage she began to wonder what she was doing in a corner in the first place. They first dated when she was sixteen or seventeen and Dad was twenty-five, and from courtship they followed the then respectable, well-trodden path of engagement to marriage four years later.

My suspicion is that the reason I am an only child was that Mum didn't want to deepen her connection to Dad any further. She didn't want the prison wall around her to be built any higher. In her eyes she had voluntarily (and naively) entered a prison, and she would serve her sentence until her parole date, which was when I left home.

This makes my parents' marriage sound dramatic and awful, but it wasn't all bad. They rarely argued in front of me, and I can remember good times. Times when they sat and watched TV together. Laughing at *Doctor In The House*, crying at *The Forsyte Saga*. As far as I know my dad never struck my mum, but there was a stifled despair that followed them around. It's sad looking back on it. When she upped sticks and went and moved in with her sister I was shocked and upset. I was eighteen years of age and experimenting with living in a flat, but their separation cut the feet from under me. I now had no home to return to if I had wanted to.

Dad didn't waste his time. He and a pal from the golf club went to Thailand, and Dad came back raving about it and revealed he had fallen in love with a Thai lady called Piti, twenty years his junior. Dad said her name was Thai for 'joyful'. Mum said she *pitied* her for falling into Dad's clutches. Although Piti was perfectly pleasant to me, I never took to her. Her devotion to my dad didn't ring true. She was a looker, still very youthful. He suddenly looked and acted ten years older than his fifty-something years.

'She washes my feet, son. Your mother would never do that.'

I should fucking hope not, I thought but didn't say. He hinted about having energetic sex with Piti and I cringed. The thought of my dad having sex at his advanced age shocked me – and the fact that his partner was not too much older than me made me shudder. The whole Thai-bride phenomenon was a very new thing then.

I made little effort to keep in touch with him, and that fills me with regret and guilt, knowing what happened next. Piti left my dad, too. Once her passport was secure and she had laid some foundations in this country, she summoned over from Thailand a grown-up daughter – whom I don't know whether Dad even knew existed – and soon the pair of them had left him. His relationship with Piti endured just three short years.

Me and Mum even had a laugh at his expense down the phone

at his naivety. I regret that now as well. Tragically he declined rapidly after Piti pissed off. He was ultimately found dead in bed, in his flat, having drunk himself to oblivion within a few years. He had just made sixty. He had always drunk heavily, and I think this is why I never have (heavily). Drink made him morose and even more negative than when he was sober. Dad was definitely a glass-half-empty man. In fact, after his slow-motion suicide, I remembered that he used to say 'We'll jump off that bridge when we come to it' rather than 'We'll cross that bridge ...' I only realised how odd that saying of his was after he died.

Those last few years were miserable for him. Mum remarried, to Bill, and was very happy. The happier Mum was, the more unhappy Dad became. We had a birthday party for Holly at the house, and Mum, diplomatically, did not bring Bill. Dad turned up unshaven, possibly having had a drink and looking awful. He did his best to appear and act as if he was together, but he wasn't. I noticed stains on his trousers and dirt underneath his fingernails. He had lost his last real job soon after Piti joined him in the UK, and, despite his cabinet full of Salesman Of The Year trophies, nobody wanted him. At Holly's party I noticed him looking at Mum with longing and regret. It was so sad, and I became haunted about the time I nearly hit him when the world he knew and felt so secure in was collapsing around him. I thanked God that I hadn't struck him that day.

I was so glad that I worked for myself. I've never understood corporate loyalty. You could work for a company for years, but once you hit the wrong side of forty you were on borrowed time. Few people these days survive in an office environment to the traditional retirement age of sixty-five. Companies themselves have shorter and shorter lifespans. Even the person who made you redundant gets made redundant in the end. It's like water cooler *Goodfellas* in the office now. Once a made man's usefulness expires he gets taken out. Dad had been trebly rejected in a short space of time: Mum, job and then Piti. Applying for jobs and not even getting replies, let alone interviews, drained his self-esteem. I guess that's when he started drinking in earnest.

It makes me angry now when I think about Mr Gage. Dennis Gage. He ran the typewriter-and-office-equipment business that Dad worked for. He may even have owned it, I'm not sure. Dad used to talk about him a lot when I was very young. Mr Gage this and Mr Gage that. And then it was Dennis. Dennis says. Dennis thinks. Dennis has gone here and Dennis has gone there. Dennis deigned to come to our house once, and it sickened me to see Dad fawning all over him and even Mum practically curtseying to him. He was Dad's boss, for fuck's sake, not King Constantine of Greece.

When they got rid of Dad it became Gage. Not Dennis. Not Mr Gage. Dad couldn't believe they would 'let him go'. He'd thought he was part of the inner circle. The title of director meant nothing at the end of the day. I asked Dad why he didn't go around to Gage's place and bash him up in front of his wife and teenage kids. That would make him feel better.

'You can't go round doing things like that, Paul.'

'You can,' I replied. 'What have you got to lose?'

'Oh, let's see. Maybe about three years of my liberty ...?'

I wanted to go round and do it. I wanted revenge for my dad and to restore some of his dignity. I'd do three years for my old man at the drop of a hat. But I knew instinctively that if I did it would make him feel worse, not better. Possibly push him over the edge.

My dad paid the price for Dennis Gage's business incompetence. He should have seen the direction in which things were moving. He should have prepared the business to adapt, to shift into new markets, but he didn't. Too busy swinging a golf club or shagging his secretary probably. So my dad had to go. I bet Gage is still around now. He probably rode the recession and is back on top. But did he ever think of phoning my dad and offering him a job? Did he fuck.

*

First, Jan and I moved into a tiny flat in Whetstone, and then, when Jan's money from Mr Jacobs landed, we put a large deposit down on a semi-detached house in Thornton Heath, Surrey. Jan knew the area well as she had grown up in Purley, down the road. She felt it was here we could make a fresh start, and I was happy to be guided by her. In the June of 1981 we were married. Jan was by now forty years old, and I was twenty-two.

'Just think,' she laughed, 'we wouldn't be allowed to go on a Club 18–30 holiday together.'

I worked briefly for a local builder in Croydon, but Jan insisted I went out on my own despite my relative youth. It was now or never. She took me out, and we purchased a nearly new Ford Transit van, which she then had signwritten GARFIELD & CO. BUILDERS. I puffed up with pride when I saw it, although the adult responsibility and fear of the unknown weighed me down.

'What have we got to lose, sweetie?' she counselled. 'If it doesn't work out, and it will, but if it doesn't you, just go back and work for someone. It's logical. If you're hardworking, honest and good at your job you cannot fail. How many builders do you really think are out there that have those three attributes?'

Put like that I could not argue. I was struggling to think of any. Meanwhile Jan had taken a job at a high-street building society, and her wage was just about enough to cover our bills. She also got a subsidised fixed mortgage. As interest rates rocketed that became more and more important. She was astute, this woman.

Jan's foresight and determination paid off. Through the building society she found a surveyor who would work with me on drawings. I already knew plasterers, plumbers and roofers I could call upon and soon replaced those contacts as we found better ones. We placed advertisements in the Yellow Pages, Thomson Local and local papers and went out together each night pushing leaflets we had had printed up at Prontaprint through hundreds of letter boxes all around the Croydon area.

Jan answered every telephone call with 'Garfield and Company, can I help you?' just in case it was a potential client, and very soon one did call. An elderly couple in Birdhurst Rise wanted their front garden slabbed over as they were becoming too frail to tend to it. I went to see them and quoted them £500. I charged myself out at a labourer's wage and knew this would be competitive because anybody else would be putting something on the materials, charging a tradesman's daily rate and estimating five days. I got the job and worked from 7 am to 7 pm. I was finished in two and a half days and told the couple that the actual cost would only be £390. They were thrilled and confided in me that my quote had been only around half the next nearest.

'I think I diddled myself,' I complained to Jan when I went home with the cash. 'I should have quoted more, and I shouldn't have charged them less when I finished.'

'Not at all. What are they going to do? I'll tell you what they'll do. They will be raving about you and telling everybody they know. Who has ever heard of a builder coming in below the estimate? Or even sticking to the estimate? You've hit on our USP! You clever little boy.'

'USP?'

'Unique Selling Point. They talk all this gobbledegook on the courses the building society sends me on. What you did today was smart. Very smart. Phone won't stop ringing.'

It didn't quite work out like that, but more jobs did arrive, and I learnt not to quote so leanly and most of the time was still able to come in under the estimate. The goodwill this generated with the customers was highly disproportionate to the pain that we needed to absorb to achieve it. Within a year nearly all jobs were word of mouth, and as my confidence grew so did the scale and complexity of the jobs I was able to take on. This was a good thing, because by this time Jan had given birth to Holly and had to go part-time at the building society.

Through the 1980s and 1990s Garfield & Co. grew solidly.

The name was changed to Garfield Design & Build to reflect the business's growing stature and sophistication. At peak times I had twenty people working for me. Jan took us into the property-development game. Through her contacts at the building society she was getting to hear about repossessions in the local area, and we were buying them direct from the lender before they even reached an estate agent or auctioneer, tidying and toshing them up, sometimes whacking in a new kitchen and bathroom and then selling them on. When the values fell and property became harder to move, we left it alone. From Thornton Heath we bought a larger semi-detached house in central Croydon, and from there a detached in South Croydon and finally a smart mock-Tudor detached place in Purley. When the time came we were able to put Holly on the property ladder, buying a flat in her name in Sanderstead when she was just sixteen, but were a bit miffed when, just a few weeks later, she announced her intention to move into it immediately. We had a Jeep each, and, once Bubbles flowered and we could rely on him to keep the business running, we holidayed as much as we could. It had become a wonderful life until the day that Jan came out of the bathroom, ashen faced, having discovered a lump in her breast.

8
JANICE AND HELEN

IN 2003 A scandal broke in the tabloid press that caught my attention. It was a resurrection of one of a clutch of high-profile crimes that I remembered from my childhood and youth that had shocked and appalled the country but were nevertheless eagerly devoured by the public. There was the Black Panther, who kidnapped and murdered teenage travel heiress Lesley Whittle and imprisoned her in a drain with a rope around her neck for days; then we had the Cambridge Rapist, who terrorised the university town for months breaking, entering and raping sleeping girls and women; and, most notoriously, a little later the Yorkshire Ripper, who waged bloody war on defenceless prostitutes and innocent, helpless young women. They were nonentities, these scum – Donald Neilson, Peter Samuel Cook and Peter Sutcliffe – losers who wouldn't stand out in a Friday-night fish-and-chip queue. Nondescript men with nondescript names, but the media elevated them by awarding them titles like 'panther' and 'ripper'. Bestowing criminal kudos. They undoubtedly loved the notoriety and their 'celebrity' status, and their media-driven identities emboldened and flattered them and probably encouraged them to commit more crimes than they otherwise would have done.

What did they have in common these panthers, rippers and rapists? They all murdered girls and women. They were cowards and bullies, every one of them. These serial killers don't normally stalk men. Women and children first. Despicable pond-life. Bottom feeders. They should be exterminated, yet we pamper them in prisons, swallow their bullshit about mental illness – and sometimes we even let the fuckers out.

Not among the aforementioned was another dirtbag who had aroused my ire a few years before. Even prior to dealing with Stuart Hinds I had imagined, but never seriously planned, killing him. His name was Russell Bishop, and he was notorious for murdering two little girls down Brighton way, and he had got away with it. A jury somehow contrived to reach a not-guilty verdict, and there he was cruising around his council estate in his Ford Capri like butter wouldn't melt in his mouth. I had considered driving down and running into him and giving him the hiding of his life. Bash-the-Bishop time. Even to the point of kicking the life out of him. But I was happy with Jan and Holly and knew it would get me time rather than brownie points. I couldn't comprehend why his own people hadn't dealt with him. Whatever happened to rough justice? When he was eventually imprisoned for the abduction and attempted murder of another terrified young girl I assumed that somebody would get to him in prison.

After Stuart Hinds I thought about Bishop again – more and more. I guessed he would come up for parole at some point, and those ridiculous, supine wankers on the Parole Board would likely grant it. I took some comfort from knowing that if he ever did get released, and I was still alive and fit, that I would murder him. Indeed, it began to frustrate me that by being in prison Bishop was escaping *my* justice. I considered targeting the jury that acquitted him of slaughtering those two poor girls. I fantasised about taking them out one by one and the media and the police not catching on until number three had been executed. Can you imagine the frenzy that would have been unleashed? A sort of *Kind Hearts And Coronets* scenario but all too real. That would have made future juries think carefully before finding child killers not guilty. I abandoned the notion, however, when I realised that not only would it be hard to identify the twelve but some on the jury might well have argued for a guilty verdict. I even thought about his mum. She had a public profile as someone who showed at Crufts dog show, and I knew hurting her would really, really hurt Russell Bishop. But I couldn't hurt a woman, and she was innocent, and my aim was not just to hurt my victim it was to achieve something wider.

In 2003, however, it was Frank Cox all over the front pages and in the news bulletins once more. Reading about him again took me back to the impossibly hot summer of 1976. I had by then left school and was working on the building sites in my cap-sleeved T-shirt and Levi cut-downs as the sun scorched everything in its wake. 'Misty Blue' by Dorothy Moore and Candi Staton's 'Young Hearts Run Free' captured the time and the place. There was a water shortage, and a hapless minister of drought was appointed, an early indicator that governments were beginning to fantasise they could influence the weather. No shortage of lager, though. The customers of steaming, sweaty pubs spilled out on to the high streets like human puddles, and whooshing and streaking briefly became fads. The former involved people throwing pints of beer over each other, and the latter removing all one's clothes and running around naked, particularly during sporting events. The drought and heatwave were a crisis that most openly enjoyed; only those who felt that the banning of hosepipes for watering gardens was an infringement of their civil liberties protested.

The fun, games and browning of the population was interrupted by a dark event. Two hitchhikers, Janice Jarvis and Helen Flannery, were thumbing a lift to a large open-air concert headlined by the Rolling Stones at Knebworth, deep in the Hertfordshire countryside. It was a big event, and eventually more than 200,000 people were said to have attended. Tragically, Janice and Helen never made it. The two Yorkshire teenagers – Janice was seventeen and Helen nineteen – stood in a layby on the A1 near their homes in Doncaster and stuck their thumbs out, as hitchhikers do. It was hot even at 6.30 am when they set out. Both girls carried backpacks and were dressed in T-shirts and shorts. Helen's shorts were very short – 'hotpants', the press insisted.

Frank, a twenty-seven-year-old double-glazing salesman, picked them up in his silver Ford Cortina, replete with a black-vinyl roof. He told them he was headed south and could drop them some way further down the A1. Janice and Helen never made the event, never got to see the Rolling Stones, 10cc or the breakout band on the bill, Lynyrd Skynyrd. Cox was the only known living person who had any idea of what exactly happened that Saturday morning, but the facts are that about halfway to Knebworth he left the main road and ended up in a farmer's field on a country lane near the town of Bourne in Lincolnshire. Somehow, he managed to rape and strangle the two girls and leave them face down in what had been a small stream before the fearsome sun had drunk all the water. Their parents did not report them missing until the Monday morning, assuming they had continued their open-air rock-concert adventure late into Sunday, but they had been concerned that neither girl had thought to search out a phone box and contact their families.

The two girls' broken and defiled bodies were discovered on Tuesday by a couple out walking their dog. Both Janice and Helen had suffered severe beatings, although it has never been clear how their attacker subdued the other while battering, raping and killing the other. There were no signs of gagging or any form of restraint. 'The Hitchhiker Murders' was splashed all over the media. The black-and-white image of the innocent, laughing girls together – taken in a booth at a Boots in Doncaster – was beamed into front rooms across the country. The tabloids made a meal of the fact that the young women were 'sparsely clad', ignoring the fact that half the population were as near naked they could lawfully get away with during the heatwave. One heartless tabloid stooped so low as to gratuitously label one of the murdered girls 'Hotpants Helen'.

The owner of the roadside café from which Janice and Helen had set out remembered them well and was able to give police valuable information. 'They sat there,' she told ITV, pointing to a table in one corner. 'The taller one went to the juke box and put on "Heaven Must Be Missing An Angel", which caused a few of us in to look over. You don't really expect that at the crack of dawn. Not that I've got anything against the song. I wondered where they were going. I guessed a pop festival. We had a few in that day, I think, going to the same place. Hippy types, some of them.' The café owner, who didn't miss a trick, said she watched them through the window as they laughed and joked and stuck their thumbs out at the passing cars. She then saw a silver Ford Cortina with a black roof stop, and, after some brief words were exchanged, they very happily climbed in. They couldn't believe their luck, thought the lady.

I remember reading about that record Helen was putting on the jukebox. I pictured her in her hotpants and T-shirt nodding her head in time to the music and felt such sadness that within literally a few hours, heaven *would* be receiving two angels. I borrowed that line from a *Sun* crimewriter.

The murders dominated the news for the rest of the week. The focus moved from the implied flirtatious recklessness of the girls' choice of clothes to the wisdom of hitchhiking in general. They were not the first hitchhikers to meet violent deaths – there had been several instances in America, and there was also the awful case of the Surrey schoolboy in the 1960s who had innocently thumbed a lift home from school only to be picked up by a murdering child-molester – but this horrific double murder high-lighted the dangers of hitchhiking, particularly by lone females. It was always considered especially foolhardy to undertake a journey alone, but it was one of those risky things many teenagers tried, and most – male or female – had a story of a driver coming on to them. These attempted and often fumbled assaults were jokingly referred to as 'wandering-hand trouble' in those days. We had a tendency then of giving certain behaviours harmless, jokey names belying the gravity of the offences, flashing and joyriding being prime examples. For a person to be the victim of indecent exposure was no fun, and for owners of cars that were stolen and often smashed up there was not a lot of joy. In the late 1960s, not so very long before the double murder, there had even been a pop song, 'Hitchin' A Ride', which celebrated the practice of thumbing a lift. After Janice and Helen, such happy-go-lucky attitudes didn't seem appropriate and the song no longer suitable for airplay.

On the following Friday, with his car and various descriptions being aired to the nation, Frank Cox walked into his local police station in Wetherby and confessed to the murders. He worked for Igloo Double Glazing, the replacement-window company with a poor reputation for pressurised selling to older folk. They'd only recently been exposed on a consumer programme on the BBC. Cox was married with a toddler. He had a put a lot of thought into his version of events.

Cox claimed he had been out drinking with his colleagues the night before in town and took his car out early Saturday morning to clear his head after a restless night. He saw the two young women hitching a ride and pulled over. He said he'd agreed to take them around halfway to their destination. The girls, he claimed, immediately started flirting with him, Janice leaning across and switching his eight-track on and turning the volume up to full blast. He had a tape of Rod Stewart's *A Night On The Town*, and all three of them sang along to the hit single 'Tonight's The Night', which they told him was about a girl losing her virginity. They kept on at him, Cox claimed, to take them all the way to Knebworth. They said they'd make it worth his while.

'You take us all the way, we'll go all the way,' he claimed Janice had offered.

'Ever had it off with two girls at the same time?' Helen allegedly added.

Cox says he agreed enthusiastically to their offer and pulled off the A1 looking for a secluded spot. When he found a place behind a large hedgerow in a field, he said he climbed into the back and tried to have sex with Helen, but the cramped situation and the audience (Janice) prevented him from getting a sustainable erection. Helen had laughed at him and called him Mister Softee, and Janice in the front had joined in the goading. Cox lost his temper and punched Helen in the mouth. Janice got out of the front, opened the back door and launched an attack on Cox, who says he panicked and began to throttle Helen with his bare hands because she was screaming. Janice was beating Cox from behind and shouting and flailing at him, 'Leave my friend alone!' Helen went quiet and limp, and Cox got out of the car and faced Janice, who tried to run, but he tripped and fell on top of her and throttled her, too, until she went quiet. He said he went back to Helen, and she wasn't breathing, and then he looked at Janice and she was choking a bit and then also went quiet. Panicking, he said, he lifted them one by one under their arms and dragged them to the dry stream, got in his car and drove home. He had concocted a scenario where he admitted to the double murder but made it sound like he was driven to it and that he was only trying to silence, not kill. Despite forensic evidence to the contrary, he denied double rape.

I didn't believe Cox's account, and neither did the rest of the country. I bet somebody *had* once called him Mister Softee, but it wasn't either of those two girls. The humiliation of not being able to sustain an erection probably lay behind his general hatred of women.

Although Cox pleaded guilty to murder at his trial, he inflicted further pain on the two families as he piled blame on to the two girls during his evidence. They led him on. They suggested three-way sex. They laughed and mocked his inability to perform and the size of his manhood. It was all too much to bear. He had little choice but to kill them. What does a girl expect if she wears hotpants? What does a girl expect if she initiates sex? What does a girl expect if she makes fun of a man's penis? Such was the mentality of the time that girls and women could be said to be 'asking for it'. Of course, as the victims' families were keen to point out, there was only Cox's account of what took place that dreadful Saturday morning, and they didn't believe a word of it. The girls were unable to tell their stories.

'Janice was an innocent young girl of just seventeen years,' said her father. 'She was not sexually active. I am convinced of that. She would not have consented to, let alone initiated, the activity Frank Cox describes. Somehow he overpowered or terrified those two poor girls into yielding to his perverted will. I dread to think – and it tortures my mind when I consider it – what really happened in that car.'

I can remember chatting about the case with the workers on the Barratt building site I was briefly on. It was tea break, and one of the hod-carriers was reading extracts from the evidence aloud from his *Daily Mirror*.

'I don't see how he could overpower the two of them. They'd have screamed the house down, and one would have got away, surely? I mean they weren't tied up or anything,' I thought out loud.

'Two of them. That'll be it. Your man, he had an accomplice.' This from Donny, the chippie, who rarely spoke, but when he did it was normally quite profound or revealing of a *Mastermind*-level bank of knowledge. And the Irish were painted as the daft ones in the building game.

'No. It was just him.'

'How do you know that? Because he was seen alone with the girls?'

'Yes.'

'Say he had a chum. Say he had a chum, and they had planned to go out and get some girls. Say they knew there would be hitchers that day, going to the festival, like. Well, two girls are less likely to get in a car with two men, but two girls and one man, well, that's something they thought they could handle. His mate gets in the boot until he's got them off the motorway, like, and then he lets him out. The proceedings don't go to plan. The girls are having none of it, so matey grabs one and wrenches her arm up her back and threatens to break it if she moves or screams. The other one rapes the other girl, and then they reverse roles. The girls by this time probably do not resist, but after it's over the two slobs realise they've gone too far and know they are in serious trouble, so they decide to silence them for good. It could have happened like that. Throttled the poor dears.'

We were astounded that day. Dublin Donny had unravelled the case like Kojak, Frank Cannon and Colombo combined. It was a compelling scenario. It made sense.

'Why didn't Cox grass the other one up?'

'Why would he? Unless he was completely innocent in the attacks, which we are pretty sure he wasn't, why get someone else life as well?'

'Or he was shit scared of the man in the boot?' volunteered the hoddie, who was also transfixed by Donny.

'Who knows?'

His assertion stayed with me, but I assumed the theory must have occurred to the police and they had had good reason to discount it, and I was young, it was before I realised how thick the police actually are and how keen they are to wrap cases up that garner a lot of media attention and so avoid any suggestion they aren't up to their job.

Frank Cox was tried at the Old Bailey and sentenced to life with a minimum of twenty-five years to serve. The judge said he was a despicable man and a menace to women, and society needed to be protected from him. Cox, who had played to the gallery throughout the hearing, saluted the judge on sentencing, clicked his heels and turned to be taken down. He had not helped himself at all during the trial. He had waved to people in the public gallery and had laughed and whistled during evidence. Despite being a murderer, he was also a knob.

After the sentencing the press let loose with the information on Cox they had been accumulating but had been obliged to sit on lest they prejudiced the trial. At Igloo he had been a top-performing salesman, although it emerged the company had received complaints about him from female customers with whom he had been overfriendly. His wife, who announced their marriage was over and she would immediately be filing for divorce, revealed that Cox had been unfaithful to her many times. She said he had a voracious sexual appetite and had attempted to introduce 'play strangulation' into their sex lives. She revealed that only play-acting during sex would fully arouse him. The police disclosed that Cox had three convictions for sexual assault dating back ten years and one had been on a female hitchhiker. That fortunate girl had fought him off successfully.

The reason Frank Cox was back in the news in the summer of 2003 was that the *News Of The World* had splashed an exposé of him living as a free man in an 'English coastal town'. What had these seaside resorts done to deserve being a dumping ground for society's misfits?

Cox had been up for parole a couple of years earlier, but following a public outcry and lobbying the notion was quietly dropped. In 2002, however, and with no fanfare, he was released, as the Parole Board concluded he was a 'model prisoner who has shown genuine remorse over his crimes, and we believe no longer poses a threat to society'. That's all right then.

It was a year before those sleuths at the *News Of The World* caught up with him. He was pictured emerging from a chemist's, where he had collected a prescription and again swigging from a plastic bottle as he took a break from riding his racing bike, clad in Lycra and wearing a helmet. At fifty-four years old he looked fit and lean, hardly the ageing, powerless, remorse-filled husk the Parole Board description implied.

'He is not an old man being released to see out his final days in an old people's home. He is a fit, healthy, middle-aged man with thirty years or more ahead of him. Our girls had not even come of age. They had their lives extinguished nearly thirty years ago to satisfy this man's wicked lust. The judge gave him life. He should die in prison, and that's too bloody good for him,' pronounced Mrs Jarvis, pictured on television clutching a framed photograph of Janice to her chest, challenging the viewers.

Mr Jarvis and Mr Flannery, the fathers, we were told, had both died during Cox's incarceration, neither man ever recovering from their anguish following the awful fate that befell their precious, beautiful daughters.

A friend, Eve, was tracked down. She had been due to attend the concert with the pair, but her dad, luckily for her, hadn't allowed her to go. 'Janice and Helen were lovely, bubbly girls. Jan worked in Woolworths, but she was going to attend a secretarial college after the summer holidays and Helen worked in a cosmetics factory. We all loved Rod Stewart and the Faces, and one of the reasons we wanted to go to Knebworth was that Ronnie Wood from the Faces had joined the Stones, and this was his first big gig. They were not naive by any means, but no way would they have led that monster on.'

Cox issued a statement to the paper. 'I have served my sentence. I have paid my debt to society. I would just like to live my remaining years in peace. Plastering me all over the front pages of national newspapers helps no one.'

It was a cold statement, devoid of empathy and remorse. Paid his debt to society? His equating the brutal sex murders of two young women to a debt – like he had pinched the milkman's money bag – angered me. The Parole Board and the government – for it is they who ultimately control the Parole Board – incensed me. Where is the justice? Where is the fucking justice? I pushed it away. I had to. Another misfit arsehole was burrowing into my brain, and he kept coming back.

I had killed Stuart Hinds, but, apart from giving me the personal satisfaction of avenging Wally Tombs's murder, it hadn't changed anything. I cannot pretend I took a dangerous man off the street; if he was going to kill again, he would have done by the time I got to him. It also didn't change anything, because nobody knew there was a murder – even the police, it seems – so no messages would be getting through to government and society. But here was an opportunity. The public were disgusted by Cox's surreptitious release, yet the government and the establishment didn't care. They did as they pleased. They knew best. It wasn't one of theirs who had been slaughtered. They were prepared to play Russian roulette with other people's lives. They'd already done away with capital punishment, now time served for life sentences was becoming shorter and shorter. We needed to hit back. Tell them enough is enough.

Good people like Jan have died, not had a full and fair crack of the whip, been dragged screaming from us in pain, yet people like Cox, who have slaughtered innocents twice, are still here. Him having his post-prison life being rebuilt for him. New name, new home, new money. Brick by brick. Pound by pound. Will certainly have counsellors, social workers, help in so many ways at his beck and call. It made me tremble with rage. I wanted to wreak havoc on him and those who facilitate – no, promote – this sick society.

9
FRANK

I KNEW IT was Hastings the second when I saw the photograph. The *News Of The World* had closed in on the background, in a weak attempt to try to preserve some anonymity, but I thought I recognised the actual step Cox stood on. Frank Cox had dismounted from his bicycle and swigged his water before lifting his bike to descend the steps when the photographer snapped him, I guessed. They had said a seaside town, so it could have been anywhere. More likely up north where he hailed from. Scarborough or Whitby perhaps. That visible step, though, I was sure was in Hastings, on the West Hill just below some prehistoric rocks where I had played as a child on holiday, and they dropped steeply down to George Street below. Day-trippers and older people may take the lift down, but locals would use those steps.

The *News Of The World* had been censured by the Press Complaints Commission for compromising Cox's anonymity, so I assumed others beside myself would have worked it out, too. They dropped the story along with their feverish indignation over the double murderer's liberty. I, however, became convinced that I should do something. I saw the Hastings connection and my hunch as a sign. I had been given a nudge. I tried the name-and-address databases again, now even more powerful since I first used them to find Stuart Hinds. No Frank Cox on there in the Hastings area. Of course, he probably had a new identity – the authorities go to such lengths to protect and cosset scum like that. It's a sick world. I had looked and was about to abandon and ignore the signals from whoever it was guiding me when it occurred to me to dip into a few Sussex-based cycling forums.

There were a number of members-only sites, and I joined a few to see if I could pin down anyone called Cox. Members posted their stats – including distances, duration of ride and sometimes climbs – along with photographs of their routes drawn on photo-copies of Ordnance Survey maps, sometimes focusing on the contour lines of particularly challenging elevations. I couldn't really see the point of all this. There was a time when Jan and I had taken up cycling together, but I had pretty much dropped it after her death and, anyway, would not have been interested in sharing the details of our trips with anyone else. We would ride all over at weekends, cherishing our time together in the Surrey countryside. We sought out canal towpaths, as we figured we wouldn't come across any unexpected hills that way.

Cox seemed committed, though, the sort of bloke whose vanity would be stroked by the chorus of admiring comments from fellow cyclists. After logging into the fourth forum that had accepted me as a member I started to trawl the archive. Sure enough – and to my amazement – there was an f_cox who'd been a member for only six months and whose rides started and ended in Hastings. Things were looking promising. He was a regular poster, almost a daily correspondent, and he seemingly detailed all his rides. He was going out most days and covering twenty, sometimes thirty, miles of Sussex countryside and beyond. He was drinking in the freedom he had been deprived of for so long. It suggested to me that he didn't have a job. I was sure it was him. His posts were pretty in-depth, and within a short time I had worked out from various clues that he almost certainly lived in a particular Hastings cul-de-sac with only a few houses that I'd located on an OS map of the town. This Yorkshireman had been resettled a long way from home when they gifted him his new life. He probably couldn't believe his luck. I decided I was not going to give him the chance to prove the prison officers, the Parole

Board and the social workers wrong by attacking and possibly killing another defenceless, innocent young girl. I decided that I would dispense justice to the bully and make the do-gooders think again. Somebody had to do it. And why not me? I had nothing to lose. A suicide-in-waiting with some personal experience now in settling scores.

A plan formed in my mind. From the descriptions and a couple of maps he put up on the blog it looked like one of his regular rides took him very close to the sea and presumably the cliff edge. He climbed up the East Hill and travelled through Fairlight Glen and the Fire Hills on to Pett Level, Winchelsea and finally Rye, where he took a road route back to Hastings. From memory I could recall that the cliffs were high around the East Hill and a place called Ecclesbourne Glen, not far out from Hastings. I judged that he likely went close to that edge at two or three points. His posts also showed he went in the other direction towards East-bourne and Beachy Head, and the latter would have been perfect, as the cliffs there are over five hundred feet high – which is why it has become the suicide capital of England. I figured it would be harder to do what I had in mind at Beachy Head, with all manner of security and the military wing of the Samaritans hanging around looking for poor souls to save.

I took my bike down to Hastings on the train, and, after looking at the house in which I believed Frank Cox resided, followed his route through the Old Town and up the steep track and through to Ecclesbourne Glen. It was a challenging hill ride, and I, being a little out of practice, had to get off twice and walk the bike. However, I found the perfect spot, where the footpath, which was not designated for cyclists, was reasonably remote and close to the cliff edge. I peered cautiously over that precipice, and it was nearly sheer and at least three hundred feet above the beach. I remembered from childhood holidays that down in the valley there had been a house, maybe two, when I was a kid. Mum and Dad and I had looked at them in wonder as they perched precariously on the cliff back in the 1960s. I wondered when the sea had finally fully claimed them, for they were no longer there.

I saw a post that suggested I had missed an Ecclesbourne trip just a couple of days after I'd visited and during which he'd passed my planned spot. So I went down the following week on the first train out of East Croydon and rode back and forth without stopping past the entry to the cul-de-sac until Frank emerged from his house. Conveniently, he came out just after 8 am. He was dressed in cycling shorts, tight-fitting top and helmet, but I got a good look at him. In the quarter of a century since the press photographs he had worn well. I recognised him. I followed him down into the town. Hastings splits itself into two towns, old and new, separated by the West Hill. The old town has preserved its old-England character, with ancient fishermen's cottages and narrow roads and a good selection of eclectic and artistic folk living there, while the new town had been scarred by 1960s architecture and with a selection of the socially submerged, mentally ill and a few crack rabbits leaning up against walls and gathering in knots clutching cans of White Lightning cider.

I followed my quarry out on to the promenade behind the ice-cream parlour, where he took the path and headed right. I managed to keep discreetly behind without losing him. We passed Warrior Square on our right, through St Leonards and Bulverhythe and past the old holiday camp, where the Garfields had once had a family holiday, into Bexhill. At the De La Warr Pavilion Cox stopped at a café and sat outside. I pulled over past him and did the same. I was convinced he had not noticed me at all. Why should he? I couldn't hear what he ordered, but a toasted cheese sandwich and a coffee were soon placed in front of him. He had removed his helmet. He wore his hair longish, and it was now streaked with grey, but there was plenty of it, and he tossed it back every now and then reminding me of a hippy French type. There was a touch of the David Ginola about him. His hands were delicate and thin, his legs and waist muscular, and I had to remind myself he had used those hands to throttle the life from two terror-stricken young girls. Sandwich devoured, he finished his coffee with a cigarette. I expected him to tap it out from a packet of Gauloises, but it was a ready-made roll-up from a small tin. Old prison habits die hard. I bet he's a mean table tennis player, too. After extinguishing the fag he paid the bill, mounted his bicycle and continued in the direction of Eastbourne. I had seen what I needed to for one day and headed back to the railway station.

The following week I decided to take the bike down on the train early each morning, struggle up to Ecclesbourne Glen and hang around until 10.30–11 am and wait until, with luck, Cox passed by. He seemed to have a habit of setting out between 8 and 9 am, and he used this route at least once, sometimes twice, a week. I would keep this up until I had had my showdown with him.

On the Tuesday, the second day, I had alighted from the train just before eight and was waiting at my designated place by twenty past the hour. I spotted him in the distance coming over from the road to the pedestrian track where I was plotted up. I quickly turned my bike upside down, sat beside it and surveyed the area. There were some early-morning ramblers ahead of me heading towards Fairlight. They had walked parallel to me earlier, and I had swerved out of their view, pushing my bike over to the cliff edge as if I was seeking a sea view. Other than the walkers now receding into the distance, the vista was deserted. Now Cox was bumping down the hill, squeezing his brakes, as the descent into the valley was steep. There was nobody coming from the East Hill, but I could hear the cars on the road in the distance. Time was knocking on, and I knew that whatever was going to happen had to happen quickly.

'Excuse me, mate, any good with chains?' I called out as he drew level and as I knelt and fiddled with my chain that I had deliberately unhooked from its cogs.

There must have been a minute shred of decency in him,

because he dismounted his bicycle, stood it on its stand and squatted down beside me.

'Hang on a minute,' he said and walked back to his bike.

Cox carefully removed his fingerless gloves and put on a pair of full gloves. Hurry up, I was thinking, looking behind him to check nobody was approaching over the horizon.

'Don't want to get caked up with oil,' he smiled.

'Thanks. I *cannot* get it back on. It just *will not* go back on.'

Frank Cox crouched down again, and I stood up and stepped back as if to offer him space. He looped the chain on to his forefinger and began simply to rehook it. Crack! I unleashed the hardest vicious kick I could muster. If I had had a run up it would have been like a Peter Lorimer penalty. My foot caught him under the jaw as I had intended, and Cox fell backwards, not unconscious but in severe shock.

'What the fuck?' he muttered.

I then pounced on him, battering his face with my fists, but not all were landing because of his blasted bicycle helmet. He tried to push himself up, but my fists were pummelling fast.

'No, no, no,' he cried as tried to adopt a foetal position, protecting his face and head. I put my hands under his arms and dragged him backwards as fast as I could – before he realised what I was doing – towards the cliff edge. Blood covered his face and my hands. He wriggled free of my grip and tried to stand, but I jumped in front of him kicking and punching him relentlessly nearer to the cliff edge.

'Please. Please. Leave me alone. What have I done?'

'What have you fucking done? You know what you've done, Frank. Did you think you could kill Helen and Janice and get away with it?'

He was on all fours now right at the cliff edge. Raising his arm to parry my kicks. Snivelling, blood dripping off his chin.

'I didn't get away with it. I didn't kill them.' He was holding his hands in front of his face, palms facing outwards, in surrender mode. I don't honestly think he realised how close to the cliff edge he was, and he didn't seem to perceive what I was trying or going to do. His main objective was to stop me attacking him.

'I didn't kill them. Honestly.'

To paraphrase Mandy Rice Davies, he would say that, wouldn't he?

'Really? Who killed them then, Frank?'

'Bernie Hogsden killed them. He was with me when I picked the girls up. I thought we were going to pick some hitchhikers up and have some fun. Know what I mean? Bernie turned violent. He strangled them. Both of them. Because he said they'd tell what we done.'

'No, I don't know what you fucking mean. There was only you when you picked the girls up. You were seen.'

I didn't have time for this now, but I was curious. I booted him in the face again to keep him submissive and looked up and down the path, and it remained clear as far as the eye could see. My kick had moved Cox back a bit closer to the edge.

'Bernie was in the boot!' he cried.

'Oh yeah? So how come you didn't tell the police? So how come you served twenty-five years for something you didn't do?'

'I would have got the same sentence even if I did grass him up. Accessory. Joint enterprise. I was there, but on my mother's life, I didn't kill those girls. I tried to stop him! I did. Honestly. I didn't tell the police because Bernie would have killed me and my family. He would have killed my wife and child. Bernie is capable of anything. He's dangerous. Extremely dangerous.'

Coming over the hill in the distance was a couple with a dog running ahead of them.

'How do you spell Bernie's name?'

'B-e-r ...'

'His second name, you cunt.'

'H-o-g-s-d-e-n.'

I suddenly lunged forward, scooped my arms under him and

literally rolled him off the cliff. He didn't even scream. His brain hadn't computed he was being thrown into the void. In films there is always the elongated cry, and when it stops you know they've hit the bottom. There was not a sound. I didn't look over the edge; I'm scared of heights. I walked back to our bikes, checking the path both ways, and lifted his up and returned to the cliff edge, raised the bike over my head and chucked that over, too.

As I rode downhill into the valley, I wondered if he was dead. He had a crash helmet on, for fuck's sake, and the contours of the cliff face could have broken his fall. Nevertheless, he would be extremely lucky to escape serious injury if he did survive and now knew for sure that he hadn't got away with murder.

I went to the toilet at Hastings railway station and, looking in the mirror, noticed some blood streaked on my face, also on my shirt, where I had wiped my face with it earlier, and, when I removed my gloves, more on my hands, where I had connected so many times with Frank Cox's helmet. My knuckles were torn and bruised. I washed everything off and caught my train home. I hoped I hadn't looked too conspicuous as I cycled through the town.

I would have preferred there not to have been so much violence, but I had to overpower him fast. He was a fit man – what with all the cycling – and capable of fighting back. I was not going to give him the chance. I was avenging Janice and Helen and meting out justice for all their friends and families who were appalled and distraught at his release. I didn't want to muck it up and knew that everything needed to be done in seconds. There was no time to impress upon him why it was happening, like I did with Stuart, but I did at least tell him. He knew.

I didn't know what to make of the Bernie Hogsden stuff. The fact that Cox had claimed this man, whoever he was, was in the boot, as my Irish colleague had posited all those years ago, made me think. However, it was most likely a desperate attempt by Cox to buy time, or mercy, or both. However, I decided that at some point I'd investigate this Hogsden character and, at least, see if he was still alive.

Nothing on the lunchtime news. Late afternoon a small item on the *Hastings & St Leonards Observer* website merely saying a body had been found and police were investigating. 'A body' – that meant he was dead. Hurrah! I sat back in my armchair waiting for the shit to hit the fan. It was the second item on the *Ten O'Clock News* behind some general panic over tumbling stock markets. I was curious as to how Huw Edwards would present the news – good news or bad news? In the event he managed to be very neutral: 'The body of the double murderer Frank Cox has been found at the foot of cliffs near Hastings in Sussex. Cox was convicted in 1977 of murdering hitchhikers Janice Jarvis and Helen Flannery. He was paroled last year after serving twenty-five years in prison. Police believe Cox had been involved in a struggle before falling from the cliff. His bicycle was also found nearby,' read Huw.

The following day's newspaper furnished more detail:

Police have revealed that Cox suffered severe injuries consistent with a fall from such a height. An eyewitness saw what she thought was two cyclists struggling on the cliff edge and one pick up a bicycle and throw it off the cliff. She was a long way away, and when she refocused saw only one, who rode off towards Fairlight Glen. She did not get close enough to offer any descriptions. Police are appealing for witnesses.

Blimey, I missed her. Where was she? The *Sun* followed up a couple of days later:

THE MYSTERIOUS DEATH OF
DOUBLE KILLER FRANK COX

Frank Cox, whose body was found at the bottom of cliffs at Sussex seaside resort Hastings, is one of Britain's most notorious double murderers. In 1976 he strangled, raped and killed teenagers Janice Jarvis and Helen Flannery after picking them up in his car on the A1. The girls were on their way to a Rolling Stones concert. Cox was released from prison last year amid great controversy after serving twenty-five years. He was said to have been a model prisoner who had shown 'significant remorse' for his crimes. On early Tuesday morning Cox, a keen cyclist, went for a ride as he regularly did along the coastal paths between Hastings and Rye. An eyewitness saw two men struggling and shouting on the cliff edge from a distance. She then saw only one cyclist ride away. That cyclist was not Frank Cox. Later that day he was found dead by children with his bicycle close by. Who was that mysterious cyclist? Nobody has come forward, and the witness has been unable to provide a description other than 'an average-sized male'. Were they riding together and an argument ensued? Were they strangers who had clashed on the path? It is notable that there has been some consternation in the town about Cox being housed there, and Cox is said to have complained recently about paint being daubed on his garden wall. Neighbours we spoke to who wish to be anonymous suggest Cox is the victim of a vigilante attack.

Alan Jarvis, Janice Jarvis's brother, who was six at the time of the murder commented, 'Frank Cox was an evil man. I hope this was *not* an accident and somebody has done away with him. I hope he suffered, and I hope he knew why. My only regret is I didn't do it myself.'

Sussex Police say their inquiries are ongoing, and, although they are treating the death as suspicious, they have not 'yet' launched a murder investigation.

The newspapers became bolder as the days went by with headlines such as WAS HITCHHIKER MURDERER THROWN OFF CLIFF? and TEEN DOUBLE MURDERER WAS KILLED BY VIGILANTE, SAY LOCALS and, my favourite, WHO KILLED

THE KILLER? But, as the days and then weeks rolled by, evidently no progress was being made. Appeals for information drew no new witnesses, and the one they did have appeared to backtrack, saying although she could swear she saw one man lift a bike over his head and throw it off the cliff, she could not say with 100 per cent certainty she saw two men struggling – she thinks she did, but it could have been one man struggling with the bike. A coroner eventually recorded an open verdict, even though a post-mortem found that some of Cox's injuries were not consistent with a fall from a great height and were indicative of battery. Although the authorities seemed unwilling to embrace the obvious – one police source even saying they had not ruled out suicide – on the streets, in sitting-rooms, on building sites and in the pubs of Britain it was pretty much accepted that Frank Cox had been served up rough justice.

The authorities wanted to play it down, is my opinion. If it was admitted that Cox had been avenged by a vigilante, then that could lead to others taking the law into their own hands, and where would that lead? The incident leant itself perfectly to a television *Crimewatch* reconstruction, with its idyllic and dramatic cliff-face setting, but there was none. There was not even an admission that a crime had been committed. Eventually the case was pushed out of the newspapers, never really to return.

I contemplated writing anonymously to the media and admitting to the Cox murder and to tell them about Stuart Hinds. Saying that I was Justice Killer, and until punishments were made to fit the crimes committed I would continue my work. That would ignite things and go further to achieving what I think my goal was, but I decided to stop now while the going was good. I had avenged three innocent murder victims, and I had done this without a murder investigation even being launched. That I was meant get away with it – as I was by now sure I had – was destiny.

However, as the weeks passed I got more of a sense of what I had done and what I was trying to do. I had ended the lives of two men not for my personal satisfaction or out of some bloodlust or because of some mental illness or compulsion on my part; no, I had killed them to make a point to society and to the authorities. I wanted to turn the tide, and, if I didn't exploit my actions, opportunities would be lost. I sat down and wrote a letter to the chief constable of Sussex Police:

Dear Sir

I am writing to let you know that I am a justice killer responsible for the murder of Frank Cox in Hastings. I did what I did to redress the injustice perpetrated by the government in releasing this monster from prison. He has not served life, and this is an affront to decency, an assault on the memories of the girls he killed and a fresh knife being twisted into the guts of their families and friends. Cox was also fit and able, and we released a dangerous beast to roam among us. I am one of many who are not prepared to let him claim another innocent, defenceless victim. Too often are the 'rights' of criminals placed above those of the victims and the general public. It must stop, and if our rulers will not conduct law and order fairly then it is inevitable now that people like myself will administer appropriate justice. Life should mean life. If you wish to avoid further actions of the kind taken against Cox, you need to lobby government now. I refer you to the case of Stuart Hinds in Bridgnorth in the year 2000. I am not a lone crackpot. I am part of a movement.

Yours faithfully,
Justice Killer

I composed the letter on my personal computer and did not save it when completed. There should be no record of it. I printed it out on my laser printer, a common model residing in millions of homes, I handled the letter and envelope with gloves and was careful not to apply my tongue to the stamp or anywhere else. I disguised my hand-writing style on the envelope and rode my bike to a destination thirty miles away and thirty miles nearer to Hastings and posted discreetly. I was pleased with the letter and my Justice Killer moniker. I had seen the term used in the press – the *Daily Star*, I think. IS THERE A JUSTICE KILLER AT LARGE? they had asked late on to try to keep the Cox story alive.

I fully expected it all to take off again, with my letter being broadcast and reproduced in the media on a scale like the 'I'm Jack' tape sent to the top copper in the Yorkshire Ripper investigation in the 1980s. But nothing. Zilch. At first I thought the police were keeping it close to their chests until (they hoped) they apprehended me following their investigation of any fresh leads the letter might have thrown up. Yet the weeks passed, and I realised they were not going to air my letter publicly.

Why? Had the police dismissed the letter as the work of a crank? It's not unusual for people to claim responsibility for most high-profile murders. But surely if they had checked out Stuart Hinds's demise then it would be impossible to do so? Maybe they looked at the Hinds case and decided there was no murder.

I then began to think that something more strategic was at play. That politics had intervened. What if it had been decided that they believed the Justice Killer letter was probably genuine but from someone acting alone, and they did not want to give him (me) the oxygen of publicity? That was a phrase I often heard in the seventies in relation to the IRA. There was a danger that other justice killers would emerge, they feared. An epidemic of vigilantism. A direct bottom-up challenge to the establishment that could undermine law and order. Was there an agreed policy to kill Justice Killer before it really did become a movement? I am sure they were still keen to find me, but it would be on their terms, not mine. I decided a similar letter to the *Sun* or the *Daily Telegraph* would be treated the same so left it as it was. The police were no nearer to apprehending me, but they knew there was somebody out there who had carried out two vigilante murders and was likely to do more. The establishment was misleading the public by pretending they believed that Frank Cox might have committed suicide. It was preposterous, and the people knew it. Somehow they had marshalled the media into dropping that line of speculation. I wouldn't be surprised if the police, under instruction, hadn't planted doubt in the poor eyewitness's mind, too. For the first time I saw clearly the national institutions and the establishment pulling together in a nifty move. Invisible manipulation from on high.

I had a chuckle when one of the tabloids had consulted psychological criminal profiler Ivan Hiscock for his opinion on the type of person the police might or should be looking for. I had seen this idiot on the TV cropping up time and time again imparting his pseudo-wisdom. There was a whole team of these same old parasites, like the forensic 'expert' in his white collarless coat even though he's not at work, the 'retired' detective, although he looked like he had barely passed his fortieth birthday, and the wizened, red-cheeked old hack, one of the last survivors of the Fleet Street drinking dens of the mid-twentieth century, squeezing out some late-life appearance fees.

Hiscock's verdict was that the killer 'most likely lives alone. Is between forty and sixty. He is old enough to remember the Hitchhiker Murders but not too old to be able to vigorously ride a bicycle. He may well be a local man, and if not local does not live too far away. He will be a loner, and this may be his first crime. He is angry with society and the world.'

Staggering insight. I could have told him that.

These murder documentaries incensed me. They call it 'true crime', and a whole salacious industry has grown up around it – and don't get me started on the books! *Crimewatch* excepted, none of these TV programmes were there as warnings or to deepen our understanding of murderous crime; they are pure titillation, and bollocks to the families and friends seeing their personal tragedies packaged and sold to the masses. I wouldn't put it past them to start putting advertisements for axes and hammers in the commercial breaks. People should be ashamed of themselves for watching.

10
BUBBLES BURSTS

FIVE YEARS HAD passed since my Jan died, and nothing much had changed. Time had *not* been the great healer. My emptiness, my misery, my yearning had not receded. I was still a suicide-in-waiting. Stuart Hinds and Frank Cox had provided temporary relief, but not for long. By now Holly was in a relationship, and it seemed serious, and I was pleased. Norman is a nice bloke. He worked for the estate agent's where Holly was still employed, and he was good at his job. The man who owned it was going to make him a junior partner, having hinted that on his retirement Norm could continue with the business. Houses were flying off the blocks, and commissions flowed into Holly's and Norman's growing coffers. I was pleased, though, because Norman would take care of Holly when I decide to go. And go I will. I am under no illusion that by taking my life I will be reunited with Jan, which is one of the reasons why I am so unhappy. I merely have no desire to be in the world when Jan is not. An Elton John song lyric reso-nated with me, *How wonderful life is while you're in the world*, and I just turn it on his head, *How miserable life is when you're not in the world*.

One of my first big moves in the months after Jan's death was to suggest to Bubbles that he buy me out of the business com-pletely, and, while he was reluctant to do so, he did eventually agree. 'Paul, you're far too young to be retiring. You'll go mad down there with all the carrot-crunchers'. I had made up a cock-and-bull story about wanting to retire to Cornwall. I had never been to Cornwall in my life and had no intention of going. 'You're a young, fit man. Let's carry on as we are. You don't have to come in at all if you don't want. I'm happy like this. This business is yours, not mine.'

Bubbles was honest, no side to him. Being raised in a children's home or as a temporary guest in other people's homes made him believe he was unworthy of good fortune. He was straight – old-fashioned straight – despite the negative influences in his early life. Jan and I had been as lucky to find him as he was us. We struck a deal. Bubbles would pay over all the profit of the business to me – or to Holly should I die – for the next four years, after which the business with all its assets and goodwill would belong solely to him.

'That'll be enough to keep me going until I peg it,' I told him.

I already owned our property and had substantial savings. You'd be surprised how little you spend when you eat for one, heat for one and live for one.

'Don't be ridiculous, Paul,' Bubbles had laughed, 'you'll outlive us all.'

Little did he know.

I don't need the money. I, or rather me and Jan, had done very well. If I'd had the ambition we could have done so much better, but once we had achieved a certain amount of security we decided to live our lives to the full and relish the time we had. Thank God we did. I currently spend much of my time memorising events from those golden years. I write them all down. I have created a retro-spective diary from memory, from Holly's memory, from old diaries and bank and credit-card statements. An old receipt falls out the bureau. It's for a meal on 25 June 1989 at the Harrow in Warling-ham. I look the day up in an old work diary. We keep them all. It was a Sunday, and then I remembered the day. Jan didn't want to cook, and we drove out and ate outside. Holly played in a little recreation area they had in the garden. I tried to remember what Jan wore, but that wouldn't come. I'm terrified of forgetting anything. I am thrilled when a buried memory resurfaces, and I add it to my log. I want to capture it all. I am recreating our lost life on paper – or hard disk, I should say.

I looked in the mirror. I was now well in my mid-forties, but it was still a boy looking back at me. This was not vanity on my part – everybody said it. I could pass for ten years younger. My hair was as thick as ever with no sign of grey. Although it hadn't always been easy, I had managed to keep the weight off. It gave me no pleasure, no hint of self-satisfaction. It just was. Holly has told me, more than once, that her colleagues, women in their early twenties, had said I was a dish – or was it a hunk? But it meant nothing. Sixty months on from Jan's death I felt no stirrings whatsoever, romantic or sexual, and no desire to attract female company. That side of me was to all intents and purposes pretty much dead – even if the rest of me was not. Yet.

I experimented with doing up and undoing the top button of my Fred Perry in the mirror and settled on fastened, as I always did. I was going down to a French restaurant in South Croydon to meet Bubbles. I had a good idea what it was about.

Bubbles had, to date, paid me £350,000 from the proceeds of the business, on top of the £30,000 a year 'consultancy' fee he had insisted on, and I felt that he had called the meeting to pay me my last instalment and sever his ties with me and end the profit-share from the business. I had no problem with that. It was what had been agreed, and I was financially secure. In fact, I was pleased with the prospect. It was another door closing that made things simpler and I could move forward with my ultimate exit plan.

Bubbles had moved the business on in leaps and bounds. He had won a contract with the council for refurbishing empty, out-of-date and trashed local authority homes. Learning from our strategy he bought in contracts under budget. The council were delighted, albeit shocked. Word spread, and soon Garfield D&B were working with other councils, too. Local authority contracts became 70 per cent of our turnover and offered prompt payment and predictable cash flows.

I parked the Jag outside the restaurant and could see through the window that Bubbles was the only customer inside. It was early. A couple of waiters looked hopefully beyond me as I approached the door, but, of course, I was alone. Bubbles was sitting with a champagne bottle tilted in a silver bucket in front of him.

'Celebrating?' I asked, raising a friendly, quizzical eyebrow as I took the chair offered to me by a fussing waiter.

'I hope so, Paul. I think so.'

When we settled and I ordered half a lager, ignoring the champagne, Bubbles took a folded cheque and held it out to me.

'There's a cheque here for £200,000, Paul. £150,000 the business owes you and interest you should have had on the whole amount ... but you don't want that ...' Bubbles withdrew his hand and the cheque, mimicking a Chris Tarrant routine from TV's *Who Wants To Be A Millionaire*. 'It's yours – of course it is – but I want you to stay in the business. I do. I really do.'

'But I don't do anything, Bubbles. And I don't want to.'

'I don't care. You might one day. Who knows? Stay on as a director and keep some shares. If you don't, I'll feel terrible. You've made me a rich man. Do you know how much the company is worth?'

'You've taken the business on yourself.'

'Do you know how much the company is worth, Paul? If it wasn't for you, and for Jan, you know ... my life ... my life would have been shit, man. I mean, real shit. It *was* shit ...'

'I know,' I said, uncomfortable by the turn of conversation, the discussion of feelings being something I rarely embraced.

'You don't, Paul. You really don't. And I never told you. I never wanted to tell you or Jan, although Jan asked me. She knew. She could read people. She knew. But I would never tell her.'

'You mean the children's home?'

'Yes.'

'I thought you said it wasn't too bad.'

114

'That's what I mean. I never told you.'

I put my head down, suddenly interested in some bread and oil that had been placed between us and then allowed the waiter to pour me some champagne.

'Do you want to hear?'

I didn't. I really didn't. 'Only if you want to tell me. Racism?'

'No, not racism. There was racism, of course, but us black kids at the home didn't really see it then. It was lifeism. We didn't know different. And all the kids – black or white – were treated the same, Paul. Know what I mean? Badly. I would like to tell you. I *will* tell you. I want to tell you because I want you to know what you rescued me from. You've saved my life and you've made my life. I want to tell you, and I want to tell Jan, but I can't. I missed it. I missed the opportunity to tell her, and I don't want to do the same with you. I don't want you to feel sorry for me because I don't feel sorry for me. I have no problems. No hang-ups. I don't "need to talk".' Bubbles made the speech-marks sign. 'I don't need to see a psycho-whatever. It happened. It's gone, and I'm fine. I'm a fucking lucky man.'

'Jan knew you appreciated her.' Jan was an intangible presence at the table. My words were inadequate to the gravity of the conversation.

'Appreciated her, Paul? I loved her ... and I love you.'

I winced as the honesty dart embedded in my forehead, looked around, half serious, half joking, pretending to be worried that the heartfelt declaration may be taken the wrong way by fellow diners. Fortunately, there weren't any. Bubbles smiled, but his eyes were filming over.

'OK. Here we go. I was taken off my mum when I was a baby. I don't really know why. I don't know who my dad is, and maybe she didn't either. I like to think he gave me the middle name Constantine after Learie Constantine, the cricketer, but I don't know that. One of the things you make up as a kid. I think my mother was fifteen when she had me, and I heard I was not her first. I know her name, or what it was in the 1970s, but I have never tried to trace her, and she never came to see me or tried to trace me. I have no interest in doing so. I wonder sometimes about her parents, though. They would have been mature. I wonder why they didn't look out for me. If I feel any bitterness, it's towards them – she really was a kid – although I don't even know if they knew about me, or anything really. They might not have existed. As a marriage, as a family, if you see what I mean. Anyway, I was fostered out to a white family as a toddler. I can just about remember them. Silly things. I remember fruit in a bowl that was plastic. Think I was told off for trying to eat it. I remember my "mum" brushing dog hair off me, complaining, like it was my fault. But that's about it. When I was four I went to Pine Forest. I stayed there until I came to you. The next eleven or twelve years. That foster family had me for four years, and now I wonder why, why did *they* get rid of me? What could I have done at four to make them not want to keep me? I mean four years is not short-term foster care ...'

'I'm sure you didn't do anything. One of them could have got ill. Anything could have happened. You should ask to see your file. You could find out everything, surely?'

'I probably could. I don't want to. As I say, I'm not massively interested. Not damaged. Sometimes, like now when I talk about it, mildly curious. That's all. Almost like an outsider looking in.'

'I didn't know any of that.'

'That's just background info, Paul. Now it gets interesting.'

Here we go, I thought, bracing myself.

'I've told you about Pine Forest before. How we lived in family units with uncles and aunties? They tried up there in some ways, I'll give them that. They tried to re-create the family dynamic with a sort of mum and dad, and they kept the real brothers and sisters together where they could. The auntie and uncle weren't always married, but they lived in, like us. Problem was they went off and got married or got new jobs or just left – so your auntie or uncle could change from one year to the next. Or from one month to the next. Anyway, my "uncle" for nearly the whole time was Philip. Uncle Phil. He was my uncle right up to when I walked on to your job. I had an Auntie Glad for a long time, too. She was a nice woman. And I had a West Indian "brother" called George and a "sister", Linda. That was our family for most of the time. George was two years older, and he left when he was about thirteen. Linda was three years younger.'

Bubbles paused to call the waiter over. He asked for a bottle of wine. We'd chucked back the bubbly without noticing.

'I don't know what happened to George and Linda,' Bubbles said, reading my mind. 'George came back once or twice to see us all. Full dreadlocks. Went to live in Brixton. And I never set foot in the place again after I left so I don't know what happened to Lin. She was a sweet girl. I hope she's OK. Anyway, Uncle Phil …' My face muscles stiffened. 'Yeah, you know what's coming. He started noncing me when I was about seven or eight, and he carried on until I started going to senior school at eleven. When I realised it was not right, I asked him to stop. Told him to stop. It wasn't just a wandering hand up the shorts, Paul, it was full-on noncing. He abused me, probably once a week, maybe twice a week, for years.'

I raised my eyebrows and shuffled on my seat. Suddenly I didn't fancy the entrecôte steak I had ordered.

'He didn't do certain things – thank God for that – but he got me to do some pretty horrible stuff. I won't go into details. He'd say, "You naughty, naughty boy," like it was me who was the bad one.'

'Fucking hell, Bubbles.'

'Yes, fucking hell. I was seven, eight years old when he started all that malarkey. And he was artful. He must have planned it like a strategic operation. It was gradual. He used to read me *Treasure Island* by Robert Louis Stevenson. I can remember the book now. Vividly. Every illustration. Long John Silver sitting, leaning up against an apple barrel, conspiring with another pirate, and young Jim Hawkins hiding inside the barrel and realising for the first time that Long John Silver was a bad man. I remember all that. And old Ben Gunn with his beard down to his knees who they had left on Treasure Island to rot. There was this character called Pugh, and he was blind, and he had to deliver the black spot, and if he put it in your hand you was a dead man, a goner. It terrified me, and I had nightmares. Blind Pugh coming to me in the night. With his hood and empty eye sockets. Because in the book it looked like he had no eyes. For years I thought blind meant you had no eyes. And Phil would come into my room and fetch me to his because I was having nightmares about Pugh, and he'd get me in his bed and calm me down. That's how it started. But you know what makes me angry now? It's not just the abuse – to do that to a young child – it was the whole Pugh black-spot thing, at seven years old. He planned it. Made me scared shitless of Blind Pugh and the black spot. The book was his, a well-thumbed copy with colour plates. He had done it before. It was his prop. You know what I mean?'

Bubbles had been talking faster and faster and stopped abruptly. He looked straight at me.

'Yes.'

'Yes what?'

'I know what you mean. Bubbles, I don't know what to say.'

'You don't need to say anything, Paul. I'm not laying anything on you. I don't want you to feel different about me. I don't want you to feel sorry for me. I don't want you to feel angry. I want you to realise what a massive favour you did me.'

'Did you ever have it out with him? How did you stop him?'

'Yeah, I mean no. I'll tell you. I had no idea, no comprehension that what was happening was wrong. I knew it wasn't nice. Like when an old lady kissed you sloppily, if you know what I mean. Worse than that. But I really didn't comprehend it was wrong. Criminal, like. Really. Not until I got to senior school when I was eleven. Up to then we were tutored in the home. In fact, Uncle Phil was a tutor. He taught us all English. But I think there was a change in law or policy or something, and it was decided all of us should attend the local comprehensives, and we did. About eighty of us got farmed out to about eight different schools. I loved it. We were a novelty at first – the kids from the children's homes. Some of us the only dark-skinned pupils in the school. The teachers automatically assumed we were problem kids and treated us as such. Some of us were, believe me. But our classmates soon accepted us and treated us no different. Kids are brilliant like that. There were local boys there ten times worse than any kid in Pine Forest, trust me. I can't remember exactly how, but I started learning a lot about the world. About sex. Even then, at eleven and twelve, that and football and music was all kids talked about. Tits and fannies and shagging and wanking and everything. Nobody was doing anything, but you would never have known it. And I can remember people talking about "child-molesters". That's what they called them then, child-molesters. Not paedo-philes or paedos. That came later. I object to that actually. What does paedophile mean? You need an A level in English to under-stand the word. It was a way of shielding people from what they did. What they liked. From the truth. Child-molester was better. There's no getting away from it. Child. Molester. Anyway, it dawned on me that Uncle Phil was a child-molester. And I was a molested child. One day on the bus on the way home from school I was just filled with confidence and power and happiness by the knowledge, and I knew it would end. I didn't like it. Deep down I knew it wasn't right, and now it all made sense. The next time he wanted to play with me I just said, "You're a child-molester, Uncle Phil. You've been molesting me for years. Don't ever do it again."' Bubbles paused.

'And he just stopped? What did he say?'

'He said he was sorry. He didn't try and justify it or anything. He said he was sorry, and he understood. That was the word he used – understood. Like I was ending a romance! Like I was chucking him. And he never laid a finger, or anything else, on me again.'

'And did you report him, did you get him nicked?'

'No, I didn't. I'm not sure why. I was scared about causing all the trouble, I suppose. I was enjoying life with my new friends at school, getting out of the home. And I liked him, I s'pose. Maybe loved him. The abuse had stopped. I didn't want Lin to lose her uncle and break up that little family. I thought I'd get moved off somewhere. Well, I would have been. We had another boy with us now, Stuart ...'

Again, Bubbles sensed my thoughts.

'I don't think so. I hope not. I don't know.'

'I'm not saying that. You were a little kid. You can't think like an adult when you're a kid.'

'I should have done something. I hope he didn't do anything to Stuart. I should have reported him. The bastard.'

Bubbles's enthusiasm to unburden himself seemed to have ground to a halt. He was having to stop himself crying.

'You still could, Bubbles. Is he still there?'

'God, no. He should be dead. He wasn't young when he got to me. That's why I said what I said about *Treasure Island*. I think it was a tried-and-tested technique over many years. No, he retired about ten years ago. Maybe more. Believe it or not, I was invited to his leaving party! Not by him. Another teacher, who obviously had no idea what floated his boat, she traced me through someone else and sent me an invite. I didn't go.'

'I should hope not.'

'Funnily enough, there was this bloke on Friends Reunited a couple of years ago. He was older than me, but I can remember him. Barbadian boy called Edward. Anyway, he put this message up appealing to people to get in touch with him. He said he was writing a book about Pine Forest in the 1970s and 1980s and its "dear little rituals and ways. Would love to talk to anyone who still has the memories." Something like that. I knew straight away what he was getting at, "dear little rituals and ways". Outsiders wouldn't. He wasn't even in my house. It must have been rife there. And nobody said anything to each other. That's the amazing thing. Edward meant he wanted to talk to anyone who was still haunted by the abuse. That's what he meant.'

'And did you? Did you contact him?'

'No, I didn't. I wanted to because I didn't want him to think nobody cared or he was the only one. But I'm happy. I have a family of my own. I have a great business. With you and thanks to you. When you have not had a family and you get one you don't want to upset the applecart. I don't know how to explain it. I rose above it, I really did. And if I revisit it, even in my mind, it's like I'm allowing Uncle Phil to ruin my life. I'm allowing *it* to define me. Oh look, there's Bubbles – the one that got nonced when he was a kid. Phil, if he's alive, he's too old now to be noncing. So what's in it for me? Only revenge. I'm not interested in revenge. Revenge gets you nowhere. I'm not sure it even makes you feel better.'

I thought of Wally Tombs and how getting revenge for him, certainly made me feel better. I wanted to tell him about Frank Cox and how getting revenge for those poor girls made me feel fucking wonderful – for a while, at least.

'Anyway, to finish my story I carried on living at Pine Forest with Phil, Auntie Glad and Lin and little Stu. But it was uncomfortable. That was when I started going out and absconding and getting in trouble and sniffing glue and breaking into places. It was eating away at me, and I was getting bigger and stronger and more streetwise by the day. The time was getting close, with how I felt then, when I might have gone for Uncle Phil. He knew that the knowledge of what happened was festering in me and that I had the ability to destroy him, and when the police would bring me back to Pine Forest he'd persuade them to not to press charges. And we'd be in a room. Me, Phil and the policemen. And I knew and he knew that one word from me could change both our worlds. I enjoyed the power of that. The policeman would ask, have you got anything to say? And I'd say, actually I have, and I'd watch Phil physically shrink before my eyes and hang his head literally with shame, and I'd say, "What time does *The A-Team* begin?" and start laughing. And then, at sixteen, I had to leave school, and the home just said that we had to find jobs and when we found jobs we had to find digs. We were put on notice that we were being turfed out into the big, bad world with not a lot of notice. We knew then, more than ever, this was not our home. It was *a* home, but not *our* home. And that's where I was when I walked on to your job. Poised to be put out into the real world. Sixteen years of age. Chip on my shoulder. Mixing with the wrong crowd. On nodding terms with Mr Plod. Riddled with guilt. That was a clear fork in the road. And you and Jan took me by the hand and led me up this one. I'm so, so bloody grateful to you both.'

Bubbles leant back in his chair and exhaled, blowing his cheeks out, and then buried his face in his serviette. He started crying. The waiters averted their glances as I leant forward and put my hand awkwardly on his shoulder. It hit me how his miserable upbringing had damaged him, and the evidence was never much below the surface.

I thought back to that first summer he worked for us. I had seen him shovel sand into the mixer. His shirt was off, and he straightened up to beam a smile at me. For the first time I noticed a tattoo on his chest. Bubbles saw my eyes alight on it.

'Good, innit?' he said, looking down proudly at his own chest.

No, it wasn't. Above his nipple, crudely carved and inked, was the laurel wreath used by Fred Perry as an iconic logo on his shirts. It was lopsided, wrongly positioned and, frankly, looked pathetic. I guessed he'd had it done it to impress his friends. It was sad.

'Don't worry, Bubbles. Don't cry, mate.'

Bubbles's head was still buried in his serviette. 'I'm sorry. I'm sorry, Paul,' he spluttered, composing himself. 'I miss Jan so much.'

'So do I, Bubbles. So do I.'

'I'm sorry, Paul. It's awful for you. It's ... it's ... Here's me jabbering on about me ...'

'It's all right. I didn't mean that. What was his surname?'

'Whose surname?'

'Uncle Phil.'

'Why? Beake. Mr Beake, to most of the children. Uncle Phil to us.'

I made a mental note.

Jan and I had discussed Bubbles many times. His reticence in discussing his previous life led us to believe there were things best left alone. We'd even wondered aloud to each other if he had been abused. But for me, at least, I preferred to believe that the abuse, if indeed there had been any, had been physical or mental rather than sexual. There was no foundation for that assumption – it just made the scenario more palatable – for me, that is. Now that Bubbles had unburdened himself, I felt burdened. Although there was not a parental age gap between us, I regarded Bubbles as a son. Here I was passing my business to him. Bubbles was a part of Jan, like Holly but not like Holly. This new knowledge would have eaten Jan up. I wanted to take the revenge that Bubbles said he had no desire to take himself.

I found myself thinking about Uncle Phil, and from the minute we walked to our cars and shook hands firmly outside the restaurant I knew that in some way I would do something. Working with the limited details that Bubbles had revealed was bad enough, but I knew that there was so much more unsaid. That the devil really was in the detail. That this man had led a little boy into his den of evil and pain, and the little boy had been helpless. It was cruelty and despicable bullying of the worst kind. Jan would understand why I could not let it go.

11
BLACK SPOT

I FOUND A Philip Horace Beake in a few keystrokes online. He was listed as seventy-five-plus in age and appeared to live alone in Great Yarmouth, Norfolk. There were other Philip Beakes, but none of the others really matched. If he was still alive, Uncle Phil could only be Horace in Great Yarmouth. I then went on to an ancestry site and tapped in 'Philip Horace', and there he was, Philip Horace Beake, born Great Yarmouth, 1929. Bingo! He'd been born in Great Yarmouth, came south to earn his living and when he retired returned to his childhood town. Perhaps he had inherited his parents' house on their deaths?

Three weeks passed as I waited to see if time reduced my compulsion to confront the man. It was a loose thread I wanted to tie off before I sorted myself out. Holly and Norman were now happily living together, and I was slowly and deliberately withdrawing more and more from her daily life. I was doing this for her, to help negate the loss she would feel. I had decided that when I did finally take my life it would be done in such a way that it wouldn't necessarily be obvious that it was suicide, as I felt Holly would deal with that more easily. I was now feeling some pressure to do it sooner rather than later, as Holly had more than once mentioned the possibility of future grandchildren, and I did not want to form another earthly attachment. That would be complicated and hard.

Great Yarmouth was not a part of the world I'd ever visited. I had it down in my mind as a lively, colour-postcard, working-class, traditional holiday resort. A Pathé newsreel in my mind of donkeys on the beach, a bustling pier, men with rolled-up trousers slumped in deckchairs with newspapers spread across their faces to keep off the very sun that their wives and children were worshipping, tousled-haired, giggling teenage girls with kiss-me-quick hats. As I drove into the town on a rainy October day I was greeted instead by a morose, grubby, apologetic town. The promenade stretched ahead of me – wide but empty. A couple of dog walkers, a jogger, some youths battling time in a bus shelter. The sea to my left looked cold, dark and forbidding; the large houses and hotels to my right not trying very hard to hide the fact that their best days were long behind them. This was not just a seaside resort out of season – it was a seaside resort out of fashion. I drove up and down three or four times and then took a parking space on the promenade. Close by was a blue plaque claiming that Charles Dickens had once stayed at a certain hotel while writing. This transported me back to Sunday afternoons as a kid. Just me and my mum and dad when they were happy – or, at least, I thought they were. The black-and-white TV was on, and we were all engrossed in a BBC adaptation of *David Copperfield*. This in a time when the BBC entertained and educated us. It broadcast *to* us, not *at* us. Young David was staying with his down-on-their-luck but contented relatives in an upturned boat on the desolate Yarmouth beach. Dad would make toast for the three of us and share daintily cut pieces fanned out on a grown-up's plate. I was momentarily and unexpectedly filled with longing for that innocent, happy past.

I knew from my Multimap printout that the street I wanted was only a three-minute walk from the front. I passed another plaque, this time for a long-forgotten boxer, Jem Mace. I knew all about him, because when I was boxing I went through a stage of reading up on all the British fighters before and after Queensbury Rules. He had been playing the fiddle outside a Yarmouth pub for farthings and coppers when he was attacked by three inebriated fishermen. He despatched two and the other ran away, but it was here that his pugilistic skills were spotted by an entrepreneur and his extraordinary career began. His last fight was reputedly when he was aged seventy-eight.

Once I was behind the empty, sea-facing, soulless hotels, hostels and bed and breakfasts – most now housing the forlorn and the homeless – the properties became quite charming and, in some spots, positively Christmas-card Dickensian. There was still a run-down feel about the place, but the existence of a functioning community, not evident along the front, emerged. A corner café seemed to be doing good trade with customers talking to one another across tables and smiling. I heard the jangling of a pulsating pinball machine as I passed the open door of a small bookmakers and the chirruping of a budgerigar – a lost sound from my childhood – from the open door of a terraced house.

Drummond Street was a long road of Victorian terraced houses with small front gardens and one bay window each. Every house said something about the owner. Most were neatly kept, a few with twee names mounted on slabs of cheap wood and possibly bought from the local pound shop – *Nosferatu*, *Hollow's End* and *Sea View* (the latter, of course, being wholly inaccurate). Some houses were falling to bits, with rotten window frames, overgrown gardens and with exhausted cars collapsed on to their wheel rims in their front gardens. Number 75 was among the neatest. Possibly *the* neatest. Low, trimmed-level hedges either side of a little iron gate led into a token lawned front garden, edged with a flowerbed, currently barren. The bay window had net curtains, and you could not see in fully, unlike some of the neighbouring properties. It had the original heavy Victorian front door with grand brass-plated knocker. No obvious car. It suggested to me that Uncle Phil was still mobile and able to maintain his property. I walked past three times before deciding to go to the café and think through what to do next. Philip Horace Beake had not conveniently decided to break cover at the precise minute I was outside his house, as I had vainly hoped he might.

The Albatross Café was a shrine to Formica. Workmen in overalls sat in pairs, gnarled hands fingering fag packets in front of them, passing a copy of the *Sun* – unashamedly folded open at page three – across the tables with knowing grins. It reminded me of how the building sites used to be not so long ago. I never really believed that the cult of political correctness and over-zealous health-and-safety concerns would penetrate the sites, but they had. Now you couldn't move for hard hats, high-vis jackets and no-swearing policies. On some sites (not mine) radios were banned.

A man lit a cigarette, and the lady from behind the counter called out to him, 'Charlie!'

Charlie smiled and inhaled and then lovingly blew out smoke rings.

'Charlie, you know I don't allow smoking in the caff.'

'Door's open, Viv,' said Charlie, still not turning around.

'Doesn't matter, Charlie. My rules.'

'You smoke.'

'Not in here I don't.'

Charlie pinched his roll-up between thumb and forefinger and leant on the door frame and blew the smoke outside, grinning from ear to ear. 'You're probably ahead of the game, Viv. Government'll be banning smoking in caffs and pubs and maybe even your own bleeding home one day.'

'Yes, they probably will.'

'First seat belts. Then fags. It'll be bacon next. You mark my words. If it's enjoyable they'll ban it. I'd be better off living in bleedin' North Korea.'

'Oh, shut up, Charlie.'

'What did we fight two world wars for, Viv? To be told when we can piss and shit?'

'Fight two world wars? The only thing you've ever fought, Charlie, is poor old Carol when she's trying to carry you up the stairs to bed on a Friday night.'

Charlie snorted.

'Yes, love?' asked Viv, looking at me now.

I glanced up and down at the menu. I wasn't hungry. 'A slice of toast and a cup of tea, please.'

'That it?' No attempt to hide the disappointment in her voice.

From my seat I could see down Drummond Street. I couldn't see the houses, but if someone emerged on to the street from roughly where I knew number 75 to be, I would see. If they walked this way they would pass the café window. If they walked the other way, I'd have to move fast to drop in behind them. I congratulated myself for a second on my strategy and then thought better of it. I should not have come into the café. People had seen me, and, should something untoward happen to Uncle Phil, police would undoubtedly ask questions in here. Would Viv remember a stranger? Many of her customers would be strangers. She might recall a day or two before but not weeks. I relaxed. There was a pen on the empty table next to me, and I leant across and picked it up and began to doodle in the margins of a second copy of the *Sun*. The pen was an annoying little stumpy black biro of the type you find in the bookies. Charlie had probably 'borrowed' it from the Joe Coral next door.

'There you go, Pablo,' smiled Viv, as she placed a mug of steaming tea and a plate in front of me.

I looked up, puzzled. Viv nodded to the vine leaves that I had decorated the borders of the newspaper page with.

'Sorry?' I queried, smiling.

'Pablo Picasso. No worries, I might frame it.'

She was a feisty lady. Divorcee or even a widow, I guessed. In good nick for a lady in her late forties or early fifties. I didn't like the 'no worries', though. Hated the Australianisms that had crept into the English language since the arrival of *Neighbours* on TV in the 1980s. Thought she would have known better.

I started. A man was walking towards me, but, being distracted by Viv, I hadn't seen him come out on to the street. He could have come out of any house in Drummond Street, but he *was* the right side of the road and he *was* elderly. I scribbled quickly with a final flourish on the newspaper and tore a strip off. Got up and placed a five-pound note on the counter.

'Keep the change,' I called, attracting Viv's attention.

'Oh, thanks,' she said, and when she saw the blue note called after me as I stepped out the door. 'You can come again.'

I was thinking fast now. Started walking quickly and was soon within touching distance of the man, so I slowed and dropped back. We turned a corner into a busier road with more cars.

'Phil!' I barked.

The old man stopped in his tracks and slowly turned. I noticed a folded-up orange Sainsbury's bag in his hand. 'Yes?' he said, politely.

It was him. I stepped into his personal space.

'I have something for you.' I held out my arm, fist facing downwards and motioned for the man to accept. Uncle Phil appeared confused, not scared.

'What? Who are you? I'm sorry ...'

'Here,' I said, nodding at my clenched fist.

Uncle Phil slowly extended his arm and spread his spidery fingers, looking at me in the eyes, searching to see if he recognised my face. To see what this strange interlude could be about. I opened my fist and a small piece of torn newspaper dropped into Phil's hand. It said nothing. Just a black spot, crudely scrawled in biro.

I longed to tell Bubbles that I had bumped into Uncle Phil and frightened the granny out of him, but knew I could not. Phil had looked down at the black spot in the palm of his hand, then slowly and deliberately lifted his head and faced me. His hand was still open, the offending scrap of paper sitting in his palm. His body trembled and his facial expression conveyed terror and resignation at the same time. I calmly took his hand and closed it around the black spot, nodded, turned away, crossed the road and walked off. I did not look back.

If the matter were to end there then, perhaps, I could have told Bubbles. For some days I felt that the matter *would* end there. Uncle Phil would have realised the significance of being presented with the black spot by a stranger. He had read *Treasure Island* enough times for the black spot to resonate. Indeed, it was an important device in his grooming of the children he would subsequently abuse. I was sure Bubbles's feeling on that was right. The old man would have made the connection, thought that the messenger of impending death was a grown-up victim and would be worrying himself sick with fear. Was that revenge enough?

No, I decided, it was not. I thought of Bubbles and the others before and after. The horrors that Bubbles did not tell me. I would try and re-create in myself the abject, description-defying fear those assaults would instil in a seven-year-old. The hopelessness a child must have felt being treated in this way by an adult. Old age should not protect this man. Nazi war-murderers were pursued relentlessly into their dotage; the same should happen to Uncle Phil.

I wanted to leave it a couple of months. This time I planned, I hoped, meticulously. Knew I must not get caught, if only to protect Bubbles's privacy and, of course, Holly's. I had decided on a method, and it was a method I could live with. Unlike Hinds, Uncle Phil was not a young, aggressive man, and the thought of committing physical violence on him did not appeal, although I could not rule it out. I kicked myself for leaving that fiver for the lady in the café. She had said I could come again. It was a flourish of unnecessary largesse that could be the difference between remembering me or not.

Planning my Yarmouth appointment got me thinking about murder generally and how easy it was or could be. The killing of strangers especially. Most murderers kill people they know. Most become emotionally involved. Peter Sutcliffe killed strangers, but he was emotionally or sexually involved, and that compulsion led to his downfall. Contract killers often get away with it. Proper ones, at least. Obviously, the smackhead lowlife who takes a bullseye to kill someone will likely be detected, but professional assassins generally are not. I cannot prove that, but I bet I am right. As I explored this train of thought it did not occur to me then that, should I murder Philip Horace Beake, I was myself about to become a triple murderer. I was progressing from being a one-off manslaughterer to double murderer to serial killer.

There was another factor that worked in favour of the committed murderer, and that was the police. I had had only limited dealings with them over the years and did not dislike them. But, for such an important job, I did not understand why they recruited from such a low-calibre pool of talent. Accountants, lawyers and doctors need to pass real exams and learn their craft diligently, but detectives destined to solve the most serious crimes in the country are generally drawn from the uniformed branches, and, as far as I could see, the only disqualifications from becoming a uniformed copper were lack of inches, tattoos and a criminal record. I had long suspected that promotion and progress through the police ranks depended on many things other than ability and intellect. I didn't agree with the school of thought that police officers were intrinsically bent or racist. Most of them were probably thoroughly decent citizens. I remembered feeling that at the height of the Stephen Lawrence affair when an inquiry judge branded them 'institutionally racist' he was off the mark. 'Institutionally stupid' would have been more accurate.

My personal interaction with the police had been positive until one night in High Barnet when I was walking back from the pub with two new pals I had met. We were larking about as we made our way down residential roads to our respective houses. Lee, who was a small lad, momentarily jumped up on a low garden wall, and a front door burst open, and a man in pyjamas came charging down the drive. He was big and was wielding a truncheon and jumped on Lee, bringing him to the ground and placing him in a stranglehold.

'What do you think you're doing?' I shouted as Lee was in no position to protest or breathe easily.

'I'm arresting him for criminal damage. He was kicking my wall down. I am a police officer.'

'He wasn't kicking your wall down, you idiot.'

Me and Jeff closed in around the pair on the floor. He shouted to his wife who stood on the doorstep in her nightie.

'Call the police. Tell them to get here fast.'

'Where's your ID?' asked Jeff. 'You can't arrest him without ID.'

'OK,' boomed this clean-shaven, brutish Brian Blessed look-alike. 'I am making a citizen's arrest.'

'In that case,' I replied, 'I'm citizen-arresting you,' and I grabbed him around the neck falling on top of the two of them. Jeff then began to try and prise open Brian Blessed's grip on Lee's neck. A Black Maria came flying in, bumping up the kerb, lights flashing and siren mewing. They must have been close by, eating hot dogs.

'This bloke's a nutter,' explained Jeff. 'He rugby tackled our mate and has been hitting him with a cosh.'

The four policemen untangled the bundle, and Brian Blessed stood upright, steaming, looking ridiculous in his pyjamas.

'These vandals were kicking down my wall. I saw them from my bedroom window. I'm Sergeant Ridley from Hackney nick, by the way.'

'Didn't touch his wall,' Lee protested.

The policemen looked at the wall, which showed no signs of damage. They asked us to get in the meat wagon, and the sergeant said he was going to get dressed and meet us all at the nick.

At the local station the three of us were put in separate cells. I could hear Ridley insisting we were charged. The Barnet officers pointed out there was no damage visible to any property. In the end they agreed to charge us with Attempted Criminal Damage – a new one on me (and on them, I think). I heard Brian Blessed ask if he could have a few minutes in the cell with the 'big one' (me), and the custody sergeant told him firmly that 'they are my prisoners in my custody, and I am responsible for their wellbeing'. We all knew what the fat bully had in mind. Sergeant left in a huff. Good and bad police illustrated starkly in one incident.

A few weeks later the three of us were up at the magistrates' court. We had been allocated a solicitor on legal aid. He was a sharp cookie. He asked Sergeant Ridley why he didn't show his police ID to us.

'I didn't have time. I saw them about to kick my wall down from my bedroom window and rushed out to stop them.'

'But you had time to pick up your police truncheon?'

Touché. The magistrate had had enough, expressing bafflement as to how one can attempt to damage something and not do so and very sensibly dismissed us with a 'no case to answer'. Ridley was fuming that the forces of law and order had not stuck together. As we left the court we hummed *The Sweeney* theme tune as we passed him. He looked set to explode.

I was still smarting over the fact that he had tried to get into my cell and rough me up and how he had lied and had assaulted Lee and I with a truncheon, so I wrote a letter to the A10 Department at Scotland Yard, which allegedly handled complaints against police officers. A few weeks later, following a friendly telephone call, I was visited by a retired officer who wanted a 'chat' with me. He wore an anorak and Hush Puppies and was a warm, charming old guy. He explained that if I pursued the case Ridley could lose his job and pension. Pointed out he was married with children. Said he was under enormous pressure at Hackney, where violent crime and mugging was exploding. I almost reached for my violin. I signed a form dropping my complaint and only in later years realised I'd been well and truly played.

My low opinion of the general calibre of the police was regularly reinforced on TV's *Crimewatch* and, in earlier times, *Police 5* presented by Shaw 'Keep 'Em Peeled' Taylor. *Crimewatch* normally depressed me and made me angry as I was treated to the terrible things human beings do to each other. The reconstructions were far more compelling and chilling than any film or TV special. Many a night I went to bed hoping that someone *would* break into my house, and I could then legitimately batter, torture and perhaps kill them. I contemplated hanging around building societies in the hope I could intervene in a raid. However, it was the policemen and sometimes women who appeared and appealed that had me shaking my head. They seemed incapable of speaking in a spontaneous and engaging way, instead reverting to a ridiculous monotone *witnessboxspeak*. People didn't walk anywhere, they proceeded, times were always approximate, not around or about, and cars were vehicles. I just knew these individuals nearly all lacked perception, nuance, intellect and talent. The notion of detectives all coming from the uniformed force seemed as daft as expecting the executives of railway companies all to have served time as train drivers or ticket collectors. If the robotic characters on TV news broadcasts and *Crimewatch* had not got into the police they would have been traffic wardens. Any self-respecting criminal should be capable of running rings around this self-serving, insular bunch of dunces.

If I were to commit a crime, I mused, I would get a kid's transfer tattoo of a swallow on my hand or even on my cheekbone. It would just not occur to the police that someone would go to such lengths, and suspects who did not have such markings would be overlooked. They would be for ever foxed. I would wear clothes I never wore before and would never wear again. I would feign an accent. Walk with a limp. Speak with a lisp. Wear a distinctive rare aftershave. Apply a skin-tanning product. I would plan carefully, just as I would the renovation or conversion of a house, anticipating the potential pitfalls along the way.

While I was still working out what to do about Phil, I had a visit from Holly. We sat and talked. She was full of herself and the place that she and Norm were going to buy. I offered her money towards this next step up the property ladder. 'I'm offering *you* the money, Holly,' I stressed. 'Nothing against Norman, but we need a legal agreement that you owe me the money. I don't really want it back, but if, God forbid, you two split up then he gets half, and that's not on. If you are still together in ten or fifteen years then, of course, we'll forget it.'

'Thanks for the confidence in our relationship, Dad,' said Holly, resting her hand on my forearm to reassure me she wasn't really offended.

'You know what I mean. If I give you £50,000 – that's a lot of money.'

'Fifty grand, Dad? We, I, don't need that much. We've got a small deposit between us.'

'Well, now you've got a big deposit.'

Holly leant over and kissed me on the cheek and practically skipped across the kitchen to flick the kettle switch back on.

'Now then, Dad, do you watch afternoon telly?'

'Not if I can help it.'

'Yes, thought not. Well, there's this bloke, a psychic called Howard Plume. You heard of him?'

I shook my head.

'Well, I know you won't have any of it, but he's a psychic, as I said, and he's really good. No, seriously, he is. Watch his programme, Dad. Just watch it. He really does get messages from the other side.'

'Does he?' My reply laced with scepticism. Apprehension rising.

'Yes, I think it's genuine. I've sat and watched it and tried to work out how he does it. Trying to suss out if it's a hoax. But I can't see how he does it. I really can't. The other day he had this woman's husband talking to him, and he said to this woman, "Your husband had an industrial accident when he was a young man." How would he know that? He also said, "Who's Willow?" and she started crying; it was his pet name for her. I mean how can he get that sort of thing?'

I looked at Holly and smiled cynically. 'Holly, I have seen some of these programmes. These people ... It's all bollocks, it really is. When these people come through do they ever say their second names?'

Holly thought. 'No, I can't say they do.'

'There you go. Why wouldn't they? Why would Howard whatever-his-name-is say, "I've got a man here. His name begins with J. John." No reply. "Johnny, Joe, Joseph." A hand goes up. "Joseph, that's it." The hand belongs to a young lady. "It's your father or father figure." He's covering himself here for father, grandfather or uncle ... it's unlikely to be her husband, too young ...'

'OK, OK, I get your drift ...'

'No, I'm serious. If this Joseph fellow was actually there – from the other side – would he really say, "Hello, Mr Psychic. I'm here to contact my loved ones. My name begins with J." Wouldn't he know his own name? Wouldn't he say, "Hello, Mr Medium, I'm Joseph Jones, and my daughter is in the audience, and her name is Caroline Rogers née Jones"?'

'You've got a point.'

'It's more than a point. It's a fucking scandal, Holly. These people profit from the misery of the bereaved. Create false hopes. Lowest of the low if you think about it.'

'There are still some strange things, there's still stuff you can't explain.'

'I bet *I* can. Why do you ask? Don't tell me he's moving into the area and Norman is his estate agent?'

'No. He's on at the Fairfield Halls next month, and me and Norm have tickets. Come with us.'

I smiled and shook my head. 'I'm washing my hair that night.'

'But I thought you believed in life after death?'

'Do I?'

'When I was a little girl, you used to tell me that lovely rhyme. Remember, about the robin? How did it go?

'An old Norfolk angler told me when I was a lad,
That the robin sitting on his rod was his dear old dad
And if he were lucky and the kingfisher do come
That's sure to be his lovely old mum.

'I love that, Dad. I walk the canal and the river looking for a kingfisher. I really do. I've not seen one yet. But if you believe that, why wouldn't you give Howard Plume a chance?'

Holly looked like she was about to cry.

'Ummm,' I said, expressing scepticism and disapproval in a single sound.

The conversation had danced around something or someone unsaid. Jan. And I began to feel cross. Very, very cross.

12
HOLLY

It was not long before Christmas, and there was an urgent rapping at the door one wet Thursday night. It was gone eleven. I had been making coffee. I'd got into making filter coffee. Took longer. Filled time. Time was dragging. Sometimes when I contemplated how empty the day ahead of me was, I panicked. Walking filled an hour. Reading the paper another. I had even started going to the pub, even though I didn't really like drinking. Normally I'd go to the Retreat by the station, where I'd sit and watch the world go by.

Question Time was running on the television, and, as usual, it was infuriating me. Full of platitudes and patronising talk. Promising and pretending. It was party lines and party lies. These people are running the country. I only knew Clare Short – whinging old cow. Change the record. There was a young Tory MP called Osborne. Quiffed hair. Superiority complex. Confident in his position and destiny. Face you'd like to punch. The token Lib Dem was called Barney or something equally stupid. You call a horse Barney, not an innocent, newborn baby. They're all promising a new dawn in a way only people who know they will never be in power can. Something about Barney, though, that I didn't like. I distrusted the Lib Dems as much as the others, even though they were irrelevant. And finally, there was the TV presenter, who had been worming into my brain for a few years. He was a young chap and looked like a decent, inoffensive guy. He was called Ned. What sort of parents call their new child Ned? Attention seekers, that's who. Ned played to the audience, saying what they wanted to hear and was less combative and offensive than he was on his own morning-TV show. He was puffed up at getting the offer of high-brow television and wasn't going to blow it. I had seen him a bit for a couple of years now; I knew the bile, hatred and insecurity that lurked beneath the 'man of the people' persona he was keen to portray. He has positioned himself as being on the side of the people. A champion of the working class despite never having done a proper day's work in his life.

Nobody normal knocks on your door at 11 pm. I thought it might be the police. Stuart Hinds and Frank Cox came into my mind. For the first time in a long time. Or somebody seeking to harm me. I took a carving knife, the sharpest I had, from a drawer and tucked into the back of my jeans, feeling the cold Sheffield steel against bare buttock. I opened the door with a fast flourish thinking that if there was hostility on the other side it would give me a degree of surprise advantage.

'Dad,' sighed Holly as she fell into my arms. Norman stood behind her and swivelled his eyes from side to side transmitting that she was in an emotional state, not him.

'Dad,' she said, looking up, mascara smudges rendering her panda-like.

'What's happened, Holly? What's happened, Norman?'

Softly to Holly, with an edge in my voice to Norman.

'No, no, it's good. It's good. It's wonderful. We've got a message for you ... from Mum.'

Holly tumbled into the lounge, tripping up and righting herself such was her excitement. Told me to sit down. Told Norman to take over making the coffee. She patted the space next to her on the sofa, like she was encouraging a dog. 'Sit, Dad, sit.'

My facial muscles tightened.

'We've been to see Howard Plume, the psychic off the telly, at the Fairfield Halls. Remember, I told you? He was on tonight.'

I nodded, anger rising within me.

'Well, you'll never going to believe this, Dad, but it's true.'

Holly started to sob, swallowing gobs of tears in her throat. 'Well, Mum came through.'

'No, you're right, Holly, I'm never going to believe it …'

Holly held up both hands and patted them downwards in front of my face. 'Hear me out, hear me out, Dad, please. Mum came through. I'm telling you. I swear. I promise. She came through. She did … and she had a message for you. Howard made me promise I'd give you the message.'

Howard? They're on first-name terms now? I took one of the three cups of coffee Norman was proffering and carefully placed it on the table. This time I raised my hand.

'Holly, I don't want to hear this. Came through? Came through? It's bollocks. I told you that, and the man is a menace upsetting people like this. You've paid him to upset you. He's a bad man.'

I was rigid. Adrenaline powered around my body. The muscles in my upper arms started to pop. I could feel a pulse above my eye. I wondered if it was visible.

'He hasn't upset me, Dad. He's made me happy. Seriously happy. Mum has spoken to me. Didn't she, Norm?'

Norm nodded and shrugged at the same time. He really wished he were somewhere else.

'And she wanted to speak to you. Dad, let me tell you from the beginning. Let me tell you and then see what you think.'

'Go on then.' Face burning. Sitting forward.

'Well. It was like the TV programme. You know *The Other Side*. It was a full house, though. Wasn't it, Norm? Before, in the foyer, there is like this goldfish bowl thing and you can put a photo in and write on the back who'd you like to get a message from, that type of thing.'

'That's handy,' I said cynically.

'No, we didn't do any of that. Walked straight in. Howard Plume came out and just stood there. Straight away he had a boy come through who had been killed in a motorbike accident eighteen years ago. What was his name, Norm?'

'Darryl.'

'That's it, Darryl. Not a common name. He said, I've got Darren here. Darren or Darryl. Lady in front of us put her hand up. Darryl. Why do I get the figure eighteen? he says. Was he eighteen when he died? No, she says, he was twenty-three. And then she says, but it's eighteen years ago this week that he was killed. We all gasped. Didn't we, Norm? Did he die suddenly? asks Howard. Yes, says the lady. It was his neck, wasn't it, my love? says Howard, and she's crying, this lady, and she says yes. He broke his neck, didn't he? I see a tree, says Howard. Yes, she says, he hit a tree. But he wasn't in a car, was he? No, he was on a motorbike, not his, though. Yes, he was on the back of a bike. That's right, says Howard, and you told him about mucking about on bikes, didn't you? Yes, yes, I did, says this poor woman. You told him so many times, didn't you, dear? And she told him that very night he died. Who's Brett? She shakes her head. Brad? She shakes her head. Then she shouts, BRADSHAW – that was the boy driving the bike. You could have heard a pin drop, Dad. Did they call him Brad? I don't think so, says the woman. His nickname was George, although his real name was Marcus. He died, too. Yes, I know, says Howard. He's with your son. And if you ask around, you'll find they called him Brad. Anyway, Dad, there were a few more – not as good as Darryl – but still stuff you can't explain, and then he looks up to where me and Norm were sitting. It was weird. He pointed at us. Or, at least, it felt like us.

'I have a mother figure, he says. A young-looking, pretty mother figure. We kept quiet. Never moved. She's not giving a name. What's your name, my darling? he kept saying. Like he's talking to her. I've got Mum here, he suddenly says forcefully. And he pointed right at me. Is your mum spirit-side, my love? he says, and I nodded. Dad, I was shaking like a leaf. I thought I was going to faint or be sick or something. Norm was squeezing my hand. Stand up, he says. And he told Norm to stand up next to me to support me. And we stood up, and the spotlight swings round on us, and we are also on the monitors up on the stage. Because we are far back Howard talked to us in the monitor, which was weird. Mum's not been gone long, has she? I nodded. Her problem was here, he said, and he motioned his hand around his chest in a circular fashion. Yes, she died of breast cancer, I said. She wants you to know she's happy. She wants you to know that she's watching over you. She said, watch your drinking. Cheek! The audience all laughed. Not because she says you're a drunk. Everyone's laughing now. She says you both know you have to watch the pounds.'

I sighed, my eyes rolling to the back of my head. My fists clenching.

'Hang on, Dad, hang on. Then he went all serious. Went all quiet – didn't he, Norm? – and looked up and said, Dad's still with us, isn't he? Dad, still this side of life? Yes, I said. Your mum's worried about him. She's got a message for him. Will you give it to your dad? Yes, I said. Well, your mum says to your dad, I'm OK, let me go. Stop fretting and get on with your life. I want that more than anything. If you want me to be happy you must be happy. That's what she is saying, my love. Will you tell your dad? So, I'm telling you.'

Holly had got it all out and sighed heavily. I slumped deeper into the sofa and winced and jerked up. I had forgotten the knife was tucked into the back of my jeans. I tried to get up. I was angry.

'No, hang on, hang on,' pleaded Holly, now holding my forearm, pushing me back into my seat. 'Guess what he said then? This will do your fucking head in! I'll tell you what he said. He said, is your dad nicknamed Bubbles? I nearly collapsed. That's when I knew it was Mum – definitely Mum. Norman had to stop me fainting. I said, no, but our very close family friend is called Bubbles. He lived with us for a few years. Well, says Howard Plume, your mum wants you to tell Bubbles she loves him, too. I will go and see him tomorrow, I said.'

Spent, Holly sat back on the sofa looking at me expectantly. Smiling broadly. Her eyes were sparkling with joy. Waiting for my reaction. She really believed she had spoken to her mum. My Jan. I reached behind me and slowly produced the carving knife from my trousers, a smudge of blood visible on the edge of the blade. I laid it carefully on the coffee table. Holly and Norman looked at me, bewildered and shocked.

'I didn't know who was at the door this late. I tucked it in my trousers.'

'You answer the door with a knife down your trousers? Who are you expecting? Son of Sam? Frankie Fraser?'

I smiled weakly.

'Well?'

'I don't believe it, Holly. I believe that you believe it. Don't get me wrong. This man has deceived and duped you.'

'But how do you explain Bubbles? It's not the most common of nicknames, is it? How many Bubbleses in the entire country? Ten? Twenty? If he had said John or even Paul, then fair enough. But Bubbles, Dad? Come on, think about it.'

'I don't know, Holly, I don't, but there will be a way. He has found that family connection somehow. I cannot answer that. But, think about it, Holly. Think about this. If Mum wanted to talk to us, or, should I say, *could* talk to us, she would contact us privately not through a fucking panto act in front of hundreds of people.'

'But, Dad, what about if there are only certain people who have that ability to receive messages from the other side? What about that? Mum would do whatever she had to do to talk to us, wouldn't she?'

Holly had a point.

'He might look at who has booked, I don't know how. He might then pick one or two to find out some history about them and they'll be his star turns. Like the motorbike boy, Darryl, and maybe you. I don't know, but you'd be surprised what you can find out on the internet about someone from 192, Ancestry, newspaper archives and so on.'

'Dad, you're not going to find the name Bubbles on a family-tree database or a newspaper report, are you?'

'Maybe not. Maybe, maybe this bloke had a spy in the audience or in the foyer and overheard a conversation?'

'We never mentioned Bubbles. We walked straight in and sat down. Dad, you've got to face it. There's something in it. I want to go and see him and have a private sitting, and I want you to come with me.'

'Over my dead body.'

After Holly had left, I turned her account over again and again in my mind. I dissected it. Plume opened up with 'I have a mother figure' here. 'Mother figure': here he is casting his net wide. Could include mother, mother-in-law, grandmother, even aunt. Holly said he pointed at her, but he pointed in their direction. He could have read her body language, seen how she tensed and leant forward at the mention of a pretty, young-looking mother. He motioned in the rough area of his chest and suggested that who-ever he had with him had died of breast cancer. This was no big deal. If it's a younger mother who has died, then there is a reasonable chance breast cancer could be the cause. In fact, it was Holly who had volunteered breast cancer, Plume just circled his hand around his torso. That could cover a whole gamut of lethal complaints. Jan allegedly saying you both have to watch the pounds. Well, he could guess that by looking at her and Norman standing there. Most people in the country could do with losing some pounds. And then the message for me. That would be an easy call – the chances of Holly having lost both parents at an early age would be slim. Poor widowed Dad, of course, could benefit from a message. Unpicked, Howard Plume's deceit and shameless exploitation is stark. In the heat of the night, Plume's stabs in the dark are carried along, developed and bolstered by the raw emotion and grief that swirls around the auditorium. He has a grieving, expectant audience longing for a message from their departed loved ones. It's cruel, immoral and should be criminalised. The one bit that has stumped me, though, is how he pulled up the name Bubbles. It's not a name you might hit lucky with like George or Dave. How did he do that? Logic tells me that he either does possess some powers or he has employed some subterfuge somewhere along the line. My every instinct tells me it's the latter not the former, and that means the evil bastard has been doing some detective work on my family. How fucking dare he?

13
UNCLE PHIL

I WALKED PAST 75 Drummond Street, slowing up and taking in as much as I could without looking like that's what I was doing. It was past 9 pm and dark, and there was nobody on the residential street, although I had passed a lady in a garden further up encouraging her dog shrilly to 'do his doings', but she had not looked up. I was wearing a Parka-type coat so I could be hooded without being a hoodie. I had grown a beard and played with my hair. The living-room light was on, and through a chink in the curtains and net I could see the glow of a television and a flicker of moving image. Uncle Phil was in and watching TV. Was he alone? Most probably, as he lived alone as far as I knew, but there was a chance a neighbour or a friend could be with him. A relative could be staying. There was no vehicle directly outside, so if there were any visitors, I decided it could only be a neighbour on foot. I turned all this over in my mind as I about-turned at the café end of the road and proceeded back up towards number 75.

It had been nearly half a year since my previous visit, when I had presented Phil with the black spot. Had he been to the police since? Probably not. Not easy to walk into a police station and say a man approached you in the street and pressed the black spot into your palm. The black spot? Yeah. You know the thing in *Treasure Island*? Have you not heard of Blind Pugh? The police officer behind the desk would be discretely online searching for the Alzheimer's Hotline. No, Uncle Phil would have got it. Got it, straight away. His past had come back to haunt him and taunt him. To threaten him. Uncle Phil would have had nearly six months of mental suffering and mind terror. Not too terrified to carry on, though. To sit in an armchair and watch TV on a Wednesday night. I would have come sooner – making Phil's life highly uncomfortable, terrifying even was not enough – but another equally enraging development had been unfolding at home. Howard Shitcunt Plume had seriously crossed my radar.

I opened the garden gate, and in three or four steps was close enough to the window to see through the chink in the curtains and net to inside number 75. Uncle Phil was in an armchair, as I had imagined he would be. He was wearing a tie, shirt and short-sleeved pullover, which I thought was a tad formal for an evening alone watching Alan Sugar on television, for that was who was on the small screen: bull-necked, grey-flecked beard, wire-brush hair and berating a group of besuited, bouncy-haired young men and women in front of him. Later he would be jabbing his sausage forefinger at one of them telling them they were fired, even though they weren't in his employment. I walked back a few steps, then took a large stride forward on to the doorstep and pressed the bell. Looking at my watch, I noted the time was 9.05 pm.

I pulled down my hood. Phil fiddled with a chain behind the door. He had got to the door surprisingly quickly. I stepped back a pace. He opened the door slightly and cautiously put his head into the space.

'Hello, Phil,' I said, smiling widely to disarm him.

'Oh, hello,' said Phil nervously, polite.

'It's me, Phil.' I stepped forward and proffered my hand, feigning relaxed familiarity. The door did not open further.

'Who?'

'Me, Phil,' and at the same time, bang! Barging the door, and I was in the hallway, door shut behind me with a swift back-kick worthy of Bruce Lee. I grabbed Phil as he fell backwards and helped him, almost kindly, regain his balance.

'It's me, Phil, Blind Pugh.'

I led the older man into the lounge and eased him back into his armchair. I sat on a two-seat sofa opposite.

'Phil, do you know why I'm here?'

Phil's frailty and passivity had fazed me. I was competing with Alan Sugar, so I leant forward and attempted to turn the TV off but could not find a button. I signalled to the remote control on the arm of Phil's chair. 'Turn it off. No, turn it down. Now, Phil, why am I here?'

Phil's veiny hands were visibly shaking, and he was blinking furiously.

'Phil, come on. I'm not playing games. Why am I here?'

Phil still did not reply. He sat, head bowed, submissive.

'*Uncle* Phil,' I said slowly with a deliberate slow emphasis on the *Uncle*.

Phil looked up, a film of fear tears obscuring worried eyes. 'Are you from Pine Forest?' he murmured eventually.

'What do you think, Phil?'

'I don't remember. It's a long time ago.'

'You don't remember Pine Forest? Or you don't remember *me*?'

'I don't remember you.'

'You remember Pine Forest, though?'

Silence, then, 'Yes. Yes, I do.'

'So, you know why I'm here?'

'Yes, I've known since the day … the day someone put the black spot in my hand. I've been expecting you. Expecting someone. Expecting something. I'm truly sorry for what I did. I'm truly sorry. I regret it all. Regret anything I did with you. I have spent a lifetime regretting it.'

'Hang on, Phil, let's not get ahead of ourselves here. You didn't do anything *with* anyone. You did it *to* them. They were tiny children, remember? You were a man. A middle-aged man. A big man. An adult.'

'I'm sorry. I am truly sorry.' Phil was sobbing and tangling his fingers nervously.

'And you didn't do anything to *me*. I'll tell you who I am. My name is John. You can call me John. I work for an organisation that seeks justice for abuse victims. We're called SOAK: Survivors Of Abuse Kinship. But we're different. We are underground. We don't whine about our lot. We don't go on the telly. We don't rely on the system to right the wrongs. Because the system will not. We do it ourselves. We're the military wing, if you like. And we do not deal with our own cases – that makes it too personal and makes mistakes more likely. I've been assigned to your case.'

Where this all came from, I really don't know! SOAK? Military wing? Assigned to his case? I was pleased, though. Thinking on my feet and firing out that menacing and believable bullshit. I almost believed it myself. Made me feel credible. Elevated me above vengeful, unbalanced nutter category. Why hadn't someone started up SOAK? I had not in the heat of the moment mentioned Bubbles. I had not connected myself to this man and realised now I did not *have* to kill him. From the moment I had burst through the door I had been thinking that I was going to take this man's life because I had to. Because he had seen me. I had pulled the situation back unplanned to something I had a degree of control over. I relaxed. I was pleased with my impromptu, sharp but lucky thinking.

Phil was leaning forward in his armchair. Wiping away tears. I could see his hands were trembling, as were his legs. Maybe he didn't want to sit back in his armchair in case it looked like arrogance.

'Phil,' I said quietly, 'I am not going to hurt you.'

'I am so sorry. So sorry for what I did,' the old man sobbed.

'I need to understand why you did it, Phil. I mean, personally I like women, but I manage to restrain myself from sexually attacking them. And, do you know what, Phil? If I had a sexual attraction to children I would be disgusted. Distressed. Worried. I would suppress it. Whatever it took, Phil. I would suppress it, and if I couldn't I would kill myself rather than interfere with a little child. What did *you* do, Phil? You got yourself a position where you had unfettered access. You made it happen, Phil. Uncle Phil.'

'It's not like that. Honestly. I worked with children because I genuinely loved them. I became genuinely fond of some of them and let my feelings escape. I'm deeply ashamed. And yes, I have thought about suicide many times ...'

Phil's eyes begged me to believe him, but I tensed up.

'Feelings escape? Don't give me that utter shit. It's not about feelings is it, Phil? It's about lust. Perverted lust. Bollocks! That's maybe what you have told yourself to make your life a tiny bit bearable. There is no wiggle room here. You were a man. A man with a man's prick. Playing with it around little, defenceless children in your care. Children who looked to you for love and security. There is no defence.'

'No, there isn't.' Phil leant further forward and put his head into his hands. 'What happens now? What must I do? What happens now? Are you going to call the police?'

'Am I going to call the police? No, I'm not going to call the fucking police. We've got beyond that, Phil. I think you know that.'

Phil nodded solemnly.

'You know what, Phil? You have an opportunity here to make some amends. Do you know what I mean?'

'How? Do you want money?'

That angered me, and I stood up abruptly. I was not going to strike an elderly man, but I wanted to hit out. I wanted to shake him.

'Money does not compensate for blighting childhoods and lives. You don't get it, do you? It's time for you to try and put some things right. You have ruined lives. I don't know how many, and I don't want you to tell me. For all you know some of those children may have killed themselves – some may have repeated the abuse on their children or other kids. Who knows? If I were you, I would write a letter to the children you abused. An open letter. Tell them how you feel. Tell them what you are going to do and that you hope it gives them some small comfort.'

Phil was keeping up. He knew exactly what I meant. He sat quietly for a moment. Blinking. Gripping the arms of his chair.

'What have you got to do, Phil?'

'I need to write a sincere letter of apology.'

'What do you need to do, Phil, to show them you are genuinely remorseful? What do you need to do to give your victims closure? Genuine closure.'

Phil sat nodding. His nervous twitch was getting worse. 'Give myself up to the police?'

'Give yourself up to the police, Phil? What, a slap on the wrists? Maybe a year or so in an open prison? Come on, Phil, you can do better than that.'

The old man thought for a bit and started nodding as if he was confirming to himself an inner decision. 'I need to end my life to show them how sorry I am.'

'Yes, Phil. I believe you do.'

We sat in silence – the two of us – considering the enormity and finality of the conclusion that had been reached. After a short time Phil seemed to relax, and he sat back in his chair. The upshot and the articulating of it giving him strength.

'Can I go the bureau?' Phil eventually said firmly.

It was like the decision had unburdened him. I nodded. I noted that age had bent the man over as he strode to the bureau. I believe that the burden of what he had done *did* weigh heavily. Here was a man with genuine remorse. The house smelt of remorse. No plants. No colour. Framed photographs of long-dead relatives from the past. Parents who mercifully had no idea of what their son had become. Phil pulled up a wooden chair, flipped down a lid and found a pen and pad and began writing. And kept writing. Finally, after fifteen minutes Phil turned to me and proffered his letter.

'I've written this letter a thousand times in my head.'

I waved his letter away. 'I'm sure you've said the right things. Can I make a suggestion?'

'Please do,' replied Phil, whose voice was becoming stronger and stronger.

'Why don't you add a postscript? Why don't you add a change to your will? Why don't you express the wish that the proceeds of your estate are gifted to the NSPCC?'

Phil nodded. 'Yes, I will. My nephew was due to inherit. I hear from him once a year when he rings to check whether I'm dead yet.'

Phil smiled. I smiled.

'I would like to leave a sum to my sister. She has been a good sibling, and she has no idea what I was.'

I felt like a bully, with him pleading to be able to leave part of his estate to his sister.

'Of course. It's all your decision, Phil. Not mine. I will not read your letter so you can address it to Inspector Morse and tell him all about me and what's happened if you like. I know you will not, though. You will do what is right.'

Phil nodded and wrote some more and then sealed the letter in an envelope. Stood it up on the bureau. I could see he had addressed it TO WHOM IT MAY CONCERN – WITH THE DEEPEST REGRET. Phil returned to his chair and sat down. He reached for the remote control and turned the television off.

'How shall I do it?'

'You said you had thought about it before.'

'Yes, I thought paracetamol, but sometimes it doesn't work.'

'True.'

'I thought that,' Phil said, pointing to the banister of the wooden stairs. I looked around.

'Yes. Could do.'

'I could tie a rope around the top part of the banister, put it around my neck and jump. Or you could kick the chair away for me?'

'No. I will leave shortly. This is your business. Your decision.'

'Strange isn't it? I have decided to take my life, and it has just occurred to me where the saying "kick the bucket" comes from. It's from this. Poor, wretched souls in their kitchens or sheds turning over an old tin bucket and kicking it away.'

'I guess so.'

'Can I ask you something? How do you know that when you leave I won't just tear the letter up and contact the police?'

I smiled and shrugged my shoulders. 'I know that you won't. I think what you are going to do shows courage. You are giving some closure to the people you have mistreated. You are giving something back. It makes some amends. If I were you, I would get the signing of that letter witnessed by a neighbour. If you have a will, make an amendment and get that witnessed, too. And then, when your affairs are in order, you will do what you need to do.'

'Yes, I will.'

We sat in silence just looking at each other. Uncle Phil smiled and shrugged as if to say there was nothing more to add. I stood up.

'Goodbye, John. And thank you,' Phil said, offering his hand.

Incredible. The guy is thanking me for encouraging him strongly to take his own life.

I shook Uncle Phil's hand. Turned and let myself out the front door. As I walked down the path I looked back and could see Phil lowering himself back into his armchair. I wondered if he was going to switch *The Apprentice* back on.

I monitored the Norfolk and Yarmouth online press for news of Uncle Phil. I knew I shouldn't. If I ever got connected to Phil's fate or Phil did go to the authorities, here I was leaving a trail of online interest in Yarmouth and deaths. Again! I was becoming conscious of my digital footprint, but how else would I discover whether my plans had worked? On the other hand, what had I done wrong? Persuaded somebody he needed to take responsibility for his actions? Signposted a road to redemption? I had no idea how the law would view my role. I still don't.

The law deems it an offence to commit an act that encourages somebody to take their own life, but is having a civil conversation with somebody an 'act'? I doubt it. Personally, I have never heard or read of anybody being charged with that offence. And, if Phil went through with his act there is only one person left on the planet who knows what went between us. Phil could have even put in his letter what my role was, but it's still my word against his, and he will be dead so he will not be elaborating. As with Stuart Hinds – about which I now figured the worst charge I could face in that case would be manslaughter, and I would have a good chance of getting off that – I felt that, although I had been instrumental in ending two lives so far, I could imagine a scenario where that could not be proved in law.

Finally, in July I found an inquest report:

YARMOUTH PENSIONER PLANNED SUICIDE

Philip Horace Beake, aged 75, from Great Yarmouth was found dead by a neighbour who had received a letter in the post from him, Norwich Coroner's Court has heard. The letter contained a key to his house. Mr Beake was taken to Gorleston Hospital in April this year but was pronounced dead on arrival. His medical cause of death was recorded as hanging by the neck. Police have confirmed there are no suspicious circumstances. Mr Beake had shown no signs of mental illness and had 'prepared assiduously in taking his own life' concluded the coroner 'and had left correspondence for various friends, relatives and institutions confirming his intentions'.

The report suggested that Uncle Phil had done the right thing, and I could not help feeling a tiny bit of admiration for him but quickly tried to suppress that. He was a bad man. Advancing age had rendered him harmless, but that's all it had done. I wanted to rush over and show Bubbles, but how would I explain the coincidence of finding that online? I guessed he would hear about it one way or the other. I hoped that Uncle Phil had followed through with the bequest. I believed he had. The police would have to act on his confessions, wouldn't they? They'd have to launch an investigation. I hoped so, but I could not be sure. What I do regret is not instructing Phil to mention he had met Justice Killer and reference Stuart Hinds and Frank Cox. That would have set the cat among the pigeons. Instead, they're probably investigating this underground vigilante group SOAK as I write.

14
IS ANYBODY THERE?

One evening Holly dropped in. I knew she wanted to talk to me again, and I knew what about.

'Have you been to see Howard Plume yet? He's on at Epsom again soon, at the Playhouse.'

'Is he? No, I haven't been to see him, and I won't be going.'

'Go, Dad. I really think you need to go.'

'I really think I don't. He's a fraud. I told you.'

Holly looked at me like she was dealing with a cantankerous grandparent. A slight raising of the eyebrow. Like her mum used to.

'Holly, think about it. These people could go on Friends Reunited and find out about people. Message boards. MySpace, or whatever you call it. There are ways of doing it. I'll tell you what, I watched one of those shysters the other afternoon, because you told me to. I watched it. Shevell or something was his name. And at the end the television company had a disclaimer, basically saying that they relied on the bloke's word that everything was above board. They are not risking getting sued. And at the beginning they had a voiceover saying, "The following programme is clairtainment," joining the words clairvoyant and entertainment. Clairtainment? I ask you … The television company is clearly saying, "This is bunkum, but you might enjoy it nevertheless."'

'I understand,' she said eventually, not shocked at my rant. We talked and laughed about other matters, and just before she left Holly took my hand again.

'It's good to see you laugh, Dad.'

'Thanks,' I said, not sure what the right response was to her remark.

'I think you're coming out the other side. I really do. I think you're happier.'

'Maybe I am,' I lied. How do you tell your daughter that you've drowned a man, chucked another off a fucking cliff and bullied, frightened, coerced, terrified and shamed an old man into murdering himself and were seriously considering slaying another, and that it was that and that alone that had provided some purpose to my life? Seeking and executing justice had made my days bearable. How do you tell your daughter that?

When she left I called the Epsom Playhouse and asked if I could turn up on the night to see Howard Plume. They said they were expecting a sell-out and I should book now. They would, wouldn't they? I booked. Again I knew this could all be leading somewhere it should not – at least in law and in terms of my personal freedom – but I still used a credit card to book a show by Howard Plume and therefore connected myself to him. I was being reckless.

A few weeks later I hung around in the foyer of this theatre in Epsom that jutted out the side of a concrete multi-storey car park like a broken bone. It amazed me that so many of the old pop music acts from the 1960s and 1970s were still going and attracting audiences. 'Coming Soon' posters that I studied on the walls betrayed the fact that most of the members could not be originals. Not a hearing aid or Zimmer frame in sight. I was so old that even the first generation of tribute bands probably had tribute bands of their own. I was early and collected my ticket from the booth, but already the foyer area was teeming with people. There were more women than men. Plenty of mother-and-daughter combos, groups of younger female friends, but there were also a few men. One, about my age, struck me. He was alone, and I studied him. Why hadn't he gone into the auditorium and to his seat? Was he moving adjacent to one group and then another? Was he eavesdropping? Then I thought he could say the same about me. My fraud antennae well and truly over-stimulated.

All the time the foyer filled, people chatting excitedly, until a disembodied voice emanated from the walls and asked the audience to take their seats. The building excitement was palpable. I sat next to an elderly lady on one side who clutched her large handbag protectively to her lap like it was a matter of life and death. My imagination was running wild, and I wondered if the bag contained an urn with her husband's ashes inside. On my other side sat a couple. From the husband's expression and body language he was there under duress. A bit like myself.

The spotlight picked out a table on the stage. Only a glass and jug of water and a box of tissues sat on it – the first tissue half pulled-out ready for action, signalling there would be tears. The beam lingered on the table, silently demanding the audience stop their whispering and the rustling of Haribo bags.

'Ladies and gentlemen, please give your warmest welcome to the clairvoyant to the stars ... the one and only Howard Plume.'

A wave of goodwill and applause cascaded down the tiers and across the rows. At the front, a line of women was up on their feet applauding like Tom Jones's groupies, and this encouraged others to stand, cheer and whistle. From stage left, bathed in the spotlight, the man himself emerged.

He was a ridiculous-looking figure. Five feet five inches in heels, wearing a blue crushed-velvet three-piece suit and a fat tie. I reckoned he was about fifty. He had a round face, with a full head of long, greying hair, parted in the middle. He could have been walking on to the stage of *The Wheeltappers And Shunters Social Club* circa 1975. If he reminded me of anyone it was the comedian Mick Miller from the 1970s TV show *The Comedians*. He luxuriated in the adulation, smiling broadly, waving, recognising – or pretending to recognise – an audience member here and there.

I had read up on him beforehand. He had worked for years in

an Inland Revenue office in the Midlands where, allegedly, his 'gift' first manifested itself as he started receiving messages from the 'other side' for his colleagues, and it went on from there. This nonentity could not believe his luck. His moribund, lowly clerical career from tea boy to retirement carriage clock had been mapped out, and here he was playing to an audience of three hundred devotees who had shelled out £25 a pop. The nobody had become a somebody in middle life, and Howard Plume, the so-called 'Telepathic Taxman', was wallowing in riches, adulation and who knows what else based on a diabolical deception.

'Good evening,' he said in a telephone voice. 'Welcome to Epsom. Hello Epsom! How are we tonight?'

What does he think this is? A Radio One Roadshow?

The audience murmured back.

'Some of you will know the ropes of how tonight will flow ... hopefully ... We are dealing with spirits, remember, and they are a law unto themselves. Sometimes they are late ... sometimes they are truculent. Basically, how they were in life. Well, their personalities don't change because they are spirit-side.'

The audience laughed. This bonhomie regarding the alleged mischievous spirits turned out to be a running theme. He then stepped forward. The lights dimmed. And he put his hands together pointing upwards like a dedicated Thai waiter. He smiled and nodded. Eyes closed.

'Yes ... yes ... yes ...'

A spirit has turned up on cue.

'That's good. I get you. I get you.'

The spirit is talking to him.

'Hang on, hang on,' he laughs.

Cheeky, excited spirit must settle down.

'Calm down, calm down.'

He's channelling his inner Harry Enfield now.

He shields his eyes using his hand as a visor and surveys the audience.

'You. Yes you. The lady in the red blazer.'

The lady in the red blazer looks to her left and right checking for other ladies in red blazers.

'Yes you, my lovely. Do you mind standing up? Are you with her?'

He addresses the people sitting next to her.

'I'm her mum.'

'I'm her aunt.'

'Good. What's your name, my lovely?'

'Janet Tr—'

'No, no. Just your Christian name. Janet, that's lovely. Ladies can you please support Janet. Physically, I mean. No, not now. In case she needs it.'

'Janet. I have a male figure here. Older figure.'

Janet is nodding vigorously. She wants it. Bad.

Why doesn't Mr Spirit tell Plume his name? He's here and he has identified Janet, but he cannot remember his own name?

'Janet, is dad spirit-side?' He cocks his head to one side.

'Yes,' she says before Plume has even finished. She is squeezing her fists shut and opening them again like an excited child. She cannot wait.

'He's here with me. Right now.'

An audible gasp from the audience. Janet buckles slightly, and her mum and aunt stand and hold her upright, one arm each. All eyes are on the three of them.

He's taking a good look at the mum working out her rough age searching for clues.

'Yes, yes …' Plume says, ostensibly carrying on a conversation with Janet's dad. 'He is trying to tell me his name.'

Why can't he tell you his name, Howard? Has he got a speech impediment?

'I'm getting Patrick.'

No response from Janet or her mum, who should be getting excited, too.

'No, Pat. A short name. Pat.'

Janet's family are shaking their heads as one, willing the reluctant name to come.

'Pam?' volunteers the aunt.

'Yes, I think your dad is saying Pam.'

The three ladies look at each other.

'Pam was my dad's first wife.'

Howard Plume laughs and chides the spirit by wagging his finger.

'Whoops!' he says, and the audience chuckles at the indiscretion.

Naughty, naughty spirit. Dad bringing up his first wife in front of his second.

Mum looks distinctly uncomfortable.

'Dad is kneeling on the floor ...'

The audience stops laughing.

'He's spreading newspaper across the floor. What on earth is he up to?'

The ladies look at each other knowingly.

'He's cleaning his shoes. He's saying, "Get me yours, and I'll clean them, too."' Plume looks down at his shoes. 'Mine are OK, thanks all the same, Dad.'

Notice he has given up on the name and has moved to Dad. Patrick or Pat was a guess. Can cover both sexes. Good try.

'It is Dad,' squeals an excited Janet. A theatre attendant belatedly tears down the aisle to pass her a microphone. 'It is my dad. He did that all the time. He loved cleaning his shoes and did ours, too, didn't he, Mum? It's Dad.'

Plume has pulled it back. It's a good hit. But he knows Dad will be of a certain age. Lots of dads did this. Mine did. Dads who were soldiers or who did National Service had a thing about cleaning boots and shoes. It was drilled into them.

Plume adopts a solemn voice. 'I think he suffered with his chest.'

'Yes.'

'His chest hurts. He is patting himself here.' Plume pats his own chest.

'Yes. He died of pneumonia.'

'Yes. Yes.'

Millions die of pneumonia. They might be suffering with cancer or heart disease or Alzheimer's, but often it's a bout of pneumonia that finally carries them off.

'He sends his love, Janet. He said you have been worrying about something.'

Who hasn't?

Janet is nodding vigorously. She is sold. Hook, line and fucking sinker.

'Dad says he's not going to embarrass you here.'

Oh, he knows we are in a theatre then?

'Dad says he knows you are undecided. It's a yes or a no? Isn't it? Dad is certain the answer is a yes. It's yes, Janet. Go for it, girl. That's the phrase he's using. "Go for it, girl."'

Janet leans forward to her mum and aunt as if to say, 'That's Dad, that's Dad talking.' Aunt cuddles her, but Mum has sat down.

The audience applaud Dad's advice to 'go for it, girl', although none of them, nor Howard Plume himself, has the faintest idea what 'it' is.

'He's sending his love to you all. You, Mum, and you, Aunt, too. He's got to go, but he wants you to know he's OK and he's happy. God speed.'

That's it? He's got to go? He comes all the way from the 'other side', and his daughter, second wife and sister are there, but he cannot remember his name or theirs and he only wants to talk about shoe polish. He barely acknowledges his wife or his sister. And he's in a fucking hurry! What's so busy on the other side? It's a piss-take, yet the crowd are behaving like they are at a Barry Manilow concert.

Plume changes tack. An older lady is standing next to him (allegedly). We cannot see her, but Howard can. She's confused about her name, too. But she's very elegant, Plume tells us. She's dressed up to the nines.

'Stop fidgeting, dear,' he says to fresh air, now channelling his inner Frankie Howerd. 'Why is March the tenth an important date?'

A couple of hands in the audience are quickly raised like eager schoolchildren. Plume takes one.

'My mum was a very smart woman, and her birthday was March the tenth.'

So this twat in the audience has walked into it. How many chances of 10 March and an older female figure matching up? Birthday, death day, anniversary?

'Are you Susan?'

'Yes, my middle name is Susan.'

Your mum rocks up, but she calls you by your middle name. That figures.

'Mum says she misses shopping with you.'

'She loved shopping.'

'Tell me about it. Oxford Street? Yes. She's showing me department stores. Yes, dear. Very nice. She's in the changing rooms now. How *did* you cope with her?'

The auditorium is smiling and murmuring along with the lady who thinks she is in a conversation with her dead mum.

'She suffered so much at the end, didn't she, my lovely?'

Susan is moved from laughter to tears in one swift and ruthless Plume stroke.

'She did.'

'It was here wasn't it?' Howard moves his hand in a circular fashion over his chest, but it could be as low as the waist and high as the neck. The evil bastard.

'Yes, she had breast cancer, and it spread.'

'I know, darling, I know.'

This is pitiful.

And so it continued. There were some misses and a couple of big hits. One set of parents had lost a son. Plume got the name right – Peter – and said he died in a motorcycle accident? Was he riding pillion? he asked. The distraught parents explained that it was a motor car not a motorcycle he perished in, but, yes, he'd been the passenger. 'I have the name Carl,' said Plume. The couple explained Carl meant something, but they'd rather not say what. 'Of course,' said Plume. You could have heard a pin drop. I don't know how he did that. But there *will* be an explanation. To see those tragic parents believing their son had crossed over to give them a few words of comfort tore me up. To know that it was an evil con man financially exploiting their grief made me mad.

'I have a Grace. Who is looking for Grace?'

Nobody claimed Grace. He tried again.

'It's definitely Grace,' he said, tetchily.

Stupid, obstructive audience.

I stood up.

'My mother was Grace.'

It wasn't, of course.

'Yes, Grace is a little shy. A shy woman. But a determined woman.'

She's a little shy, is she? But she's standing on the stage with you talking to three hundred people. She prefers to come to her son in a packed auditorium, not the privacy of his own home.

'Did Grace pass over recently?'

'Yes, last year.'

'She's showing me a canvas. Did your mother paint? Or did she collect art?'

She's come from the other side, but she's showing him a canvas. Did she carry it in under her arm? Give me bloody strength.

'Yes, she did,' I replied, with false shock and wonder. 'She was a good artist. Can you ask her if Dad is with her? Arthur.'

This was the best bit. Plume turned as if to talk my 'mum'

and was nodding and laughing. He turned back to the audience.

'OK, dear, OK. She's not so shy now. Yes, Arthur is with her. He's not here, but he's there, if you see what I mean. She's telling me Arthur passed some time ago.'

So, Arthur, my father, cannot be bothered to turn up and communicate with his son. I expect he's watching The Antiques Roadshow.

'That's right. Nearly twenty years ago.'

'Yes, she says. She wants you to know she and Arthur are happy ...'

'Can you ask her if she's cross with me about Sally, our dog?' I interrupted.

I could see the first sign of Plume feeling uncomfortable. He needs to control the narrative.

'She says not. You had to do what you had to do. You had to have her put down?'

Was Howard Plume a tiny bit psychic, after all? Something from somewhere was telling him I was not kosher. The dog unnerved him. Did he start to suss Arthur was a set-up? My psychic powers tell me that Howard was worried I was from the *Daily Mail* or another cynical media outlet. He thought I was leading him into a trap.

'Your mum has gone now,' he announced, hurriedly, 'but there's a big, big smile on her face.'

I bet there was.

I was dismissed, but the groupies clapped loudly. There was no doubt whatsoever in my mind now that the man was a fraud. I had proved it to myself. Beyond reasonable doubt. An evil fraud of a human being who had pretended to my daughter that her mother – my Jan – had come to her. As I left the theatre, threading through the chattering throng all marvelling at the supernatural experience they had been privileged to witness, I knew I was destined to derail the toxic, telepathic tosser taxman one way or another.

*

Bubbles sat opposite me in my front room. Through the window I could see his gleaming brand-new Range Rover on the drive. He was excited and happy, and it made me happy to see him like this. The business was doing great, booming, he said, and he was telling me about plans, running things past me. He was buying a new house and said he had his eye on a place in South Croydon. Then he changed the subject abruptly.

'Remember I told you about my "uncle" at Pine Forest? The nonce. Remember?'

'Uncle Phil?'

'Blimey you've got a good memory. Yes, Uncle Phil.'

That was a mistake. Why would I remember the name? I was too quick off the mark.

'Well, listen to this. He hadn't died, as I thought. He's alive. Well, he was. He committed suicide. Hanged himself.'

'Fucking hell. How do you know that?'

'They were all talking about on that Pine Forest internet group, Pine Forest Survivors. I'm not on it. But I go on it. Know what I mean? Well, they reckon he hanged himself and left a note apologising for abusing children there.'

'Fucking hell.'

'I know. Yeah, he left a note apologising and admitting everything, but get this, he left his house and his money to the NSPCC! According to someone on the group, and I don't know how they know but they seem clued up, he confessed to all sorts and wanted to make amends.'

'Fucking hell.'

'And ... and ... apparently the police and several London councils are looking into it. Looks like an inquiry. A big inquiry. They reckon loads of compensation. One of the posts on there claims she's been told that the councils are going to settle with all the victims. They're not even asking for proof. They are going to believe us.'

'That's brilliant. I've not seen anything on TV or in the papers.

Your uncle's money should have gone to you and the others. Anyway, you might get some compo.'

'He's not my real bloody uncle, Paul. Or he wasn't my uncle. I don't want his money. Wouldn't touch it with a bargepole. I won't get involved in this inquiry. I don't want to know. But you know what? I feel better, like a weight has been lifted off me. That man suffered. Suffered to the extent that he took his own life. He must have had some concern about us, and he tried to make amends. Late in life, I grant you, and he was probably sweating on meeting his maker, but after doing what he did there's not a lot you can do to make amends, but he did do something. It makes me feel better that he had some humanity – a smidgeon of decency. I've never heard of such a thing. People like him struggling with guilt and trying to put things right. Or as much as you can do in a situation like that. Have you?'

'No, Bubbles, I haven't.'

'There you are. At the risk of sounding like some Hollywood luvvie, I feel like I got *closure*. I don't need to think about it any more. I will not think about it any more. Uncle Phil wasn't all bad. There was a little trace of goodness in him, and it grew and grew like a positive cancer until it overwhelmed him. That's what I'd like to think. Anyway, thought you might be interested.'

'I am. I'm pleased. I'm pleased you feel better about it.'

'Happy ending, mate? Not many of them.'

'Yeah, happy ending,' I said and patted Bubbles's shoulder.

Bubbles was right. What he had heard was not mere gossip or speculation. I came across the following article in the evening paper a few weeks later:

Police have launched a wide-ranging inquiry into historical abuse at the former Pine Forest Children's Home in Surrey, which closed in 1988 and has now been demolished. It is understood that the detailed allegations that have been made by a former worker in the home form the basis of the inquiry. An internet group of former residents at the home have passed on to police over one hundred individual allegations against this man and several others. A Surrey Police spokesman said: 'Complaints from former residents and workers about physical, mental and sexual abuse are being actively investigated. We urge any former residents of Pine Forest to come forward. Your accounts are important and will be believed. It is not too late to receive justice.'

At least three London councils are cooperating with the investigation, and a cross-council inquiry has been launched. The local authorities have pledged to make compensation available to victims.

Kim Wild, a spokesman for the Pine Forest Survivors Group, commented: 'We welcome the police investigation and the commitment from the councils to make amends where they can. What happened at Pine Forest is a national scandal. A horrible stain on our care system. Paedophiles moved from home to home, so to imagine that the sustained abuse was limited just to Pine Forest is fanciful. Whatever the outcome, lives were blighted for ever. It is a matter of national shame. Having said that, there were decent people working in the children's homes who devoted their lives to loving and nourishing the lost children of London, and it is important not everybody is tarred with the same brush and that the actual offenders are named and shamed.'

A police spokesman confirmed that several allegations have been made against staff at children's homes in three different counties.

The confirmatory news filled me with pleasure and a strong feeling of achievement. The chain of events that began with me slapping the black spot into Uncle Phil's palm that day in

Yarmouth now looked like giving not only my dear Bubbles closure (he said so himself) but hundreds of abused children, now adults. It was bringing to account not only a bunch of evil people, dead or alive, but a rotten system. I had achieved more for these people in several months than our so-called system ever had. Had it not been for Uncle Phil's dramatic actions, their plight would have been kicked into the long grass for years longer. Probably for ever. I had been responsible for that 'national stain' being aired publicly. Indirectly, granted, but I had, most definitely, saved further children from abuse, and I hadn't had to kill anyone! The quiet hand of Justice Killer making a real difference. It made me feel great. Filled me with pride and hope for what could be achieved. I am not blowing my own trumpet here. I don't want thanks or praise. I am demonstrating that strong action delivers results, and weak action normally does not.

15
MOTHER'S DAY

IN THE DAYS, weeks and months after my visit to the Epsom Playhouse I became an expert on Howard Plume. The first thing I found out was that his name was Howard Plumb, not Howard Plume. Wonder why he changed that? He said the name had dogged him since childhood and that he changed it as soon as he was able. In my part of the world we called someone a 'plum' if they were generally an idiot and a fool. I enjoyed finding this description of him in a Coventry newspaper from one of his former Inland Revenue colleagues:

Howard Plumb was an odd fish. He didn't mix much. Never came to the pub after work. Never seemed interested in girls (or boys). Or football. Or darts. He said he was keen on amateur dramatics, which was odd for someone who barely spoke and appeared chronically shy. But sometimes he came out with weird stuff. He said that dead people spoke to him, and he wished they didn't. What, I said, people like Napoleon? No, he said, ordinary people like the lady in the chip shop. He could also visualise how places looked years ago. Before this pub was built, he'd say there was a row of weather-board cottages. That sort of thing. Next thing I heard he was doing readings for colleagues. I never had one. He said he earned more from the readings than he did from his day job. And then a few years ago he just resigned. The next thing he's on the TV. I couldn't believe it. None of us could.

Later press articles showed that the Inland Revenue tried to disown him to the point they issued a cease-and-desist order banning him from using the title 'the Telepathic Taxman'. The Revenue argued he was no longer a taxman, and Plume countered that it was a name coined by others, not by him.

Plume's career took off, though, around ten years back when he gave a one-to-one reading to Heather Jenkins, the respected breakfast-TV presenter. Heather told her viewers that she was sceptical about mediums, clairvoyants and psychics, but Howard had put her in touch with her recently departed mum. 'He told me things that only me and my mum knew. Personal things and silly things. The whole episode has given me great comfort and closure. I am not saying any more than that. It has worked for me. I have no plan to consult Howard again. It's happened and it's done. I am so glad I did it. And I am so grateful.'

Plume, the cunning bastard, had written to Heather after he had read about her grief over her mother's death in a women's magazine. Heartless, exploitative and greedy. I suspect strongly that Plume researched Heather's life and garnered the information that she believed was not in the public domain. I, too, had started thinking like that and discovering how you can find things out about people.

Heather's prime-time-television testimonial was the making of Howard Plume. Celebrities and the public clamoured to 'reach over spirit-side' via the conning conduit. He got a spot on an afternoon television show that showed edited readings he had done for audience members. Russell Grant and other TV mystics must have been fuming as their innocent horoscopic musings were being pushed out by this new breed of snake-oil salesman. Plume was soon packing out provincial theatres, and then his celebrity was confirmed with his very own afternoon TV show, *The Telepathic Taxman*, which was made up of heavily edited readings with minor celebrities. It was the perfect relationship. Failing or desperate Z-list celebs exchanged their integrity for perpetuating the myth of Plume's ability to glide among the spirits. The live shows then fed off the TV and so on. It was a charade, but a charade dipped in a cauldron of evil.

Plume became a rich man. He drove a deep-red Bentley, kept a London 'bachelor' flat in trendy Camden, but his main residence was on the banks of the River Wye just outside the bucolic border town of Ross-On-Wye. He was a celebrity supporter of nearby Hereford United Football Club.

He revealed in one newspaper interview that his mother had died a few years before. 'Ironically,' he said, 'I have never tried to contact my mother spiritually. If she wants to come through she will. I miss her every day. On her birthday and Mother's Day I go to her grave – pull up a chair and just talk to her.'

A chair in a graveyard? Thanks, Howard. All I needed to do now was identify his mother on ancestry websites, which would not be hard. Not many women in the Coventry area married a Plumb. I would then have her birth date, and the genealogical history site would probably give me a steer as to where she died and was buried. I decided it was time to get up close and personal with Howard Plume.

Mother's Day fell first, and I travelled over to the churchyard in a village called Thorley in Essex, which was where, I had learnt, Plume's mother had been laid to rest. It had been her childhood home. I picked up a bunch of languid-looking flowers in the local petrol station. I aimed to arrive by ten, thinking it highly unlikely my man would attend any earlier. Of course, I had checked he was not appearing anywhere this Sunday night but had also considered he would not show. His devotion to his dear old mum could well have been sick and dishonest PR exercise.

Getting through the Dartford Tunnel was unusually easy, and when I pulled up alongside Thorley Church at about 9.30 am there was nobody in sight. It was a windy, rainy morning, but the sun was threatening to disperse the clouds. I clutched my daffs and started to walk through the graveyard that wrapped around the ancient, charming church, looking for a stone with the name Doris Plumb on it. Half an hour later I had eliminated almost every stone in the churchyard when I found it. A small and modest memorial beneath an old oak tree. There was a withered bunch of flowers laying in front of the headstone. I searched further until I found the grave of another female whose lifespan dates could have been my mum. About fifty feet to the side of Doris I found one and dropped to my knees and placed my flowers on Winifred 'Winnie' Vyse. By 11 am there was no show from Plume, but a handful of other relatives of the dead were dotted around the churchyard. I decided if he didn't turn up by midday he wasn't going to, and I'd head home.

I killed time by wandering around looking at the inscriptions and reading the epitaphs. Being a village, the same surnames cropped up again and again. Very few recorded ages north of seventy, which made me contemplate my own mortality. Most memorials were neglected. It occurred to me the majority of graves are lucky to receive care or visits beyond the generation below the person who had died, 'His/Her memory will live for ever' being the most often repeated but patently untrue epitaph in this graveyard as in all others.

I was reminded of an old rhyme that a teacher told us at junior school. She was an old country lady herself, and it touched me then and it touched me now how an old dying mum wanted to convince her son that she'd still be having fun when she died. It went something like this:

> I should show some respect, I s'pose
> Here in the churchyard where the dead repose
> For, tho' their living loved ones wail and weep
> The dead are alive and not really asleep
> They rise from their tombs and dance and sing
> Run round shrieking, laughing and everything

And how do I know this ain't all a lie?
My dear mum told me on the day she die.

I peered over the low wall and spotted Howard Plume easing his near-corpulent frame out of his red Bentley, which he had parked as close to the entrance as he could get. I walked quickly back to my 'mother's' grave. Plume was well wrapped up for an early-spring day, with a heavy coat, scarf and one of those Russian hats that had been briefly popular in this country in the 1960s and 1970s and popularised by Michael Caine in a couple of spy films. He walked past me on the path as I crouched down rearranging the daffodils in the vase. Glancing sideways I watched him flick open a canvas chair, the kind a country angler might use, and sit down. There were more mourners here now, arriving laden with flowers. The church bells were ringing out, and people were entering the actual building. It hadn't occurred to me they'd be having a service.

I walked over to Howard.

'Excuse me, is there a water tap here?' I asked.

Plume looked up. 'Yes, around the back of the church. Should be some watering cans, too.'

He was perfectly pleasant.

'Lot of people here,' I continued.

'Yes,' he nodded.

'I guess it's because Mother's Day has fallen on a Sunday.'

Plume lifted himself up a little in his chair and turned to face me fully. 'Mother's Day always falls on a Sunday.'

'Does it?'

'Yes, that's why it's called Mothering Sunday.'

'Of course. Silly me.'

I shrugged and set off for the water tap. I shouldn't have been so cocky as to strike up a conversation with a man I was stalking, but I couldn't resist it. My ignorance was now probably implanted in his brain, and our little exchange may well become a dinner-party story for him – or, worse still, be incorporated into his act.

More importantly, though, Howard Plume's general affability and his failure to declare 'Don't you know who I am?' had made it a little harder for me to hate him and weakened my resolve to confront him and kill him. I had to sit down and remind myself that this man had deceived my daughter and tried to deceive me, through her, into believing her dead mum, my beloved wife and soulmate, was talking to us. He did this to hundreds of people every year. He was an exploiter of grief on an industrial scale. Abusing their trust and milking their grief to the extent that his deceptions had bought him a Bentley and a posh riverside home. I made up my mind that the crowded little churchyard in Essex was an inappropriate venue for my showdown with the Telepathic Taxman, so I sloped off to my car. I took a final glance over at Howard Plume. He was ensconced deep in his chair, a Sunday red-top spread across his lap. Little did he realise that the idiot he had just exchanged pleasantries with was a man who was plotting to take his life.

16
GENTS

MEANWHILE I WAS drinking even more regularly down the Retreat, the former wine bar down near the station. Although I had never been a big drinker, I knew pubs and how they worked. When I first went into business on my own I had to recruit workers, and the way it got done in those days, before mobiles, was in the pub or via the evening paper. Brickies, labourers, sparks, plasterers and painters went to the Swan & Sugar Loaf on a Friday night not only to spend their wage packet on early-evening beer but to fix up work for the following week. I'd ask one bloke if he knew a brickie who wanted a start on Monday, and it would go from there.

I first ventured into the Retreat on impulse late one afternoon after I'd paid my road tax at the post office. I needed a change of scenery. I had to fill the time. Living alone and not working was a solitary existence, and I craved activity more than company. Thinking about Howard Plume and others as well as the state of the world in general was frustrating me and winding me up. Television had left me years ago. Every programme had an angle, or was it me? I felt I was being dug out for being older, white, working class, British, heterosexual, wealthy. I had recently picked up cycling again and occasionally went out, but that particular day I fancied a drink. I had a couple of pints of lager and watched and listened. I enjoyed being surrounded by others and started visiting once, twice, even three times a week for a while. I loved people-watching. Especially, these people. The clientele was predominantly males aged between twenty and fifty. They all seemed to know each other and were mainly late-afternoon and early-evening drinkers. I became fascinated with the group as I slowly built up an understanding of who was who and what they were all up to. I was the anthropologist Desmond Morris but dressed and looking like them. Ted was the main man in here, and he intrigued me. Considering I was a stranger to them I was surprised they were so relaxed and blasé about their drug-taking and dealing and loose talk around me. A bloke sitting on his own with a newspaper. How could they know I was not the police? Perhaps the police are so remote from real crime nowadays the routine cocaine trade has been downgraded to Category Blind Eye.

Ted would roll in about 4.40 pm. Being the first in would not have been his choice. One: it didn't look good. Didn't want people thinking he needed a drink. (Not like Jason. Red-faced Jason. Boring Jason. Where was Jason? It was gone five – nearly past postie bedtime.) Two: Ted does like an entrance. I soon noticed that about him. He appreciates the heads turning – the heads of those who know *of* him. He likes the nods from those who *actually* know him. He likes the offers of drinks from those who *want* to know him, and he likes the mafia bearhugs from his friends – the anointed. And on the rare occasion someone calls in who is higher up the tree than Ted, he might get the respectful mafia kiss on the forehead. *The Godfather* went down well in Croydon all those years ago. A people-watcher would observe that the sub-groups normally settle around the bar area, unwittingly perhaps, in inverse proximity to the man himself. Well, the Retreat is Ted's headquarters, and his table at the mouth of the corridor to the toilets is his desk.

Barman Geoff pours Ted his golden pint of San Miguel in the stylish San Miguel glass. Ted thinks the glass sets him apart. No word is exchanged, and neither is any money. Ted has a slate that is settled erratically and normally at times of cocaine-fuelled benevolence when he has been bestowed with particularly large amounts of fifty- and twenty-pound notes. He likes to hand it over to Geoff in a wad at peak times in full view of the jostling clientele. Slapping it on the counter and sliding it over the bar.

'That's my slate, Geoff, full and final settlement,' he shouts above the cacophony. 'If it's over, keep the bunce for yourself. Your service, sir, has been impeccable.' The last sentence is uttered in a Wilfred Hyde-White accent and triggers grins and heaving shoulders from the acolytes. Geoff has never known Ted's 'settlement' to be over I should imagine.

Ted sits down. Back to the wall, eyes on the front door.

'Who's been in?' he asks Geoff.

'Nobody. Only opened up five or ten minutes back. Wife's away, had to pick up the kids from school, feed 'em, settle 'em down, like.'

Ted raises his eyebrows in acknowledgement. He has no interest in Geoff's domestic life. His mobile comes out, signifying the conversation is definitely over. Geoff moves to the other end of the bar to allow Ted his privacy. Wipes down the Guinness pump. Geoff and I knew the ritual well. The first call is normally to someone higher up the tree than himself – a forehead kisser. We know this because Ted laughs out loud a great deal. He asks after the person's family. Whatever is being said at the other end is punctuated with a series of 'sweets' and 'cushtys' and a few 'I make you rights'. This is who Ted reports to, I guess, or, at least, he facilitates Ted's livelihood in some way. There is deference in the air. Then he makes a couple of calls to his minions. They are not his equals, but they are the huggers. He is normally asking them when they're coming down. When? Hurry up. And then there are one or two more menacing calls. There is no laughing. No platitudes. No small talk.

'Where you been? I thought you'd have been to the office to see me. It doesn't take much to pick up the phone, Keith ...' 'I'm not a fucking charity, you know, Rog.' And then progressing on to threats. 'Stephen, dear boy, are you listening? You really need to be here tonight with my dosh – I don't care if he's swerving you – *you* owe me. Oh dear, Stephen, it's not going to be smacked-bottom time. I do hope not.'

'Smacked bottom' was one of Ted's favourite phrases. Along with 'naughty'. If someone was naughty it meant in Tedspeak that they were fucking evil, capable of extreme violence. Hard. Therefore to be admired and lauded. When Ted worked for some naughty people it was his job to dish out a few smacked bottoms. And didn't everyone in the Retreat know it? That's how Ted became Ted.

See, Ted wasn't born a south-London-suburb-mafia made man. In fact, he was born in a nice house in a nice road with nice parents. I know the story well. They were the McStables.

'I could have been a commuter,' jokes Ted, mimicking the famous Brando contender line – or it could have been a coincidence.

My theory is that at school he was drawn to the 'bad lot' and soon barged his way into their number. He got himself over-tattooed and caused extra trouble in order to compensate for his lack of council-estate and petty-criminal credibility. I'd seen it before on the building sites. He became obsessed with gangsters, devouring Kray, Mad Frankie and Richardson books by the shelf-load, no doubt. He seemed to know a lot about their careers. Ted built up his muscles in the gym. Nurtured what little violence there was within him into something he could use. He started to knock people out in pubs. Marvelling at how easy it was with his leaden arms. Raising the bar each time. Made the Croydon big time when he fought a known local face. An older man. Ted did him with a 'head, fist and foot combo' in the kebab shop. Word was out Ted was a dead man. Ted decided to take the fight to his little lot and went to their local and fronted them. The older men – the local gangsters, if you like – backed down. Ted with his snarl and serpent tattoo curled around his neck was a 'face' himself now at nineteen. There was rarely an afternoon when Ted didn't tell that story.

Ted was headhunted. He started working for Tommo. Now Tommo *was* a gangster. I saw him once when he came in the bar to see Ted. Something, something I cannot pin down set him apart. He supplied the amphetamine sulphate to the boys in Brighton and all along the South Coast, and when cocaine went mass market, that, too. Ted did a bit of small-time dealing, buying from the man who bought from the man who bought from Tommo. After a while he had to administer his first smacked bottom to a non-payer. His self-control and proportionate violence was noted. He met Tommo. Tommo liked him. Called him Rocky. A nod to the Sylvester Stallone character. Ted puffed up. Tommo found him work on the doors of the busy Brighton clubs. Ted became a well-known player. 'Game' was the word used most to describe young Rocky from Croydon. Game little bastard.

He was awestruck being on the firm with Tommo, learnt from a pragmatic man of violence and stayed with him for some years. It was then he got a three-year stretch for demanding money with menaces. He didn't grass, and this raised his stature among the chaps, but in the two years he spent in prison he decided he wanted to pull away from Tommo. He was in his thirties now and wanted to live life a little less dangerously and be a big fish in a small pond rather than the other way around. The Retreat became that small pond, I guess. Besides, he had no stomach for guns and what they could do. And now there were guns. Maybe there had been all along, but he hadn't seen them before. Brighton had become a dangerous place. South Croydon and Purley were safer, quieter.

I may be adding two and two and making seven but that's how I see Ted's trajectory from his own conversations holding court, my bit of local knowledge and hearing what others said about him.

'All right, Ted. Want a drink?' asked Jason in the essential modern-day postman uniform of short-sleeved blue shirt, shorts, trainers and white socks, even in December.

'San Miguel,' replied Ted, pushing his legs out to their full extent to prevent Jason being tempted to take the empty chair at his desk.

Jason climbed on to his usual stool. Ted texted one of the huggers to hurry up.

'Man U, eh?' says Jason, big grin, thinking that a football conversation unites all men and that the decline of Manchester United would delight all the customers of the Retreat at least.

'What about them?'

'Got beat last night. Shocking.'

Ted hates football, and he hates people who talk about it.

'Fergie has lost the dressing-room. That's what I heard anyway.' Like an alcoholic postman from Sanderstead has a hotline to Wayne Rooney. 'Did you watch it, Ted? United were absolutely shocking ...'

'Jason, shut the fuck up, please. I'm busy,' Ted shot back without looking at the pathetic postman.

Jason shut the fuck up. Andy was in soon, followed by Bruce. They sat in close to Ted. Jason was now talking to Geoff, who nodded absently as he wiped glasses. He has become adept at feigning attention since he's been in this game. Jason has tried to talk to me a few times, but I give him scarce encouragement. He's an idiot. Money was passed over to Ted by Bruce. He had made some sales. A boy comes in. Blatantly does not buy a drink and approaches Ted's counter. Ted 'serves him up' four wraps. Two hundred large quickly tucked into Ted's pocket. Others start to file in. Workmen with plaster-, paint- and brick-dust-encrusted jeans. The odd office worker, who seems to know some of the characters here, drifts in and then, finally, the scaffolders. The scaffolders are a handful. They are loud. Not averse to a row but careful not to tread on Ted's or the huggers' toes. They are also Ted's best customers, with a voracious appetite for early-evening cocaine. Don't ever ask for credit. Some of them know me from working on my sites. Their brief acknowledgement of me probably dissipates any suspicions Ted and co. may have subconsciously nursed about me.

Within two hours of arriving at the Retreat Ted had taken over a monkey in sales, and the night was still young. The amount relaxed him. He went to the toilets and then into the single cubicle inside. He calls it the Tardis. It was made for Ted's trade. The managers before Geoff had spared no expense a few years back when relaunching the Retreat, hoping to attract an affluent mix of local business people and commuters into their 'boutique wine bar'. The two sisters who had pooled their redundancy cheques had not banked on the recession, the limitations on turnover of not much space and the scarcity of appreciative imbibers. They surrendered eighteen months back, returned the keys to the landlord, £30,000 poorer, and Geoff saw an interim opportunity and rented the premises. Geoff told me all this. The toilets were tiled black with plenty of room. The sisters weren't to know; they were new to the game. The black was perfect for arranging neat lines of snow-white cocaine and enthusiastically snorting off through a £20 note or, in the case of Ted and the huggers, through their own personal coloured straws.

'There's two lined up for you,' said Ted to a couple of acolytes as he sat down.

'Nice one.'

'Cushty.'

They didn't jump up. That would not have been cool. Jason passed them. Tapped the side of his nose and grinned inanely. He was on his way to the Tardis.

'Oi,' called Bruce. 'Hang up. Give us a second.'

He and Andy stood up and pushed past Jason and entered the Tardis together. Not an uncommon sight in the Retreat.

Meanwhile a man in a mac tied around the middle with a fat belt, clutching a thin briefcase without a handle, entered the bar. (Who thought that one up? Let's start selling briefcases without a handle and make them more awkward to carry and easier to lose.

Brilliant!) I guessed he had just got off the train. He looked beyond the bar and around him. I was sure he was looking for the toilet. I reckon he'd had a drink at Victoria and was dying for a slash before continuing his journey home. Against his better judgement he was forced to enter the Retreat. Despite the pulsating discomfort of an overfull bladder, he felt he had to order a drink first, and he did. The landlord might not appreciate people using his conveniences without buying a pint, the commuter had probably figured. Half a lager shandy. Geoff poured it, noting the new customer's strained look, realising why when he pocketed his change and headed for the corridor – where a toilet sign was visible – like Zola Budd in one swift movement. The commuter was in that toilet seven minutes. His bladder must have been well full. Perhaps he had further ablutions to attend to. I watched him sink his shandy in one when he returned.

'What bitters have you got?' the commuter asked.

''Fraid they're all off,' Geoff replied. 'Guinness?'

'Guinness. Yes, Guinness.'

Geoff smiled. The commuter smiled, relieved now in more ways than one.

Bruce came out of the toilet. Bruce was small and stocky with a very short haircut, designed to confuse people about his galloping hair loss. He was unusual in this company as he had no tattoos. His parents probably forbade it while he lived under their roof. Bruce was called 'the Cockney from Redhill' behind his back and sometimes a 'plastic gangster'. This was on account of his affected cockney accent. He loved being around Ted and wallowing in the reflected glory. Worried sometimes that Ted felt he was a lightweight and knew he was prone to exaggeration and bullshit. Most of his minor criminal escapades had occurred in that centre of degeneracy and nest of naughty people – Redhill.

'You ain't going to fucking believe this,' he whined to the table generally.

Ted, Andy and Jason all looked at Bruce expectantly.

'Some misfit has only had a shit in the Tardis.' He stepped back, holding his hands high, mouth agape. The corner of the Retreat fell silent.

'What?' said Ted, incredulous.

'Someone's shit in there. It fucking stinks, and there's a skid mark down the pan. I fucking retched.'

'Who the fuck done that?' from Andy.

Ted shook his head solemnly. The stupidity of people. The disrespect. Jason leant sideways on his stool to catch the table's eye, a mildly drunken glint in his. He then swung the other way and almost comically, with index finger outstretched, pointed at the besuited middle-aged man in a mac standing next to him, oblivious to the conversation, supping happily on a pint of Guinness. Bruce pointed, too, and with his eyebrows sought confirmation. Jason nodded. It was like a Monty Python sketch. The group shut their lips tightly and shook their heads with exaggerated disapproval.

'Mate,' Bruce said, voice slightly raised. 'Mate.'

The commuter realised he was being addressed. 'Yes, sorry?'

'Have you just had a shit in there?' Bruce said, flapping his hand in the direction of the toilet.

The man realised immediately this was not someone passing the time of the day and detected by the body language the question was hostile. Instinctively, he put his glass on the bar and dropped his hands submissively down to his sides. What could he have done wrong? He didn't leave the toilet in a mess did he?

'Yes, I did go to the toilet. Sorry, are they private toilets or something?'

'Yes, they fucking are. Of course they fucking are.'

From where I was sat I saw that Bruce was standing in the stranger's personal space, little pigeon chest puffed out, and I stood up to move nearer to the situation.

'What's up, Brucie?' Geoff said, worried.

'What's up? What's fucking up? This fucking idiot has only been and had a fucking shit in the Tardis.'

Geoff's shoulders collapsed in exasperation. This was all he needed. Others in close proximity had tuned in. Despite the randomness and chatter of a bar, pub crowds have a knack of smelling trouble.

'That old geezer's only gone and had a shit in the Tardis,' one youth whispered to the bloke next to him by way of bringing him up to speed.

'You're joking,' gasped his friend.

Word spread across the room, and heads turned to look at the man in the suit. The tutting became audible. Heads shook ominously. Eyes moved over to Ted. Sitting down, looking straight ahead. Jaw grinding.

'I'm very sorry,' said the commuter, now visibly scared and not a little embarrassed about his bowel activity being widely discussed. He was still none the wiser as to what he had actually done wrong. He pushed his half-finished pint down the bar and started to button his coat to signify he knew he was not welcome. He was going. Didn't want any trouble.

'Thank you,' he mumbled to Geoff and turned for the door.

Jason, the postman, blocked his way.

'Excuse me, please,' said the frightened man, addressing a space beyond Jason and carefully attempting to step around him.

'Excuse you? You filthy bastard. You're out of order,' Jason remained in in his path and looked around for encouragement as cowards do.

He was contemplating hitting a man he knew would not hit him back. I stood up and stepped towards Jason. I was going to put myself between the dopey postman and the hapless commuter come what may.

'Liberty-taking arsehole.' Jason's fist clenched – but there was something in the look Ted threw him that stopped him. I was still watching his arm. Had it had moved fast I was going to clump Jason, the divvy postman.

Ted stood up. Jason thought that Ted wanted to deal with the man himself. He had overstepped the mark. He slid backwards to his stool and hoisted himself up. Waiting for the pissing of blood and the cracking of bones. I now knew that this was going to end up being between me and Ted. I would stop Ted striking that poor man, and where that would lead I dared not think. Ted was no Stuart Hinds.

'Don't worry, mate,' said Ted, placing his hand on the visibly trembling man's shoulder. The entire bar was now silent. 'Orf you jolly well go. We all make mistakes.'

Who knew it? Wannabe gangster Ted was a fan of Jimmy Young. The man smiled weakly, nodded, still oblivious to what offence he had actually committed – but he was not going to ask – and headed for the door, bodies parting slowly as he threaded through.

'Fucking brain dead,' said Bruce as conversations resumed and bodies relaxed.

'On another planet these office workers. Probably an estate agent,' decided Andy.

'No, estate agents know the score. Love their bit of chisel,' Bruce corrected him.

'No commonfuckingsense,' Ted concluded. 'Silly as a box of chocolates. You don't walk into a strange bar and have a shit. Asking for trouble. He was lucky it was us. Good people. Gentlemen.'

I sat back down hoping Ted hadn't noticed my positioning. He probably had but thought I, too, was moving in to bash up the perfectly innocent commuter. Sometimes I wish Ted had gone for him, and I had gone for Ted. I would have had a serious problem, but at least it would have diverted me from my pursuit of Howard Fucking Plume.

17
HOWARD PLUME

I FIRST WENT up to Howard Plume's country abode in the early autumn and rolled up at the King's Head Hotel in Ross-On-Wye, a charming, ancient building where you needed a pick and an oxygen cylinder to ascend the twisted, steep staircase. I paid in cash, which bothered me because I didn't think many people still did, and I was keen to avoid lodging in anyone's mind. I figured, though, this was preferable to leaving a credit-card trail. Importantly, though, I was mildly disguised. I wore a large sovereign ring on my middle finger – a hangover from a flashier 1980s youth, a distinctive Prince of Wales-check overcoat, which I had purchased ten years earlier and had only worn once. Nobody who knew me would be familiar with it. Finally, I parted my hair in the middle (like my target) and wore a small pair of John Lennon glasses with clear lenses that I had picked up in a junk shop years ago because I liked the old case they came in. I looked like a crank, but I didn't look like me on initial examination, and that was the key thing. I had also not used the pub car park, having put the car in a residential road outside a nearby pub called the Horse And Jockey. As I checked in at reception two young men behind me were discussing the news that a TV adventurer who wrestled crocodiles had met his end by being stung by a ray. The male receptionist was shocked and more interested in their news than in me and asked questions over my shoulder about the event. Behind him I noticed that a small black-and-white TV with a long aerial was on. He had been watching Ned Fletcher's morning show, and Ned was down on one knee, microphone in hand, in front of an uncomfortable-looking young mum, seemingly berating her for having children while claiming benefits. Horrible man. Exploiting the socially submerged to further his own vacuous celebrity. Ned was no better than Howard Plume, I mused. Possibly worse.

Finding Plume's house wouldn't be hard – I had the address – but there was only one way in and out. I drove up the winding road but missed the turning and overshot and had to turn and go back in full view of the house. Another stupid move! If Plume had CCTV I'd be knackered, but there was no obvious sign of cameras. The red Bentley was there on the drive like a flag flying over Windsor Castle when the queen is in residence. I had checked that Howard had no shows that evening. I could see from a map that his front garden descended down to a field that was all that separated him from the banks of the idyllic River Wye. He had paid around £200,000 for this charming pile, and I was shocked at what he had got for his money compared to us in the south of England. There was a small car park about a mile away, which was at the start of a footpath that threaded alongside the river, and I parked up and ambled along the track. I was soon approaching the house from the other direction looking beyond the field to Howard's back garden.

Plume had helpfully revealed in a celeb magazine health piece that his greatest relaxation was walking his spaniel along the river and that when at home he endeavoured to do this twice a day, in the early morning and the early evening. To be sure, I was walking up and down the path at 7 am the following morning, and around an hour later I spied him coming down the slope from his house with the spaniel trotting happily ahead of him. I was in front of them both which was good, as I didn't want to pass him and allow him to register me in any way. Who knows, he might remember the bonehead from the boneyard. At the end of the second field I climbed the stile into the third and headed sharp left up the slope. Plume followed without a glance up to where I was climbing the hill and continued on to the clearing where I was parked and turned around. I sat at the top of the hill and watched him. His entire walk was around two to two and half miles – there and back. The lazy, obese oaf. No wonder the dog was so fat.

Satisfied, or hoping, that this was the mystic's daily routine, I returned to the hotel for a breakfast of steaming porridge and began to formulate my plan. How was I going to kill him? I had made my mind up that I would, even though I'd fucked up big time by driving up to his house. Killing him would have to be quick, as this was a public place and demonstrably used by dog walkers (shit everywhere), ramblers and anglers, although none were about just now. Cooler weather and the time of day reducing the footfall, I surmised. Dragging him down to the river like Stuart Hinds was not a practical option, although it would be my preferred one. Plume would likely struggle, and there was a yappy dog to contend with. I had no stomach for stabbing him or beating him to a pulp. Also, I needed some time to tell him why he was going to die, and I wanted to give him fair opportunity to prove he was not a fraud. That was the whole point. Shooting would be cleaner and more clinical, but I didn't own a gun and had never handled one. I believed I could hold a gun to his head, turning away and squeezing the trigger. But what about the dog? I could never harm an innocent dog. Dogs cannot be guilty. That would be cruel.

Over the course of the next few weeks I built my plan, testing it in my head, working out how I would react in every eventuality. It was a plan I was comfortable with, but it needed a lot of things to go right. I hadn't been this excited since Suzy Quatro joined the cast of *Happy Days*.

At 4.30 am on the morning of Saturday 4 November I set out for Ross-On-Wye. The M25, M40 and A40 were empty, and I arrived in the town in record time. I was wearing my glasses, sovereign ring, centre parting and Prince of Wales-check coat. It was cold, so I added my bobble-less bobble hat. I did not take my mobile phone as it was common knowledge by now that police (and God knows who else) could track your movements by telephone masts that come in and out of range. I calculated that I would be able to get there and back on one tank of petrol. Just.

I arrived in Ross at 6.45 am, just as the place was waking up. A milk float juddered along in front of me at one point. They were practically extinct in the south. I decided to traverse the main high street and drive out of town straight towards the river car park I had visited before. My stomach was churning. I suddenly wanted a shit but decided I had to hold on. I parked in the corner of the car park and was pleased to see there were no other cars around. A council byelaws notice and a waste bin were the only indications that this was indeed a car park. A pair of carefree buzzards mewed as they floated on the breeze overhead. I walked around, sat back in the car and walked around again to kill time. All the while I was going through the eventualities. What if he shouts for help? What if the dog doesn't behave as I hoped? What if somebody else is walking a dog? Early-morning fishermen? What if he's not home? My tension palpably eased as I considered having to go home with nothing having happened.

Then in the distance I could see him coming down the track with the mutt running twenty feet ahead. I knew from last time the dog was named Hector. Hector? What else? Within a few minutes Hector was in the clearing. He half walked, half ran past me with a mildly curious sideways glance.

'Hector!' I hissed.

Hector stopped and now regarded me curiously, I produced from my coat pocket some sausages I had bought the day before from the butcher's shop near me. The dog came forward, trustingly, I opened the back door of my car and placed the sausages on the back seat, opening the paper wrapping wide to tempt him. I urged him to jump up, but he had probably been told not to get into strange men's cars. He was sniffing hard and a gentle push on his behind was enough for him to clamber in. I slammed the door shut.

'What on earth do you think you are doing?'

Howard Plume had witnessed that last act and was striding towards me with rising alarm. He was holding the thick metal dog lead like a weapon. I quickly but confidently pulled out a replica gun I had recently acquired and pointed it at him.

'Stay there, Howard, or I will kill you. I will not harm Hector.'

Calling him Howard and name-checking the dog registered, and he realised this was more than a weirdo or dognapper in the woods. Howard stopped. His expression was one of confusion and building fear.

'What do you want with the dog? I beg you, don't hurt my dog.'

'I'm not interested in Hector. He will not be harmed. Now go in there.'

I motioned with my head to a narrow pathway into the trees surrounding the car park. Howard raised his hands high, like in a film.

'Kneel down.'

Howard knelt on the ground looking up at me and the gun.

'I need to talk to you.'

'Yes, yes.'

'You are a fraud. Aren't you?'

'What do you mean?'

'Howard, we only have a little time. Just admit you are a fraud.'

'OK, I'm a fraud.'

'Are you saying that because of the situation?'

'If you think I'm a fraud, I am.'

'I want the fucking truth, Howard. Some time ago you did a show and you told someone close to me that my dead wife had appeared and gave a message to me. Do you remember that?'

'Where was it? I have done hundreds of shows.'

'Forget where it was. Did you get a message for me? Well, I'll tell you what. You get a message for me now. If you can prove you are in touch with my wife then you walk free. You can tell the police, and I will take the consequences. If you don't or can't get a message then I know it's a con. All a con. And you cruelly scammed my daughter and tried to scam me. And every fucker. You pretended to speak to my dead fucking wife! Her late mother, you bastard! Her mother ...'

My voice was rising. I was shaking with anger, and Plume was quivering with fear.

'I will try. Come to my house. It's just there. I need to prepare. I promise you we will do everything to contact your wife. I will do my utmost. I give you my word. I cannot do this kneeling on the floor trembling with a gun in my back.'

This man was desperate. Trying to remain calm and save himself. I was impressed by his relative serenity given the circumstances.

'Fuck off. If you can do it on a stage at will in front of hundreds of people you can do it now. Here!'

Howard Plume could see his life ending. There was a very angry man towering over him with a gun. He bowed his head. I could hear the muffled barking and whining of Hector from the car. He looked up at me earnestly and then closed his eyes.

'Hurry up, Plumb.' I was worried about what I would do should we be disturbed. Of course, my gun was not loaded. It was not even a real gun.

'I can see water,' he said, hurriedly. 'I cannot see your wife. But she is here. Did she drown? I can see water and a struggle, and your wife is saying enough. Enough. Walk away. She is speaking about the water.'

An awful feeling enveloped me. 'Tell me about the water.'

'I see two men fighting in the water. Your wife is shouting at you to stop. You are not listening. You are on top of the man. It's you in the water. Fighting. Your wife is crying and wants you to stop. This is what I am seeing. You asked me what I am seeing.'

'Can you see her?' I was poleaxed by what he was telling me. I buckled and felt weak at the knees. Panic filling me.

'No. I can hear her. It's like she is talking over a film.'

'Tell her, I love her.' I was crying now. 'Jan, I love you.'

'He loves you, Jan.'

He knows everything now. Her name. The show and a daughter. He may piece this together with meeting me in the churchyard and when I led him up the garden path in the theatre. And he knows about me fighting a man in water! He may know I killed him and is sensibly holding back.

'I see a ponytail,' he said, looking up at me and searching my eyes.

That was too much for me to bear. A fight in some water was too close for comfort, but the ponytail, that was definitive. I should let him go and keep my word. Let him go to the police. There was absolutely zero chance he could have known about the incident in the river. Only two people in the world know it. One is dead, and one is me. He's for real! That was not one of the eventualities I had rehearsed. Who knows what further details will come through to him? The dog is barking. It's getting later. Must be 8.15. There will be people. He's crying.

'Look down at the floor.'

He thought I was going to kill him. Big sobs were being ejected involuntarily from his body. I pushed him to the floor firmly with my foot. Picked up the dog's lead he had dropped beside him and hooked it over his head. He screamed 'Help!' as he realised what was happening and I dug into the small of his back with my foot and pulled the lead tight. I screwed my foot down and bore down on his head with the palm of my hand more to stifle his screams than hurt him. I didn't want to hurt him. He started to arch his back like a bucking bronco, and I dropped on him with my free knee into the centre of his back. He couldn't shout. He flailed with his hands at the chain. But I pressed and pulled. Pressed and pulled. It seemed to take an age. I can tell you this – time stands still when you're trying to kill someone in this way. He went limp, but he was trying to fool me, I'm sure. I could see his back move. I kept on him and kept tightening. Then I knew he was dead. It was 8.43 am when I returned to the car. I let Hector out and he ran back towards the house leaving his dead master in the woods. I was now less enthusiastic about the final flourish I had planned but thought, I've come this far.

I had a quick scan down the path and saw Hector bounding along in the distance – noticing his tail was wagging – but there was no other sign of life. Picked up the heavy stapler and the sign from the passenger-side footwell. Howard still lay there, and I could not bear to turn him over and staple the notice to his chest as I had intended. Could not look him in the eye. Instead, I knelt down and placed the notice on the back of his jacket and stapled it just above the hem. It read:

I WILL BE COMING THROUGH
TO LET YOU KNOW WHO DID IT.
CAN'T BELIEVE I DIDN'T SEE IT COMING.
JUSTICE KILLER

18
CONTACTING THE DEAD

I WAS BACK indoors by midday. I picked up my phone from next to my bed and called Holly and then Bubbles about nothing, just to have a record that I had been in Purley, not Ross-On-Wye, that morning. I felt bad. It hadn't worked out anything like I had hoped. My intention had been to use the gun to control him. If he admitted he was a fraud I was going to kill him. If he didn't admit it I was going to kill him the way I had done. What I hadn't even considered was that he would demonstrate he *wasn't* a fraud! And the way he did that freaked me out, and to save my skin I thought I *had* to kill him. I was a coward and had let myself down. I was now the bully. A bully! I hate bullies. The man was genuine, for fuck's sake. My moral high ground crumbled beneath me. Hinds got what was coming. Frank Cox and Uncle Phil, too. But had Howard Plume? For the first time I felt like a murderer. Felt bad. A bad man. Had I let my wife down? Had she tried to speak to me? Was she really there? Had she been telling me through Howard not to do it? Howard suggested she'd pleaded with me not to kill Stuart.

On Sunday morning I woke after a restless night and vivid dreams I remembered for a few minutes, but they'd gone again by the time I'd made tea. Like trying to catch the bubbles you blew from those tubes of soapy water when you were a kid. My unease was running close to panic. I had been assured in my mission. Convinced right was on my side. But now I had compromised myself. Plume *was* a man with psychic powers. What other explanation is there? He really *could* see things we couldn't. He hadn't deserved to die for benefiting from those powers. But then I pulled myself up. I felt a bit better. I cast my mind back to the Epsom Playhouse when I led Plume on, and he took the bait and took advantage of what he thought was a grieving son. He was a con man then. He was a con man throughout the show and every show and every TV appearance and every private reading. He got by on suggestion, leading, guessing, some subterfuge and dollops of luck. If I'd allowed myself the time I would have studied him in more depth and written a thesis on how he and the other charlatan clairvoyants worked, but Howard Plume got personal. He brought my wife and daughter into his lucrative fantasy world.

But how do I explain the episode at Ross? I turned what he'd said over and over. I wanted to write it down so I could never forget it or allow it to be compromised, but decided against doing so until now. He said he had seen water and two men fighting and Jan was saying stop it and crying. He hadn't given Jan's name. If she had been talking to him, why hadn't she given her name? That would be definitive. He said I was on top of the man and striking him. Why hadn't he given Jan's name? He hadn't described her. I had challenged him to produce Jan, so produce her he did. What are we left with? Two men fighting in water. He didn't say I'd killed a man. If he had mentioned old Wally Tombs that would have been a clincher. But he hadn't. If he had mentioned Stuart's name or described Bridgnorth that would, too. He was close but short of a bullseye. In matters of life and death you need a bullseye. Plume had Jan in the picture because of me. He had assumed that I was a violent man – which is not generally the case – but you can see how he'd got there. So, he'd assumed and thought there may have been times when she'd had to call me off people. Maybe he'd assumed I was a violently jealous person. He'd been thinking fast and had created a scenario that could not be disproved. His masterstroke, though, was the water. A pure guess, I'd say. We'd been by water. Next to the Wye. It had probably been the first thing that came into his panicking mind. I had made some peace with myself. But then the ponytail? That had been his 'Bubbles' moment. There must be a logical explanation. Could he have been referring to Jan's ponytail? She didn't have one, but he could have been searching around for a clincher and got lucky (or unlucky in this case). Lots of women have ponytails. Cumulatively, what Plume had said was compelling; taken apart, not quite so much.

I had expected to hear something during the course of Saturday, but there was nothing. Hector would have gone home to a locked and empty house. The dog would have whined, barked and fretted. At some point a neighbour or someone familiar with Plume's routine would see that something was amiss. They would follow his footsteps, perhaps with Hector in tow. I would have thought Plume would have been discovered the same day, as I had made no attempt to cover the body. Indeed, I left it with a fucking great message stapled to it. Plume made a big thing about living alone with his dog, but who knows? There could be a partner? A maid? A cleaner?

I knew the case would make the TV and newspapers, but I was unprepared for the furore that followed. It started as a 'just-in' item on the late ITV news that Sunday. The last of the Guy Fawkes Night fireworks were whizzing through the sky. Mark Austin announced solemnly, 'News just in. West Mercia police have reported that the body of the TV psychic Howard Plume has been found in a rural area a mile from his home. Mr Plume was declared dead later on arrival at Hereford County Hospital. Police say there is no further comment at this time. Howard Plume shot to fame in the 1990s with his TV show *The Telepathic Taxman*.'

That sounded like a suicide. A rural area. I went to bed and tuned into the radio station where Plume had worked for a while hosting a 'psychic phone-in'. I thought they'd be all over it. I listened to a couple of the hourly news bulletins, but they added nothing, with one presenter saying solemnly that it 'would be wrong to speculate'.

On Monday morning Holly rang. I saw her name flash up on my mobile and composed myself.

'You seen the news, Dad?'

'Not yet.'

'That Howard Plume chap. You know, the mystic. He's dead.'

'Is he?'

'Yeah. It's really strange. He was walking his dog where he lives up north somewhere and they found his body.'

'Heart attack?'

'Don't think so. Sounds like suicide.'

'Guilty conscience?'

'Don't be horrible, Dad. It's sad.'

'Well, he can still talk to his relatives, can't he?'

'You're awful, Dad.'

The lunchtime news had a reporter standing a few feet from where I had parked the car on Saturday. The key thing he disclosed was that police had not ruled out foul play. The story was moving up the news agenda. By the time the evening news came on a fuller account had emerged. 'TV medium and entertainer Howard Plume has been the victim of a targeted murder, West Mercia police have announced,' said the reporter excitedly. 'Police are not revealing how Mr Plume was killed or what exactly they mean by targeted but are appealing for any early-morning dog walkers and residents in the vicinity of Mr Plume's home in Ross-On-Wye and who saw anything suspicious on Saturday or Sunday to come forward. They also appeal for anybody who has any information about Mr Plume's private life to contact them.'

By Monday morning the online speculation was intense. That spot by the River Wye was, apparently, notorious as a gay meeting place. Others denied this was so. But there was a head of steam that a gay liaison had gone wrong. Of course, as some amateur sleuths pointed out, this did not fit with the police's use of the word 'targeted'. Another poster asked who goes to a planned sexual encounter with their dog? I wondered how long the police were going to withhold information about the message pinned to Plume's back.

I went down to the newsagent's and bought nearly every paper. I couldn't resist it, even though, should I come to the attention of the police, Mr Sharma might decide my unusual purchase was relevant to their inquiry. The case was the front-page story on most of them. I must admit I was incredibly excited and pleased to read the heated coverage. The tabloids were digging deep. They knew there was more to the story.

MYSTIC MURDER MYSTERY boomed the *Sun*. HOWARD PLUME SLAIN cried the *Express*. TELEPATHIC TAXMAN FOUND DEAD headlined the *Mirror*. On Tuesday it emerged that Plume had been strangled with a chunky dog lead. I glanced over at the peg where my coat was hanging. That very lead was dangling there. Plume led a solitary life, they all agreed, devoted to his dogs. (Were there more?) Unmarried and no suggestion of any partners of either sex. Former colleagues from the tax office were resurrected to tell the same stories about his mundane clerical career. The *Mail* seemed to have the best handle on the case asking:

WHO WOULD WANT TO KILL
THE TELEPATHIC TAXMAN?

When Howard Plume left his house with his beloved Labrador [sic], six-year-old Hector, had he arranged to meet someone? Or was he followed by somebody with murderous intent? The police have clearly indicated that the attack was premeditated and 'targeted', so avenues of inquiry are focusing on the television-and-theatre medium's private life. So far those inquiries have yielded nothing.

Holly called again. 'What do you think about this Howard Plume stuff? It's mental. Have you been watching it?'

'I saw something briefly on the news,' I said, glancing down at seven newspapers fanned out across the coffee table.

'You didn't do it, did you?'

Boom! That took the wind out of my sails.

'Do what? I wouldn't recognise him if I passed him in the street.'

'I'm joking, Dad.'

I knew I needed to recover fast. Had I been a bit too defensive and sharp? 'Do they have any idea why?'

'They said it's likely he knew his killer.'

'It will all come out. He's probably had someone over.'

'I don't know, Dad. I just get a weird feeling about it.'

'That's because you went to see him and he's famous. You'd probably feel the same if ... Des O'Connor was murdered.'

'No such luck,' joked Holly and changed the subject to house prices, a theme on which she and Norman (and half the country) were fixated.

I wondered if I was going to get caught. Had someone ventured into that car park, seen Hector distressed (perhaps) inside my car and noted down my number? Would police find my car on CCTV covering his driveway? If so, game over. Yet I felt no fear. I felt like I was watching an episode of *Colombo*. I knew who did it and why and was watching with great interest as the world tried to unravel it. Of course, Lieutenant Colombo always got his man or woman.

I was still uneasy about Plume, though. What he had said. I played it over and over in my mind. He clearly stated I was on top of a man. In water. Fighting. That Jan was telling me to stop and walk away. Did she mean stop and walk away from Stuart Hinds, or did she mean stop and walk away from Plume? If it were the latter, that is awful. Ignoring her plea would have meant I had gone against my love. Plume knew nothing about me. There is no way he could have known about Stuart Hinds. The distressed-wife bit, he could have just been lucky – but the fight in the water? I offered the man a deal. If you're psychic, prove it. And he had. And I still killed him. That was wrong. My self-respect was ebbing away. I was a wrong'un. A gratuitous murderer. It was not a pleasant feeling.

Crimewatch, however, cheered me up no end. The police were struggling, and only a week and a bit after the murder they were flagging a reconstruction. Several million people would be watching. I treated myself to a good bottle of Sancerre and cut myself some mature cheddar cheese and tore open the Jacob's cream crackers. At the top of the programme Nick Ross promised some important new information about the Howard Plume case. Butterflies became airborne in my gut.

A couple of robberies and some wanted faces passed through until they got to the main event. Ross described the victim as a 'much-loved television entertainer with no known enemies'. Television entertainer, Nick? Pretending you are talking to the loved ones of despairing people is entertainment? Fuck off. What have we become? The reconstruction showed Plume making and eating porridge, Hector wagging his tail beside him. That was the unnerving thing about *Crimewatch* reconstructions – the way they juxtaposed familiar domesticity and day-to-day life with the unimaginable violence and horror to come.

'Come on, old boy,' says Plume. Artistic licence, surely? And he puts the lead on the dog – I glanced over at the *real* lead hanging on the peg – and they push open the garden gate and walk downhill to the riverbank. The *Crimewatch* team have retraced his steps exactly, even having the dog run ahead into the woods and Plume follow him in. Then they show ominous feet trampling the undergrowth and stop the film. The photography was worthy of a Hammer Horror flick.

'What happened next was horrifying,' warned Nick Ross pausing for effect. 'Howard Plume was knocked to the floor, brutally attacked and strangled, police believe, with his metal dog lead. Before his attacker left the scene of the crime, he attached this note to Howard's jacket.' Ross held it in front of him and the camera zoomed in:

I WILL BE COMING THROUGH
TO LET YOU KNOW WHO DID IT.
CAN'T BELIEVE I DIDN'T SEE IT COMING.
JUSTICE KILLER

You could hear the sighs, whistles, shaking of heads and perhaps even laughing in fourteen million homes across the country.

Ross was joined by the policeman leading the inquiry, Detective Superintendent Mark Scull.

'What does this cryptic signature, if you like, tell us?'

'It tells us that the murder was premeditated, planned and targeted. The killer certainly knew who his victim was.'

'Why would anyone want to kill Howard Plume?' asked Ross. 'Does this message indicate that the answer may lie in what Howard did for a living? His telepathic performances.'

'Not necessarily, but it could do. The wording seems to indicate a disdain for alleged psychic powers.'

'What would you like to appeal to the public for?'

'First, if anybody has seen or picked up a dog lead like this [image flashed up] please approach us. Second, if anybody used this car park near Ross-On-Wye any day recently please come forward. We believe that at some point on Friday or Saturday a Land Rover Freelander Sport entered the car park. We would like to know who that was if only to eliminate them from our inquiries. Third, if anybody knows of anyone who had a grudge against Mr Plume, please come forward. All information will be treated confidentially, and your privacy will be guarded. Fourth, do you recognise this writing? The paper is torn from the empty fly leaves of a large hardback book. (They were right there. Holly had bought me a Gordon Ramsey cookbook for Christmas. Waste of money. I detest the bloke.) Have you come across a book with one of its front pages torn out? Do you recognise the writing? The author of this sign has used block capitals but the upward stroke of the top of his Ts is distinctive. Do you know anyone who writes their capital Ts with such a slant?' (I did that on purpose. I do not write my Ts in such a way.)

'Thank you. Finally, this person has signed themselves *Justice Killer*. Does that worry you? Do you think this man could strike again? I say a man ...'

'We are sure we are looking for a man. Plume was over-powered, and he was not a slight individual. The method of strangulation would have required brute strength. All murders and serious crimes worry me, Nick. At this stage we have no reason to believe this isn't more than a very, very serious isolated incident. We feel that the perceived injustice the killer implies is connected to Mr Plume alone. However, that said, we need to catch this person as soon we can, and for that we need your help. Please come forward, however inconsequential you think your information is. It is highly unlikely that the murderer has never mentioned his antipathy towards Howard Plume to others. Please cast your mind back and see if you recall anybody expressing a disproportionate dislike of Mr Plume and even so-called clair-voyants in general.'

Disproportionate dislike of Mr Plume. I liked that. Did this policeman before me know about my previous Justice Killer letter a few years back? It did not make sense to reveal the letter in the Plume murder and not connect the Cox one. Surely this Plume killing seals the Cox 'cliff fall' as a murder in the eyes of the police. Surely the public should be told there is a real justice killer on the loose who has murdered at least twice. Could it be police incom-petence? Did the Sussex Police not pass their letter on to Scotland Yard? Was it sitting in a file somewhere? I couldn't figure this out. Wouldn't the police now appealing for information want to see if anybody out there could find anyone with connections to Hinds and Plume? Handwriting tests would show, presumably, the same author of the address on the Cox envelope and the Plume sign. I had tried to mix it up and insert red herrings, to be honest, but surely they'd never fall for that.

Holly flashed into my mind. This policeman, Mark Scull, didn't seem as stupid as some of those I'd seen on *Crimewatch*. I liked the way he said, '*so-called* clairvoyants' and '*alleged* psychic powers' indicating to me he was not particularly enamoured of the way Plume made his money. When the policeman engaged the camera, I read his eyes, and he was speaking to me. He was saying, I'm on to you, I'm not quite there, but I'm on to you. But was he? It's not hard to work out that whoever killed the Telepathic Taxman didn't like him. It was obvious it was premeditated and planned. The Land Rover was a red herring in my favour, thankfully, and I guessed they'd identified that – whoever it belonged to – by tyre impressions. I again felt some unease that my Jaguar might well have been picked up on CCTV somewhere, and that, I felt, was my weak link. If my car was identified as having been in the area on that day I'd have to come up with a good reason for what I was doing in Ross, why I got there so early and came home so quickly. It might not take long for them to find out I had been to see Plume at the Playhouse. Paying by credit card had been a monumentally stupid and lazy thing to do.

I expected a call from Holly, but it didn't come. I hoped she had gone out and missed the programme. I could do without more of her speculations about Howard Plume.

I sat there and mused. If you put your mind to it, you could kill regularly and successfully if you were that way inclined. I wondered how many people were really being murdered each year. A rudimentary Google search claimed six hundred murders a year across the UK. I didn't believe that. Not even two a day? There are 175,000 people reported missing each year! Most of them turn up, but 5,000 are acknowledged as long-term missing. They have been off the radar for over a year. In this world it's nigh on impossible not to leave a trail, and it gets harder as time goes on. My gut feeling is most of those 5,000 are dead. Suicides don't as a rule hide their own bodies, so those – let's say 4,500 – long-lost people, in my opinion, have died at the hands of another. If you spread those 4,500 over ten years, that equates to 1,050 murders a year rather than the 600 quoted. That's more like it. I suspect, though, it is even higher. I also think that many murders go unrecognised. Stuart Hinds, for example. Officialdom has him down as an accident. A death by misadventure. And then there are the manslaughters. Hundreds of them every year. These are still one person taking another's life.

So those 4,000 poor people are not really a missing-people statistic, they are a murder statistic. These are the murders where the killer or killers have successfully disposed of or hidden the body. They are, therefore, planned murders. The murders we hear about are the unplanned murders, and, because they are unplanned, the perpetrators are normally caught. There could be, and I am sure there are, murderers out there – dead and alive – who have killed dozens of times and will never be identified. Bodies are buried and hidden all over the place. Ideally I'd like to have been able to identify that rump of serial killers in our midst. Become the first serial killer of serial killers. That would be fun and worthwhile.

Over the next few days there was little in the way of new developments on the case. Police appealed for an angler who was believed to have spent the night in a bivvy on the river. He came forward but said he heard no car, no voices, no dog barking, and it transpired he had been tucked up on the bank of the Wye just below the car park. I guessed that, luckily for me, copious amounts of tinned lager or inhaled cannabis – probably both – had sent him into a deep sleep, his brain conditioned only to react to a screeching bait alarm. I read somewhere else that local hotels and bed and breakfasts were being scrutinised. I could feel the police getting closer. It's like that game when you're a kid. You are getting warmer, warmer, warmer, no colder, colder, warm. Hot, hot!

However, what did happen, which pleased me immensely, was a media frenzy about psychics that broke out in the tabloid newspapers, on daytime television and on the radio. The whole Justice Killer thing ignited the story more than I could have dared imagine. The *Mail* and *Express* speculated (rightly) that Plume was murdered by a person who been upset by his assertion that he talked to the dead, and they went on to question the veracity of the industry's claims more generally. Should it be allowed? they asked. *Preying on the bereaved and grieving*. Profiting from misery. Helpfully, had I had the inclination to take out more mediums, they pictured four of television's surviving top psychics, questioning their ethics and in some cases picturing their palatial houses. The *Mirror* revealed that Howard Plume and Raymond Shevell really *were* arch-enemies, each calling the other a fraud after falling out during a joint theatre tour of the towns of the United Kingdom. Shevell had been the first psychic to break into the television mainstream in the 1980s and, seemingly, resented Howard Plume's ascendancy. Plume, in turn, had accused Shevell of trivialising what they did by featuring in a series that traipsed around the inns and houses of the land flushing out ghosts! Give me strength. However, it was the *Sun* that had delivered the *coup de grâce* by going undercover at one of Doreen Mackintosh's shows and alleging she'd been receiving messages from an assistant via an earpiece. Quite how this was aiding her performance was not fully explained, unless the person in her earpiece could speak to the dead, too. Doreen promptly issued a lawsuit for defamation of character and libel.

The public perception of the telepathy, talking to the spirit, is anybody there? industry pivoted. A man-of-the-people daytime-TV presenter challenged Shevell, Doreen and several other not quite so famous psychics to come on his daytime magazine show and be 'tested'. He seemed really angry. He said he had a very simple test to put to them. He wanted to challenge them to contact Howard, who would, in turn, tell them who had killed him. They all refused. I was half excited, not at all worried, because, although I couldn't now be sure that Howard was a fraud, I knew that the rest of them were definitely charlatans.

Raymond Shevell later went on the TV to say that he feared for *his* life. He was shitting himself. Demanded police protection. He was concerned that Justice Killer was coming for him, and he had taken extra security measures. What, for the rest of your life, Raymondo? I was tempted, really tempted, to kill him, too, but as it turned out my actions would soon put him out of business anyway.

Doreen Mackintosh pushed her luck even further by telling the *Sun* that she *had* managed to contact Howard Plume.

'He came through,' she declared. 'Howard and I were close, and I knew he would. He told me some private things, but as for the murder, all he could tell me was that it was a man, he didn't know him, and that the man has the murder weapon – the dog lead – in his home.'

I suppose that could have freaked me out, too, but it didn't. The dog lead was missing. Police had made a thing of it. Therefore, it had either been disposed of or kept by the murderer. It was a 50 per cent chance of getting that one right.

DS Scull was not too happy with the narcissistic fraudsters muddying his messaging. He responded to Doreen Mackintosh's claims by saying, 'We have an open mind on whether Howard Plume knew his killer or not. It is entirely possible that he did. It does not aid the investigation to give a platform to celebrity speculation.'

Scull damning the psychics and the tabloids in one swipe.

Nevertheless, as time rolled on DS Scull didn't appear to be getting anywhere. His determined, small, pinched face was cropping up on the TV less often. I began to believe I had got away with murder again.

DS Scull appealed in a *Crimewatch* update several weeks later. 'I want anybody who attended any of Howard Plume's shows to come forward if you can recall anything out of the ordinary. Anything particularly upsetting or any incident that sticks in your mind. Do not hesitate to contact us. Something might be worth following up. And, I repeat, if you have experienced anybody showing a strong dislike of Mr Plume, please contact me.'

It was clear to me that the investigation was faltering and that Scull was relying on his gut feeling. He had admitted there was no definitive DNA left at the scene of the crime. He was sure that Plume had upset a punter and had guessed that rather than a private sitting or the carefully managed and edited TV productions, the bone of contention had been because of a live performance. I suspected that he suspected some underhand, morally repugnant method of information gathering had been uncovered, leading to a relative of a deceased person deciding to take extreme revenge. Scull never said this, but I was convinced that was his theory. It was the only game in town.

On the other hand, of course, he may have known by now that the murderer of Plume had also claimed to be the murderer of Stuart Hinds and Frank Cox and had indicated they were justice killings as well. If he had done his research or consulted a local seasoned cop he would have known that Stuart had been acquitted of a murder he most likely did. In that case, Scull knew by now he was dealing with a serial killer who attaches himself to various causes. But the fact he didn't come straight out with it and increase the chances of solving all three cases baffled me.

ITV and other channels announced they would no longer be airing repeats of the *Psychics Three* show that had been running for years and featured Shevell, Mackintosh and, for a while, Plume. Theatre shows were cancelled amid plunging ticket sales, and those that went ahead were being picketed by protestors calling them evil. Public sympathy for Plume dissipated. My meeting with Howard Plumb – let's call him by his real name –

had, within a few months, brought down an entire industry – or shall we call *it* by *its* real name – racket. A cruel, exploitative, immoral racket. Even if Howard Plume had not deserved to die, I had done society a favour by triggering a chain of events that had destroyed that racket. This, I felt, compensated for the doubt and guilt that still nagged at me as to whether I had been fair to Plume. All in all, there was no escaping the fact that for the first time in a long time it was good to be alive.

19
INSPECTOR SCULL

OVER A YEAR after Operation Plume had fallen out of the news there was a ring on my doorbell. I was reading *The Times* online and listening to the radio. A double hit of doom, gloom and inane tittle-tattle, but it passed the time of day. Ned Fletcher now had a radio show. He had just destroyed a caller. An earnest older man by the name of Dave.

'What's on your mind, ma friend?'

'I wanted to talk about the immigration issue.'

'Ah yes. What troubles you, ma friend?'

'Well, if we keep letting people in there will be too much pressure on public services.'

'What evidence do you have for that?'

'Well, I read it. It's common knowledge.'

'Where did you read it, the *Daily Mail*?'

'I don't know where I read it. I think we all know.'

'Do we? David, we are one of the richest countries in the world. Is it really so hard to offer the warm hand of friendship to people fleeing war and persecution?'

'Are they, Ned? Are they? This latest lot are coming from eastern Europe on cheap flights for a better life.'

'And, ma friend, what's wrong with fighting for a better life?' Ned's tone hardens. Menace curls in his throat. '"Latest lot", David? "Latest lot"? Do I detect you don't like our European brothers and sisters? How do you feel about people with darker skins than ours, David?'

'What? What you on about? I'm not a racist, Ned. That's

unfair. I'm just making a point. I grew up with black people in my neighbourhood. *Some of my best friends are black* ...'

Before David could finish Ned interjected, 'Some of my best friends are black ... that old chestnut. There we have it, ladies and gentlemen. Goodbye, David. Have a nice life.'

And David was despatched into the ether with the flick of a switch. No right of reply. For ever condemned as a racist.

The bell rang again, and I turned Ned off. Not many people turned up unannounced these days, so I guessed it was a sales-person of some sort.

'Mr Paul Garfield?'

I recognised him immediately, and my facial expression and body language may have given that away. He was even smaller than he appeared on television, but his black, swept-back, slightly long hair – which gave him the look of an ageing Teddy Boy – left no doubt.

'I am Detective Superintendent Scull. This is my colleague Detective Inspector Best.'

DI Best was a smart, middle-aged lady. She gave me a reas-suring smile.

'Come in,' I said, feeling like I had watched this scene play out a million times on screens both big and small.

I offered them a tea or a coffee, which they declined, and I sat down in my chair, motioning them to take the sofa.

'Thank you,' Scull began. 'We are investigating the murder of Howard Plume last year. Are you aware of the case?'

'Yes, the spiritualist chap?'

'That's him. What do you know about it?

'Nothing.'

'Nothing?'

'Well only what I've seen and read.'

'What's that then?'

'He was murdered while walking his dog. In Wales or some-where.' At this point I was meant to say, 'What has this got to do with me, officer?' but I decided against it.

'Have you ever met Mr Plume?'

'No.'

'No?'

'No.'

'I believe you went to one of his shows at the Epsom Playhouse in …' Scull began to finger a notebook.

'That's not meeting him. Yes, I did.'

'And was there any particular reason you went to Mr Plume's show?'

Has he spoken to Holly? Has Holly told him about the 'message' from Jan? Shit, this is getting hairy. Surely, though, Holly would have called me if the police had called on her? The police are just working through all the people that they can identify who went to Plume's shows. I must stay calm.

'I go to shows. I'd seen him on TV, and when I saw it advertised thought I'd go.'

'Where did you see it advertised?'

'I cannot remember.'

'And who did you go with, Mr Garfield?'

'I went alone.'

'You went alone?'

'Yes, Mr Scull, I went alone. My wife is dead. I go to places alone.' Why did I volunteer that? I told him my wife had died. If Holly has told him something, too, I am on weak ground.

'I am sorry to hear that, Mr Garfield.'

'Thank you.'

'Can I ask if you believe that people like the late Mr Plume have the ability to speak to the dead?'

'No, I don't,' I replied too quickly.

'So why did you go to Mr Plume's performance?'

'Perhaps I was open to persuasion. Perhaps I hoped I was wrong. Perhaps I wanted to be entertained.'

There was a brief hiatus.

'I can understand that, Mr Garfield. And were you persuaded?'

DI Best beamed a wide sympathetic smile at me, cocking her head slightly to one side. The questioning was direct but nonetheless gentle and conversational, yet I had the strong feeling that DS Scull had a strong feeling about me.

'No, I was not.'

'And was there any particular reason you were not persuaded?'

'It's a racket, isn't it? Well "racket" is too pleasant a word, don't you think?'

The detective pushed out his bottom lip in a maybe-maybe-not facial shrug.

In for a penny ... 'You know. The psychic is apparently talking to some poor old lady's late husband. She's grieving. She's desperate and her lifelong partner has battled through from the other side. And what does he tell her? He doesn't say he loves her, to remain strong and they'll have a glorious future on the so-called spirit-side. No, he tells her she needs to oil the bloody garden gate. It's still creaking.'

DI Best raised her eyes, signalling agreement at the nonsense of it. I had showed some emotion there but decided on instinct to do so. To have said otherwise maybe would have indicated I was being disingenuous. A game of chess was developing.

'So, can I take it you agree with how the industry is going to be regulated?'

'I don't know anything about that. But I'm glad these chancers are off our televisions. What do you think?'

The detective paused. I was waiting for him to say, 'What I think is not what we are talking about here,' but he didn't. He actually said, 'Exploiting vulnerable people emotionally for financial gain or kudos is detestable. But some will argue that these messages from the other side, real or not real, give many great comfort.'

It was a good answer.

'But we know they are not real, don't we?'

DS Scull smiled and not in a patronising way. 'What car do you drive, Mr Garfield?'

'A Jaguar.'

'How long have you owned your car?'

'Three years, maybe a bit more. I chop it in when the warranty ends. The last car was a Jag and the one before that.'

'Do you know where you were on the day of November the 4th last year?'

'No. I guess I could find out if I made any transactions on my bank account that day. My phone bills can tell you who I rang, no doubt. I really don't know. I don't go to any bonfire parties these days,' I shrugged in an Alan Partridge so-what sort of way.

The policeman nodded. He didn't speak. I took that as *don't worry, we will find out*, or *we can find out*, or, most likely, *we have found out*.

I watched Scull look around the room. He used silences to encourage me to fill the void. I did not speak either.

'Thank you for your time, Mr Garfield,' he said eventually, folding his notebook.

'No problem. Are you going through every person who went to see Howard Plume? That will take you years, won't it?'

'Not all of them, no.'

Not all of them? What was that supposed to mean? Why was I one of them? And if the police were genuinely interviewing hundreds, possibly thousands, of former audience members, what warrants the head of the investigation coming to my place?

The two detectives got up, and, as they turned towards the door, DCI Scull, in peak Colombo mode, turned around and asked, 'One final thing. Tell me, Mr Garfield, have you ever been to Ross-On-Wye in Worcestershire?'

What if he knows if I have? What if he has a record of my registration number in the area? That's it! They are matching up the owners of cars with registration numbers. *Not all of them*, indeed. I am probably the only one! That's why he is here. I am their breakthrough. I looked at the floor and knotted my brow in pretend thought. If I say yes, do I admit I was there on the day of the murder? I can't. So much to process. So few seconds to make this call.

'I can't say I have. I went to Hereford once when I was in a boxing match, but I don't think I ever went to Ross-On-Wye.'

'You box?'

'I did as a schoolboy, but I wasn't much cop.'

'Much *cop*,' repeated Scull, smiling.

I laughed, too, at the unintended pun. Relief more than anything. I really was expecting his next line to be, 'You've never been to Ross-On-Wye, so why was your car recorded entering and leaving the town on the day of the murder?' If he had that information then now would be the time to lay it on me. This wasn't really *Colombo* after all.

'What about Hastings? Do you have any connections to Hastings? Have you been there in the last several years?'

'Hastings?' I asked, my face showing bafflement as to why the town could have possibly been brought up. 'Well, I used to go there on holiday as a kid. Took my daughter there on day trips. That's about it. Not been since she was a little girl. Could be twenty years. Why?'

'Just curious, Mr Garfield.'

The two detectives turned to the door again, and DI Best opened the front door. Scull and I were queued behind her. Next to the door were the pegs, and – along with several coats, hats and scarves – there was Hector's lead on its very own peg. The blood drained from my face. I could not see Scull's. He seemed to stand still for longer than he needed to. Then he turned. I was waiting for him to ask if I had a dog, and, when I said no, why did I have a dog lead then. Scull reached out and touched the lead. I froze. DI Best was halfway down the garden path.

'You have a dog, Mr Garfield?'

'Not any more. Died as well.'

The policeman nodded. 'Good afternoon, Mr Garfield. Thank

you for your help. If we need anything else we will be in touch. There shouldn't be any reason for us to do so. I hope not.'

I was obviously in a heightened state of paranoia, but Detective Superintendent Scull looked deep inside me. In fact, his stare was penetrating yet not malevolent or accusatory. I almost felt like confessing, 'OK, mate, you win. You got me.'

He smiled and nodded his head slowly up and down as if between us we had reached an understanding.

'Goodbye and good luck,' I said, slowly closing the door as he followed his colleague down the drive.

I slumped down on the sofa and looked at my hands trembling mildly. Fear and adrenaline pumped through me. I swallowed hard and contemplated what exactly had just taken place.

I pictured them outside in their plain clothes car.

'Did you see the dog lead, Wendy?'

I'm guessing she's called Wendy.

'No, sir.'

'There was a big, chunky dog lead hanging from the pegs by the front door.'

'Was there?'

'Yes. Did you see a dog bowl?

Wendy shook her head.

'Did you see or hear a dog?'

Wendy shook her head.

'Could you smell dog, Wendy?'

'No.'

DS Scull would have sat back in the passenger seat in controlled triumph. He had solved the case. He smiled as he was taken back to his childhood and reading 'The Adventure Of Silver Blaze', in which his hero Sherlock Holmes solved the case of a missing racehorse via the dog that didn't bark. The curious incident of the dog in the night-time.

'But who would put a murder weapon on display?' asked DI Best, marvelling at her guv'nor's powers of deduction.

'He didn't know we were coming, did he? You'd be surprised, Wendy. Murderers often keep trophies. It's a well-known trait.'

'What now, sir?'

'Slowly, slowly, catchee monkey.'

That threw DI Best, it really did.

Although that conversation never happened – at least, I don't think it did – DI Best would have been right. What sort of murderer puts the murder weapon on display? Me. That's who. I knew the sensible thing would be to chuck into the river. Not the Wye but a river down here. But from that first day I hung it from the peg I had never moved it. I wasn't getting off on it. I just did not want to move it. It's like the order of service for Dad. I came home from the funeral that day and tucked it behind a small ivory elephant ornament on the end of the mantelpiece over the fireplace. It is still there now. Nearly twenty years later. I cannot chuck it or move it to a drawer, even though it has curled up and yellowed from the sun. It's the same sort of thing. Can't really explain it. I realised that Holly might see it, but I would just say it was Cindy's – the dog we'd had when she was just a baby – and that I'd recently found it in a box and couldn't bring myself to throw it away.

Something else was bugging me about DS Scull's visit. I could not put my finger on it. Was it the look on his face when he turned around by the door to say goodbye? It was a knowing look but not a challenging one. I don't think it was that. There was something else. Something as he walked away. I went to check the doorway security camera and rewound the tape. The film starts as DI Best opens the door and steps out. She pauses a second or two as Scull is obviously bidding me farewell. She then proceeds down the path. Scull, after our dog-lead exchange, follows a few feet behind his hands clasped behind his back. Perhaps a throwback to his uniform days? 'Allo, 'allo, 'allo, and all that.

There it is! I nearly missed it. Watching the detective's hands, I see his thumb flick itself out of the clasp and stand erect for a few seconds and then fold back. Like he is striking a match or a lighter. I watched it again. It was not a thoughtless fidget or rearranging of the hands behind his back. It was a deliberate and definite action. What could it mean?

Thumbs-up normally signals agreement, approval, appreciation. I cannot think of anything else it could signify. The fact that Scull had elected to visit me personally suggests to me that there was something other than that I featured on a list of people who had paid by credit card to watch one of Plume's shows. Could he have filtered it by males who'd made a single purchase (i.e., probably attended alone) – given that it was believed to have been a man acting alone who had committed the murder? In that case I could be one of very few. Could it have been that our surnames figured twice in a few months, and the police connected me with Holly? More of a long shot.

Holly! My first urge was to pick up the telephone and ring her and tell her about the visit. Suggest she might not want to tell them about the message Plume gave her and her subsequent visits to me. For God's sake, don't mention that I cut my arse with a bread knife the day you came to me after seeing him!

Scull really could be doing a Lieutenant Colombo and be on his way there now. I can picture the scene. The phone rings just after she has invited the officers inside her flat.

Please answer it.

It's my dad. I'll ring him back.

Please answer, and put it on loudspeaker.

Hello, Dad.

Holly, the police may be on their way ...

Holly would have crumbled. The great denouement is complete. Scull has got his man. Like the Mounties and Colombo, he always does.

Because of my galloping imagination and paranoia, I didn't

ring Holly, hoping that the police had not made the connection. I decided against mentioning it at all. The next day passed with my liberty intact. And the next. After several weeks I was sure I was safe. Not because DS Scull had not joined the dots but because he *had*. I thought back to his last words to me: *There shouldn't be any reason for us to do so. I hope not.* A strange thing to say. *I hope not.* Was Scull saying, *I know you did it. I know you did the others. Don't do any more, and that's the end of the matter*? Was the thumbs-up a signal to underline this in case I hadn't got it?

I believe that Scull was routinely put in charge of the Plume inquiry, but after some days or even weeks (at least after he had revealed my Justice Killer message on *Crimewatch*) he was made privy to the information that someone calling themselves a justice killer had previously confessed to two murders in recent years. While they wanted to catch this serial killer, a decision had been made at the Frank Cox stage and at a far more senior level that the connection would not be made public through fear of vigilantism spreading. There was the potential for law and order to be undermined. Scull's instructions were to find the murderer but to not to reveal to the public that there was a justice *serial* killer at large. On the same basis, if I were found out, then it would be deemed in the national interest not to expose me. I would have to be stopped, and if the view were taken that I could not be because I was unstable, then I believe they or, more likely, MI5 or MI6 would have taken me out. I know I'm straying into *The Professionals* territory here, but I really do believe it. It's the only way it all adds up. Detective Superintendent Scull had either been ordered to warn me on orders or was warning me off his own bat.

The random mention of Hastings was his way of telling me that he knew who I was and what I had done without alerting his colleague. He knew I had killed at least three times, and the cryptic thumbs-up was him telling he knew but was not going to pursue it. The deep look in the house and the fingering of the dog's lead had been him telling me that it ends. Now. That was the deal. They won't pursue if I don't pursue. My secret was safe with him, and his secret was safe with me.

20
NED

I HAD NEVER imagined myself living in central London. Never had a desire to and never thought I would. It was an accident really. As the years passed I increasingly found that a large, detached house in Purley was becoming a headache, and I felt ever lonelier in it. Some rooms I never entered. The gardeners seemed to be a fixture. The swimming pool an expensive pain. I decided to get rid.

Bubbles and I had started investing in property again. This time not developing and selling but buying and renting. We bought three flats off-plan in a development in the Borough, SE1, and by the time they were finished I decided to move into one of them while I pondered what to do next. A big, spacious, echoey, wood-panelled house seemed to magnify my loneliness, my solitary existence, while the flat's compactness had the opposite effect. The leafy roads of Purley were very nice, but you barely saw a soul all day. Big cars swished in and out of drives and hummed contentedly outside electric gates, but walking, talking humans were in short supply. Here in the Borough it was buzzy, an area on the up; the tube station was across the road, and pubs, cafés and restaurants abounded. I didn't really talk to anyone, but knowing there were people around should I want to was a comfort.

Actually, I had made a couple of friends. Ben lived across the corridor from me, and we met in the lift, in the foyer and in the corridor. He was divorced, rebuilding his life, his wife having left him for another man when he was in his fifties. He had now turned sixty. He was bitter she hadn't done it earlier. He'd have had a chance of starting again, he said, but not now. We went to the George together, standing in the ancient courtyard putting the world to rights. Losing his wife had coloured everything for Ben. He saw the world he knew slipping away. He reminded me of me.

Ben was an IT manager. In the 1980s and 1990s he had earned big money in the City. He explained that the IT revolution happened so fast companies were caught on the hop. Anybody who even half understood the rapidly changing technologies was like gold dust. Supply could not meet demand, and Ben said that at his peak he was earning over £200,000 a year. This against a backdrop of being self-taught. He was still working, but less and less. His youthful cerebral dexterity had slowed, and his skill set could be sourced from India at a fraction of the price. Supply now exceeded demand, and the highly paid posts had disappeared. Ben was now an agency worker, sent into smaller organisations at short notice to trouble-shoot. He was, he said, unlikely to average a full working week. But he had done well climbing the housing ladder and benefited from a clutch of pension schemes from various employers over the years.

He asked me how well I knew the area, and I told him not much. He knew the City intimately and one lunchtime walked me over London Bridge and introduced me to some of his favourite drinking haunts. He was a fan of real ale and kept urging me to try different brews. 'Lovely and smooth, you can taste the hops dancing on your tonsils,' he'd say as he tipped the liquid down his throat, closing his eyes as if experiencing ecstasy. To me it tasted drab, although I'd enjoy the first waves of light-headedness that came with it. I could only drink one pint to his two or three, but I didn't have the heart to tell him I'd rather be drinking lemonade.

One day Emma knocked on my door. I had noticed her around, too, and we had exchanged a hello or two before. She, like me, was a first resident, and she wanted to know if I wanted to join a tenants' group. I said, 'Yes, of course', although I decided not to let on that I was the freeholder, not only of my flat but of hers, too. Emma worked in human resources, and, on seeing my lack of recognition of the term, explained it used to be called personnel. She, too, lived alone, having been divorced some years before. She never said, but I'd put her in her early fifties, a few years younger than me. She organised a 'get-together' in the early months in her flat so we could all become acquainted. We had a laugh and a joke, and she gravitated towards Ben and me, as she could see we were already acquainted. Only three others turned up: a Sri Lankan couple, Hashini and Jegan – one a doctor and one an anaesthetist who were working at Guy's Hospital – and a tall, imposing Nigerian man called Koko, who had one glass of champagne and left.

One early evening, as I sat staring at the television, Emma knocked on the door.

'Hi, I wondered if you'd be interested in coming to the cinema with me.' Then she laughed and brandished two tickets. 'I'm not trying to proposition you. Genuinely, I was about to pick up my coat and meet my girlfriend for a drink before we headed to Leicester Square to see *T2 Trainspotting*, and she just phoned. She has a family crisis and has to go to her parents' urgently. I'm still going and thought, why waste a ticket? But don't feel like you need to. I'm happy to go alone. But waste not …'

'*Trainspotting 2*? I haven't even seen *Trainspotting 1*.'

'Not your cup of tea then?'

'No, I like trains. Especially old steam trains.'

'You are joking?'

I wasn't. I had heard of the film and seen the book on sale but had never given any thought as to what it was about

So I had my evening with Emma at Leicester Square Odeon, and we had a drink after in the Borough. It was my first 'date' since Jan, but it was not really. Emma was charming, but I didn't detect any sense she was interested in anything more than not wasting a ticket. Perhaps some sense of being uncomfortable at being a woman alone going to the cinema was avoided. I was not hoping for any such attraction, to be honest. I was not far off sixty years of age by then, and I wasn't interested in embarking on a new romantic relationship – I'm still not. But it was nice evening. Really nice.

Weekends I was in the habit of driving south and visiting Bubbles and Holly. To my great surprise, Bubbles's first marriage, to Marcella, had fallen apart a few years back, but now he was married again, to Benita, and they had a little girl, Mia. He lived in Banstead in a smashing new-build on the very site of the Pine Forest Children's Home. It was as if he was making a statement about his past. I survived your shit, and here I am living in the beautiful houses that have sprouted from the sordid remains of your institution. He wears sharp suits, looks every bit the successful builder and property developer. Mia calls me Uncle Paul. He's happy. I'm happy. Holly's happy, too. She and Norman have a busy life. They played the property market as well, moving up the ladder with speed and investing in rentals, encouraged and some-times aided by me and Bubbles. Holly has qualified as a yoga teacher and practises Buddhism. I don't see them much, but we speak regularly. To my private relief they eschewed having children in the end. In truth, they seem to be out of the country more than in it.

'I'm happy.' There, I said it. I'm happy. No longer a suicide-in-waiting. I am happy enjoying my life. Emma is a good friend, as is Ben. We go to the cinema, the theatre, to talks. Where we live is ideally placed for so much. I still feel different from everyone else, though. But how do I know how they are feeling? I am dif-ferent. I have murdered four people – or three, depending on how you look at it. I am or was Justice Killer. That marks me out as different. But, believe me, I don't often think about it or them. I killed four people in a brief six-year period of my life. I don't let it define me. They were my serial-killer years, like someone else might have had rave years or travelling years.

My conscience is clear, and as time has passed I actually feel more than ever that I did right. Plume was the only marginal 'victim' – but look what came of it. That insidious, morally repugnant industry is no more. No more TV programmes, no more packed theatre shows, no more idolisation of con men and women. My actions drove it back where it belongs, into darkened rooms with Ouija boards and cranks pushing upturned wine glasses across a table. Stuart Hinds got his just deserts. Following the death of Uncle Phil, investigating the unfettered abuse in social care got pushed up the list of priorities, and Frank Cox's case certainly raised some questions about the way the parole system worked. But, sadly, memories are short, and they are again releasing these people back among us. Only recently there had been pushback following a paedophile killer with the eerie name of Colin Pitchfork being allowed out after thirty years. I was pleased to see the following excerpt in one of the many newspaper articles about the case:

'Police officers are often disheartened at juries acquitting guilty men – and it is nearly always men – judges imposing light sentences and the Parole Board allowing horrendous killers back into society when they still might pose a risk. The public are entitled to justice, and they are entitled to protection. Depriving them of this will eventually manifest itself in unrest and possibly vigilantism,' commented Mark Scull, a former senior policeman.

Scull's statement confirmed to me that my suppositions as to what really happened in the Howard Plume investigation were pretty much on the money. Seeing him in print was like hearing a familiar voice after so many years.

I had made a difference. I hope I did. I hadn't turned around the tide of supine law enforcement and the crumbling of our national spine, but I think I changed things a bit. Slowed them down. The overall direction remains dire, though. I switch on my television, and I see a whole channel devoted to 'true crime'. It's a genre now, like romantic comedy or science fiction. There are literally hundreds of so-called documentaries with the words 'killer', 'murder' and 'body' in their titles. Ian Brady, Myra Hindley, Peter Sutcliffe, Fred and Rose, et al. recycled time and time again with no thought for the poor souls and their families forced to watch their tragedies packaged and unashamedly exploited. What new is there to say? Shocking, for me, is that some of those victims' families choose to partake in this sick parade. If I think about it I despair. How many of these killers do so in the knowledge they will be for ever celebrated in this way? It's not genuine analysis of the murder problem we have, it's part of the problem.

Occasionally I am tempted to kill again. I had created Justice Killer, and I yearned, in my more reckless, self-indulgent moments, to let the world know that he had killed before and who he had killed and why. I thought about seeking out Frank Cox's alleged accomplice. He had still been alive some years back when I had thought seriously about looking for him. I had a feeling he'd be a handful and dreamt up a scenario in which I killed him in his local pub with a crossbow after having made his acquaintance over a period of time in disguise and as someone else. I'd have a false swallow tattoo on my neck or hand. I couldn't use a gun, and the thought of knifing someone appals me. For a few days I researched crossbows. They are easy to source and simple to learn how to use. However, I only had the compulsive liar Frank Cox's last words to go on, and after Howard Plume I lost my appetite for taking things at face value. This arsehole could be innocent of murder, but I doubt it. Whatever, he had a lucky escape.

Ned Fletcher, the TV presenter who irks me so, has developed his profile and audience gradually over the last twenty years and has come closer than anyone to bringing me out of retirement. He delights in tricking ordinary honest folk to debate with him, and then he skewers them with his intellectual dexterity, publicly humiliating them. It was the worst bullying I had ever witnessed, worse in my opinion than physical bullying. I wanted to avenge those he had toyed with, humiliated and destroyed with words and then disappeared them with his fade button as they struggled to find the language and arguments to fight back. His skills, which he had probably acquired at the debating societies of his private school and university, were being used against people who were forced to get out to work early in life to help out their mums and dads in keeping families' heads above water and were denied the opportunity of paid-for educations. This odious man's targets were decent, ordinary folk alarmed at their diminishing prospects, depressed by being demonised for wanting Britain to stand proud, for remembering their hard-but-happy childhoods. This self-obsessed man – and all his class – enraged me. For the first time I felt the desire to kill for pleasure. I thought about marching into his studio and killing him live on his show. I wanted to avenge those ordinary people who had innocently phoned in and thought they would get a fair hearing. I also wanted it to be a warning to other bullies. Then Emma and I went to the cinema at Leicester Square to see *Joker*. Somebody had beaten me to it. Bloody Joaquin Phoenix.

I have been studying this creature, and he has gained strength in recent years, openly combative to those colleagues who dare not to share his alleged ideological persuasion. The I say alleged because I am convinced he does not have a passion for a particular doctrine but has adopted one to give himself a position. He could just as easily have gone the other way.

Over twenty years his daytime TV show has gone from strength to strength. He trawled the poverty-stricken, drug-addled, alcohol-soaked towns of Britain for sad, hopeless individuals who would bare their misery for all to see in exchange for a night in a hotel and a well-stocked mini-bar. Once in the studio he would set these people against each other – wife against husband, father against son, sister against brother and boyfriend against girlfriend. It was the twenty-first-century equivalent of the bear pit. He introduced regular lie-detector tests to try to ramp up the tension, and his catchphrase – 'Get a grip on yourself, man/woman' – had entered the national lexicon. The viewing public lapped it up, and the regulator looked away. I saw only evil, and, as far as I was concerned, Ned Fletcher was corrupting and corroding the national soul.

How it didn't happen earlier, I don't know. But, eventually, one lady, mortified and ashamed following her five minutes of fame, went home and committed suicide, leaving a note apparently blaming Ned and his programme. The innocently named *Noon With Ned* was taken off air immediately, and thankfully he was toxic for a while.

I thought that was the last we'd see of him, but in recent years he has reinvented himself on radio, where has created a new persona 'fighting' for the underprivileged, 'holding power to account' and 'giving voice to the unheard'. He claims to champion the very people he had previously exploited and tortured. His volte-face has gone apparently unnoticed and unchallenged by almost everyone except me.

Ned Fletcher is only interested in himself. He is a narcissist and a broadcasting psychopath. It's meant to be a debate he conducts, but it consists mainly of monologues ('Nedologues', he calls them) where he cleverly constructs and deconstructs arguments.

I know where he lives. I know he travels to and from work on the tube. He makes sure we know that, too. He is one of the *people*, remember. No pickup car for him. Most recently he has decided he is passionately against Brexit. But he has gone further. He has labelled those who voted for it as half-wits, racists and white supremacists. He is sowing discord, unrest and hatred, and nobody is pushing back against him. He paints a picture of a country and people I do not recognise. I voted Leave, but I wasn't very sure, and, like most of the electorate, I had no massively strong feelings. Holly and Norman, for example, voted Remain. I don't think any the less of them, nor them of me, I hope. Only when I saw how the establishment pulled together to reverse a democratic vote that the public were asked to make did I become engaged and enraged. I couldn't believe democracy was going to be pissed all over so casually and openly. It was an attack by the upper classes on the lower classes. And this man demonising ordinary Joes and Joans in this evil way was in the vanguard. He declared his war on half the country.

I have decided to run into him one night as he leaves work following his address to the nation and goes to catch his train to the leafy suburbs where he is far removed from the raging fires of the more deprived areas of the inner cities that he stokes so freely. When that night will be or if it will be I don't know. As I write, I am content to carry on living.

I will wear a Leave EU badge on the day I do decide to go, so that people may think afterwards the badge would have enraged him and throw some doubt around who was trying to kill who. I will stand in front of him as the train approaches and then turn suddenly and pull him towards me by the lapels while screaming, 'Help! Help! Leave me alone,' the two of us tumbling into the deathly path of the thundering train.

My Darling Holly

If you are reading this letter, I will have left this world.

Inside this attached Jiffy bag is a manuscript I have been writing on and off ever since Mum died. This is what I've been doing when I say, 'I'm writing.' This is the 'book' I've been working on for years. It's about my life. I suppose you could call it autobiographical. Some might call it a confession memoir. I like to think it's an autobiographical novel.

You may like to read it, but you may not. It's all true. This is no Enid Blyton or Jeffrey Archer. There are things here you know nothing about. At least, I don't think you do. You will be very shocked, and the revelations within may make you change your mind about your old dad. I detail certain actions that I took in my life that are not lawful and many would argue are immoral.

I have struggled whether to leave you this letter and manuscript. One side of me thinks I am cruel to burden you with such a choice as to read or not to read. I ask myself – Why? Do I genuinely believe you have a right to know? Is it my ego? Can I not bear the thought that what I did will die with me?

All I can say is that I have no regrets and believe that what I did was right. The constructs of law, order and justice in this country are wrong, misguided, lost. These were not the impulsive actions of a wayward youth. When I did what I did I was in seasoned middle age. I hope I made a stand in holding back the tide of evil and cynicism that seems to be enveloping this country. The Western world. Humanity. However, I am not physically here now to absorb and face any shame, recriminations, accusations and other fall-out that could stem from my confessions. You are, and the last thing I want is to bring any discomfort, unhappiness or shame on you, Bubbles, Norman and anybody else connected to our family.

I am happy if you decide not to read it. Take the bag and burn it. Nobody will be any the wiser. The secrets I disclose will remain secrets. You may read it and then decide to keep those secrets to yourself. Then you can still burn it. Alternatively, you may read it and decide that you want to take it to the police. They might decide to burn it. Who knows, you might decide to publish it and make a few quid.

The destiny of this knowledge I have bequeathed to you. You will do the best thing with it, I know.

All of my love

Dad

PS Remember to look for the robin.

X

Daily Telegraph
17 November 2020

RADIO PRESENTER NED FLETCHER
KILLED IN TUBE FIGHT

Ned Fletcher, 52, the TV and radio presenter, most famous for his long running TV debate show *Ned At Noon*, was pronounced dead yesterday following a confrontation that resulted in him and another man falling into the path of a tube train at Amersham station.

Witnesses said that the presenter and a man who has been named as Paul Garfield, 61, of Borough, London, argued on the platform at around 10.15 am on Monday morning. It is alleged by one witness that Garfield's T-shirt referred to Brexit, and this may have triggered the exchange.

Doreen Harefield of Little Chalfont said, 'We often saw Ned Fletcher around. People leave him be. I heard shouting and saw Ned and this man in a clinch, and before I knew it they'd tumbled on to the line, and the train came in. It happened so quickly. It was awful.'

Mr Fletcher was declared dead at 11.55 am. Mr Garfield has suffered critical, life-threatening injuries.

Police have appealed for witnesses and are examining CCTV footage.

LONDON BOOKS

FLYING THE FLAG FOR
FREE-THINKING LITERATURE

www.london-books.co.uk

PLEASE VISIT OUR WEBSITE FOR

- Current and forthcoming books
- Author and title profiles
- Events and news
- Secure on-line bookshop
- An alternative view of London literature

London Classics

The Angel And The Cuckoo *Gerald Kersh*
Doctor Of The Lost *Simon Blumenfeld*
The Gilt Kid *James Curtis*
It Always Rains On Sunday *Arthur La Bern*
Jew Boy *Simon Blumenfeld*
May Day *John Sommerfield*
Night And The City *Gerald Kersh*
Phineas Kahn *Simon Blumenfeld*
Prelude To A Certain Midnight *Gerald Kersh*
A Start In Life *Alan Sillitoe*
There Ain't No Justice *James Curtis*
They Drive By Night *James Curtis*
Wide Boys Never Work *Robert Westerby*

BARRY DESMOND IS A WANKER

MARTIN KNIGHT

Barry Desmond is an only child. He's had a sheltered upbringing by ageing parents distrustful of the outside world. This leaves him ill-equipped to deal with the savagery of school, the trials of adolescence and the reality and politics of the workplace.

At school he is a figure of fun, excluded and picked on. At home he struggles with the eccentricities of his parents and is alarmed and confused as his hormones spring into life. He finds guilty pleasure in self-relief. Later, he follows his father into a career with the Empire Bank, a throwback organisation doomed to become extinct. In middle age, and following the death of his parents and redundancy, Barry ventures out into the wider world determined to live his life and strike up relationships. Unlike his parents Barry believes that people are fundamentally decent. Will he find the fulfilment and interaction he craves? Will society repay Barry's trust?

This novel from Martin Knight, author of *Battersea Girl* and *Common People*, explores and illuminates 21st-century suburban loneliness and the grim reality of having a face that doesn't fit. *Barry Desmond Is A Wanker* is a seductive and surprising book, laced with humour, shot through with poignancy and sensitivity.

London Books
£8.99 paperback
ISBN 978-0-9551851-9-9

NEW FICTION

CATEGORY UNKNOWN

KOUSHIK BANERJEA

Life on a London council estate leads the entrepreneurial Conrad on a conflicted journey between his ambition, his loyalty to his Jamaican nan and his need to redeem himself. The suppressed scars of a life under the Spanish dictator Franco resurface in Laura's traumatic coming of age. Seemingly comfortable British Indian girl Roxy wants something different, but isn't sure what. Then there is D, the inner-city boffin looking for more than the dubious distinction of being the younger brother of an accomplished thief. Like the others, D is not content with his allotted role in life. He'd rather be a 'category unknown'.

Four very different characters, one lifetime, the old certainties gone. And as the threads holding their identities together unravel, these intertwined lives are propelled into the heart of their troubled times. Spanning the decades from the rise of Thatcher in the late 1970s to the fall of Lehman Brothers in 2008, *Category Unknown* is a darkly comic portrait of lives in miniature flailing around the edges of the bigger questions. Who am I? How did I get here? Why am I kitted out in counterfeit sportswear? At the book's core is the simple premise – when life is precarious, perhaps the greatest freedom of all resides in refusing to be stereotyped.

London Books
£9.99 paperback
ISBN 978-0-9957217-8-4

NEW FICTION

THE SEAL CLUB

WARNER WELSH KING

The Seal Club is a three-novella collection by the authors Alan Warner, Irvine Welsh and John King, three stories that capture their ongoing interests and concerns, stories that reflect bodies of work that started with *Morvern Callar*, *Trainspotting* and *The Football Factory* – all best-sellers, all turned into high-profile films.

In Warner's *Those Darker Sayings*, a gang of Glaswegian nerds ride the mainline trains of northern England on a mission to feed the habit of their leader Slorach. Welcome to the world of the quiz-machine casual.

In Welsh's *The Providers*, the Begbie family gathers in Edinburgh for a terminally ill mother's last Christmas, but everyone needs to be on their best behaviour, and that includes her son Frank. The ultimate nightmare family Christmas looms, where secrets and lies explode like fireworks.

In King's *The Beasts Of Brussels*, thousands of Englishmen assemble in the city ahead of a football match against Belgium, their behaviour monitored by two media professionals who spout different politics but share the same interests. As order breaks down we are left to identify the real beasts of the story.

London Books
£10.99 paperback
ISBN 978-0-9957217-6-0

NEW FICTION

SHE'S MY WITCH

STEWART HOME

Strange things happen on social media, such as the almost chance encounter between a London born-and-bred fitness instructor and a drug-fuelled Spanish witch. At first Maria Remedios and Martin Cooper share their love for super-dumb, two-chord stomp in private messages, but when they meet magic happens. Maria knows that she and Martin have been lovers in past lives, and sets out to convince the former skinhead that her occult beliefs are true.

The main narrative takes place in London between 2011 and 2014, detailing riots, rock-and-roll excess, and the times of austerity leading up to the Brexit vote in 2016. In online messages Martin and Maria hark back to other eras – his immersion in London's 1970s punk explosion and her tales of teenage drug-dealing and murder on Spain's notorious Ruta Destroy party scene. As Martin gets ever closer to Maria, she constantly surprises him by detailing different aspects of her life – such as running a bar for a criminal motorcycle gang in Valencia, her seven-year stint as a professional dominatrix, and a decades-long struggle with heroin.

She's My Witch is a dark romance with an incendiary conclusion, written to reflect today's social-media world and a resurgent interest in the occult and kink.

London Books
£9.99 paperback
ISBN 978-0-9957217-4-6

MALAYAN SWING

PETE HAYNES

Aidan is different. He is small, awkward and often silent, an easy
man to ignore, mock or exploit, yet on the inside he is intelligent and
thoughtful. He speaks to the reader in a way he can't manage in
everyday life, reflecting on the world around him with great insight
and an almost childlike honesty. This is the internal life of an outsider.

We meet Aidan not long after he has moved into a room in a
shared flat, forced from the home in which he felt secure by a policy
labelled 'care in the community'. But the community is dismissive
and threatening. He becomes lonely and scared, his best friend
the radio he carries everywhere. An old shed offers a hideaway
during the day, while his evenings are often spent in the local pubs.

Aidan's physical and mental state starts to deteriorate, and when
he bumps into Joey from the home he comes to the notice of some
bad people. He wanders the streets and is attacked, his life quickly
spiralling out of control. The story ends in dramatic fashion, but it is
Aidan's decency and a sense of escape that remain with the reader.
Malayan Swing is a moving novel, a testament to those living on the
margins of society, and as such is a brave and important work.

London Books
£8.99 paperback
ISBN 978-0-9551851-6-8

SLAUGHTERHOUSE PRAYER

JOHN KING

When a boy realises the grown-ups are killing animals and that he has been eating their bodies, he gives up meat. But should he share the truth and break another child's heart? As a youth he wants to believe in the ability of words and peaceful protest to end the slaughter, while struggling to resist a desire for revenge. Now a disillusioned man trying to rebuild his life, he must choose one of two paths. Acceptance means security, but those meat-industry adverts keep taunting him and some familiar insults – *smelly pig, dirty cow, chick-chick-chicken* – fill his head.

Slaughterhouse Prayer deals in human invention and our treatment of non-human animals, the manipulation of language and the corruption of innocence. Society's pecking order is challenged as the story moves to its margins and beyond. A book of dreams, where visions are more real than reality and sentimentality is a strength, it asks a series of questions. Can a person honestly kill without emotion? Could a vegan soldier stay professional and humane? And will we ever confront the terror that surrounds us?

London Books
£9.99 paperback
ISBN 978-0-9957217-2-2